MICHAEL L. NICHOLAS

BLACK GOLD

A Detective Mathieu Mystery

ISBN: 979-8-9906265-2-2 (hc)

ISBN: 979-8-9906265-0-8 (sc)

ISBN: 979-8-9906265-1-5 (e)

Acknowledgement

To my friend and first reader, Damir thank you for your encouragement, suggestions, and wise counsel during the writing of this novel. To Katie McCune, my editor, thank you for your excellent work editing the manuscript, catching my mistakes, and making key suggestions to enhance the story.

Finally, I want to express my sincere gratitude and thanks to everyone who has read and shared their enthusiasm for the previous Detective Mathieu novels. Your support is gratifying and much appreciated. I hope you enjoy this novel just as much.

1

The Last Roundup

Los Angeles 1930s. It was the last roundup for the gentleman in the three-piece suit, bobbing up and down in the moonlight like a rodeo cowboy on the back of a pumpjack.

The metal horsehead pump was one of the smaller ones in the Inglewood Oil Field. Perhaps eight feet high at best. The victim's legs, torso, and right hand were strapped to the walking beam, leaving his left arm to flop around with the rocking horse motion.

It was a bizarre sight in an equally bizarre landscape, filled as far as the eye could see with a forest of hundred-foot-high wood oil derricks, their relentless motion oblivious to the human tragedy on display. The LA city fathers wouldn't be promoting this dystopian nightmare in their tourist posters any time soon.

Detective Theo Mathieu turned to Fred Wilson, the forensic investigator, and said, "Fred, see if you can find someone to turn the pump off so we can get Hopalong off his horse."

"Yes, sir. Right away," Wilson said as he went in search of help.

Stuart Thomas, the crime scene photographer, came over soon after and said, "I guess the moral of this story, Detective, is never ride bareback at night."

Mathieu couldn't help but laugh as he turned to Stuart and asked, "Are you upset they called you out so late?"

"Not at all … there's no place I'd rather be on a beautiful moonlit night than in one of Dante's nine circles of hell."

"When did you arrive?" Mathieu asked.

"About a half hour before you did."

"Do you know who called it in?"

"The night watchman," Stuart said, pointing to a man in work clothes standing in the shadows of a small wooden shed about twenty yards up the hill.

"He has a field telephone in the shed. He was doing his rounds when he discovered the body. Scared the hell out of him apparently, he said he thought he'd seen a ghost."

"Do you know his name?"

"Henry Walters."

"Did Mr. Walters recognize the victim?"

"No," Stuart said, shaking his head. "He said he'd never seen him before."

"Did you get photos of the victim riding the pumpjack?"

"Yes, sir."

"Was there enough light?"

"I brought plenty of lightbulbs with me," Stuart said. "I always come prepared for night shoots."

Mathieu nodded. "When they turn the pump off, climb that metal ladder on the far side of it and get some closeups of the victim's face, hands, and how they tied him to the pumpjack."

"Understood, sir. Will do."

"Thanks, Stuart," Mathieu said as he walked up the hill toward the night watchman.

Walters was nervously smoking a cigarette when Mathieu arrived.

"Mr. Walters, I'm Detective Mathieu from the LAPD. I understand you discovered the body. Is that correct?"

Walters dropped his cigarette, squashed it with his foot, then looked at Mathieu and said, "Yes, sir. I was making my rounds in the northeast sector when I spotted him on the pumpjack."

"And you didn't notice anything earlier?"

"No, sir, but this is a huge property, and I'm the only watchman on duty on this side of the canyon at night. It's over a thousand acres, the largest contiguous oil field in the United States. We've got close to 900 wells that produce over 145 barrels of oil a day. So, I patrol it in sectors."

"Who owns the oil field?"

"Standard Oil of California, but other companies lease drilling lots from them."

"Where's the main access road?"

"On Duquesne off of Jefferson, which is probably where you came in. But you can't just drive onto the property. There's a guard shack there."

"Yes, I saw it," Mathieu said. "Any other way in?"

"Not officially. There are Keep Out signs posted around the periphery of the property but no fences."

"What's the closest access to the pumpjack?"

"You could park beside that dirt road in the canyon and hike up the hill. There's usually not much traffic on that road, especially at night. There's only farmland out here."

"You mean La Cienega?"

"Yeah, that's the closest road to the pumpjack where I found the dead man."

"I assume whoever did this had to turn the pump off to tie the man to it," Mathieu said. "Is that hard to do?"

"No, sir," Walters said, shaking his head. "There's an on/off switch on the left side of the diesel engine that powers the pump."

"Why is that pumpjack so much shorter than the others?"

"Most likely because the oil is closer to the surface," Walters said. "I believe that's one of the original wells from when oil was discovered here in 1924."

"Did anything else happen here tonight?" Mathieu asked.

Walters scratched his head, trying to remember. "Yeah, around eight-thirty, I discovered a pipe leak in the southwest corner of the field," Walters said, pointing toward a distant hill. "I used one of the field telephones to call it in. The foreman scrambled two oilmen and two firefighters to the site. Pipe leaks can be dangerous. One spark can cause an inferno that could set the whole field ablaze. Fires and explosions are what we worry about the most here."

Mathieu nodded. "And you stayed with the crew until they fixed the leak?"

"Yes, sir."

"Were there any other men on duty tonight besides the ones you were with?"

Walters shook his head. "No, sir. That was the entire crew. We only have a skeleton crew at night."

"What time did you discover the body?"

"Around ten, when we got back from fixing the pipe," Walters said. "Do you think that pipe leak was a diversion?" he asked as if it had just dawned on him.

Mathieu shrugged. "It's hard to know. But it looks well-planned to me. Somebody knew a lot about this field and how you operate at night."

"Jesus!" Walters said. "Pretty scary to think one of our own crew did this."

"We don't know that yet, Mr. Walters," Mathieu said. "It could just be someone who'd been watching your operation. So, please don't start any rumors until we have more facts. Where does the crew hang out when they aren't in the field?"

"In those buildings," Walters said as he pointed up the hill at a cluster of wood-plank buildings surrounded by three oil derricks. "There's a tool shed, office, and bunkhouse up there."

"What's the foreman's name?"

"Roy Duncan," Walters said. "I saw one of your men fetch him a few minutes ago."

Mathieu nodded. "Thanks for your help, Mr. Walters. See that officer over there near the squad car? Tell him I asked him to take your statement and get your contact information."

"Sure," Walters said. "I'm glad to help, Detective. Finding that body scared the hell out of me."

"I can imagine," Mathieu said with sympathy. "Sorry, you had to see that ... it's pretty grizzly."

"Can I get on with my rounds after I give him my statement?" Walters asked.

"Of course," Mathieu said as he turned to leave.

Walking downhill to the pumpjack, Mathieu spotted Fred Wilson with a tall man near the diesel engine. By the time Mathieu joined them, the pump was off.

The tall man looked at Mathieu and asked, "Are you Detective Mathieu?"

"Yes."

"I'm Roy Duncan," he said in a firm voice. "I'm the night foreman here. I'd shake your hand, but as you can see, I'm covered in oil."

Duncan wasn't exaggerating. He looked like a coal miner. Except for a few areas of white around his eyes and nose, everything else was black with oil: his hat, overalls, shirt, and leather boots.

"No need to apologize, Mr. Duncan," Mathieu said.

"Just called me Roy, Detective. We're not very formal around here."

Mathieu nodded. "I understand you had a busy night."

"That we did," Roy said. "First the pipe leak, and now this."

"I've already spoken with the night watchman," Mathieu said. "I assume you didn't notice anything unusual tonight because you were busy fixing the leak."

"Nothing except the leak itself."

"What do you mean?" Mathieu asked.

"It looked like deliberate sabotage to me, Detective."

2

The Stock Certificate

"Have you ever had this kind of sabotage in the oil field before?" Mathieu asked.

"No," Roy said, shaking his head. "Not until just recently."

"So, there have been other incidences?"

"Yes, but none as serious as the leak tonight. The others were minor compared to this. I chalked them off to sloppy work or disgruntled employees."

"Did you suspect anyone?"

"Yes, but I never caught them red-handed."

"I'd like their names and addresses plus those for the rest of the crew," Mathieu said.

"Sure," Roy said. "I'll get them for you, but a few of them I've already fired."

"That's okay. As long as you give me all the names and addresses, I'll have them checked out by my sergeant," Mathieu said. "Are any of the disgruntled employees from tonight's crew?"

"No," Roy said, pursing his lips. "I trust all these guys."

Mathieu nodded as he thought about what it could mean. Perhaps the target was the oil field itself, not just the victim.

Just then, Fred Wilson walked over, "I finished dusting the ladder for prints, and Stuart's finished taking photos. Can we bring the victim down now?"

"Yes, but I'll do it myself, Fred," Mathieu said. "I want to see how difficult it was to get him up there."

Turning back to the foreman, Mathieu said, "Thanks for your help, Roy. I'd appreciate it if you could write up that list tonight. I'll meet you at your office after I finish up here."

"Of course, Detective. I'll get to it now," Roy said as he turned and climbed up the hill toward the office.

After the foreman left, Mathieu walked to the steel A-frame supporting the pumpjack's horsehead walking beam. Mathieu grabbed the ladder rails and climbed to the top, where he stopped to survey the landscape.

The extra eight feet in height gave him a better vantage point to study the terrain. He looked toward the two-lane dirt road at the bottom of the canyon. It was about two hundred yards away but easily accessible via a labyrinth of paths that snaked down to it. And while the slope was steep, the switchbacks would have made it easier to carry or drag a body uphill.

Mathieu turned his attention to the body. It was the first time he'd seen the victim up close. He was a dapper-looking man with a proud bearing even in death. He wore a three-piece tailored wool suit with a buttoned vest, blue tie, and starched white collars.

The man looked to be in his early fifties, slim, clean-shaven, with well-manicured hands. To Mathieu, he looked like a salesman and a successful one.

Mathieu examined the ropes holding the victim to the walking beam. They were coarse and thick, like those used in construction and ranching. He untied the hitch, loosened the ropes, and let them fall to the ground.

He descended a few rungs below the victim, then tilted the man toward him until his body draped over his right shoulder, then wrapped his right arm around the man's legs.

The victim felt surprisingly light to Mathieu, perhaps only a hundred and forty pounds. After securing the body in the fireman's carry position, Mathieu started down the ladder.

By the time he reached the bottom and laid the victim on the ground, Mathieu had convinced himself that one person could have easily carried him up the hill and then to the top of the pumpjack.

Stuart came over to take a few more photos of the victim as Mathieu turned to Fred and asked, "Has the medical examiner arrived yet?"

"Yes, sir," Fred replied. "It's the 'Walrus'"—the affectionate nickname they used for Chief Medical Examiner Thomas Marsh because of his namesake mustache.

"Why did they send Marsh out this late for something like this?" Mathieu asked.

Fred shrugged. "You'll have to ask him, sir."

Mathieu watched as Doctor Marsh approached, exquisitely dressed as usual in a tailored wool suit and wearing galoshes to protect his pant legs from the oil puddles and dust.

"Good evening, Detective," Doctor Marsh said as he arrived and extended his hand. "It's always reassuring to see the LAPD's young wunderkind assigned to a case."

Ignoring the remark, Mathieu asked, "Why did they call you out for this, Doctor Marsh? Why didn't they send your assistant?"

"I assume for the same reason you were, Detective. I was told our presence was requested."

Mathieu looked confused. "By whom?"

"Apparently, by the president of Standard Oil of Southern California," Marsh said. "Big Oil is Big Business, Detective … we have to please our masters."

Mathieu shook his head in dismay. The LAPD was so corrupt it was making case assignments based on the whims of corporate executives.

He took a moment to compose himself, then explained to Marsh where the body had been found and ended by saying in a deadpan voice, "I highly doubt the rocking motion killed him, Doctor."

Marsh laughed and said, "Then, let's see what did, Detective."

Doctor Marsh knelt beside the victim and examined his face, skull, and neck for bruising. Then he unbuttoned the victim's vest and shirt and probed for wounds to the torso. As Marsh worked, Mathieu could hear him muttering to himself.

Marsh turned the victim onto his stomach, then pulled his shirt up so he could examine his back for knife or gunshot wounds. Finding none, Marsh turned him face up again and studied his face more closely.

Spotting something, Marsh said, "Ah ha!" He bent forward, forced the victim's mouth open, and extracted a large, crumpled ball of paper. He smoothed it out and studied the document.

Doctor Marsh looked up at Mathieu and said, "It appears our victim suffocated on an oil stock certificate."

3

Lester Jensen

Doctor Marsh handed the crumpled linen certificate to Mathieu. The legal-sized document was beige with a starburst border design. The title read "Participating Oil Agreement."

Mathieu could see that someone had cut off the top portion where the Agreement Number, Date, Number of Shares, and Amount usually were. Further down in the certificate, they had also cut out the section where the purchaser's name and city should have been.

What remained was a standard boilerplate agreement for purchasing shares in an exploratory oil well leased by the Jensen Petroleum Company. In the bottom right-hand corner, above the signature of the Attorney who had executed the certificate, was the name "Lester Jensen, Leasee."

Mathieu turned to Doctor Marsh and asked, "Have you ever heard of a 'Lester Jensen?'"

A look of recognition crossed Marsh's face. "Ah, yes, of course! I thought the victim looked familiar. He's Lester Jensen. He's notorious for over-selling shares in oil wells that never seem to pan out. He comes from a long line of hucksters just like him in the oil and gas business. The California Corporations Commission has investigated him numerous times for fraud, but he always seems to wiggle out of it."

"Does he own the Jensen Oil gas stations around town?"

"Yes, those are his," Marsh said. "And this is not the first attempt on his life."

"What do you mean?"

"Several years ago, someone threw a firebomb through a window of his Los Feliz mansion, but it was a dud and didn't ignite."

Mathieu nodded as if remembering something else. "Is he the guy in those billboards wearing a cowboy hat and a three-piece suit sitting on a horse with the slogan 'For More Horsepower buy Jensen Oil?'"

Doctor Marsh laughed. "Yes, that's him. Jensen was quite the character … but it seems to have finally caught up with him."

"He must have made a lot of enemies over the years," Mathieu said.

"I heard in one of his scams Jensen sold over two million shares in a worthless oil well. So, you've got your work cut out for you, Detective."

Mathieu shook his head in dismay. "Going through his client list isn't going to help."

"I agree," Marsh said. "But Jensen was straightforward in his own way. I remember one of his billboard ads said, 'This Isn't an Investment for the Meek.'"

Mathieu laughed. "Practically told people it was a scam."

"Yes, but for most men, that's a dare," Marsh said. "What he was really saying was, 'Do you have what it takes to become rich?'"

"Did Jensen have a wife?"

"He's had several," Marsh said. "Usually divorces them when they turn thirty-five."

"The wives might be a good place to start," Mathieu said almost to himself, then, changing subjects, asked, "What's your estimate on the time of death?"

Marsh looked at his watch. "It's just past midnight. Based on the lividity I saw on his back, I'd say between 7 p.m. and 8 p.m. yesterday evening. But I'll know more when I get him back to the morgue."

"Thanks, Doctor. Let me know if you find anything else."

"Certainly," Marsh said as he stood to leave. "By the way, I saw a friend of yours the other night when I dined at your father's restaurant."

"Who was that?" Mathieu asked in a curious tone.

"Lady Caroline Astor."

"Ah," Mathieu said. The mere mention of Caroline's name still caused him pain.

"She was there with her husband and their three-month-old daughter, a beautiful child. She has her mother's red hair and porcelain skin."

"I hope my father didn't bore Lady Caroline and her husband by boasting about me," Mathieu said.

"No, Pierre was on his best behavior, but I did overhear Lady Caroline ask him to say hello to you."

Mathieu nodded. He'd be spared that conversation. He rarely spoke to his father.

"Let me walk you back to your car, Doctor," Mathieu said. "I have to speak with the foreman before I leave."

When they arrived at the foreman's shack, they parted ways. Mathieu stood in the doorway of the cramped wooden structure and peered in. Roy Duncan sat at an ancient rolltop desk, finishing the list.

Roy looked up and said, "Almost done, Detective. Give me five more minutes."

"Sure," Mathieu said as he stepped outside to look around.

Behind the foreman's shack was an open-air toolshed with a covered roof and a haphazard collection of saws, wrenches, and pipe cutters filling its only wall.

Beside the shed stood a bunkhouse with a narrow porch. Two workmen in oil-stained clothes sat on the porch smoking as they rested their backs against the peeling plank wall.

To kill some time, Mathieu climbed further up the hill, where he spotted a strange sight. At the highest point, surrounded by three pumpjacks, sat what looked like a two-story brick Craftsman mansion in the middle of the oil field.

The hulking structure had a green gambrel roof and white-trimmed windows and doors. It must have been grand once but looked neglected now with its peeling paint and missing roof tiles.

Intrigued, Mathieu walked closer to get a better view. The house had a steep driveway up to a porched entrance in the front and another driveway in the back that led to a dilapidated rust-colored garage. Next to the garage, someone had built a covered corral where two quarter horses, one paint and one bay, stood munching on a hay bale.

From his vantage point, Mathieu spotted a lone light coming from a dormer window on the second floor. As Mathieu stared up at the house, he heard the sound of footsteps and turned to see Roy Duncan approaching.

"Here's the list, Detective," Roy said, handing it to him. "Sorry, it took a little longer than I thought to find all the addresses."

"Thanks, Roy. No need to apologize," Mathieu said, then pointing at the house, asked, "What's the deal with this mansion sitting in the middle of an oil field?"

Roy laughed. "It's a long story, Detective. My men call it the haunted house, but I call it the rumor mansion."

"Why?"

"Because there are so many rumors about it. One is that it's haunted by the ghost of the man who built it. Another is that Otis Gray, the founder of the *LA Times*, used to keep his mistresses up here."

Mathieu scoffed. "What's the real story?"

"A businessman named Charles Rand bought this lot in 1910 and built his mansion on it a few years later. At the time, there was nothing up here but a sheep pasture and this magnificent view of Los Angeles and the Hollywood Hills.

"In 1917, Rand married a much younger woman who, as it turned out, was still married to her first husband. When Rand discovered that, he divorced her, and soon after, he 'accidentally' shot himself. Rand's mother inherited the mansion but sold it to an eccentric Silent Film star, Marion Gray. The actress lived here during the early twenties. In 1924, Standard Oil dug their first well up here and struck oil. The well happened to be on her property. Standard Oil dug two more wells, which were also on her property. Because of that, she became amazingly wealthy."

"Why didn't she move? Nobody that rich would want to live in an oil field."

"She did move," Roy said. "She bought a mansion in Los Feliz, but she held on to the property to retain the rights to the oil revenue. She owns three of the most productive wells in the entire field."

"Does anyone live there now?"

"Yes, she hired a caretaker who used to be her chauffeur."

"What's he like?"

"He's a bit of a character. He tells a lot of stories, some believable, some not. Apparently, when he was younger, he was Tom Mix's stunt double in all of his Westerns."

"What's his name?"

"Hank Laramie."

"Does he cause you any trouble?"

"No," Roy said, shaking his head. "Hank mostly keeps to himself, and he's usually drunk. But when he's sober, he rides the hills patrolling the property, so he's actually pretty useful."

Mathieu nodded. "I noticed the horses in the back."

"Yeah, Hank loves to ride," Roy said. "He told me before he became a stuntman, he used to be a rodeo rider."

"Did you see him riding on the property tonight?" Mathieu asked.

"No," Roy said, shaking his head with a smile. "Hank never rides at night."

"Why not?"

Roy chuckled. "He's afraid of ghosts."

4

The Lay of the Land

The next morning, Mathieu called his friend Sergeant Gus Lombardi. He asked Gus to send a couple of his officers to take statements from the Inglewood Oil Field employees.

Mathieu told him he'd leave the crew list with Enya. He asked him to pay special attention to the recently fired employees. Gus said he'd get his men on it and that he would personally interview the fired oil field workers.

After that, Mathieu called Fred Wilson, and they returned to the Inglewood Oil Field to search for clues in the daylight.

The oil field dominated the Baldwin Hills on both sides of a dirt road named La Cienega, which meant swamp in Spanish. The hills were an anomaly, an island of high ground in an otherwise flat marshy plain surrounded by open farmland.

The oil field was just as depressing to look at during the day as at night. It was essentially a factory without walls and all the uglier because of it. Acres of wooden derricks covered the hillsides, clustered in groups of threes and fours like greedy hundred-foot monsters sucking the earth dry. The air smelled foul with the stench of petroleum.

The relentless piston action of the oil derricks seemed to have a life of its own. Once started, they could seemingly continue long after humanity was gone, spewing geysers of oil in the air and befouling the land with a layer of thick black tar.

Mathieu drove his Buick Phaeton up La Cienega. He spotted a service road off to his right, which he took. The service road ended near a tar pit, where Mathieu and Fred parked and got out.

From here, a series of makeshift dirt tracks, wide enough for service trucks, snaked their way into the oil field. The paths, surrounded on both sides by low scrub and oak trees, led to clearings where oil derricks and pumpjacks stood.

Taking the path on their left, Mathieu and Fred hiked up the rutted, dusty trail as it curved right past a small shed, then switchbacked up the slope for a quarter of a mile toward the site where the night watchman had found the victim's body the previous evening.

They scanned the trail as they ascended, but it appeared a truck had driven through recently and obliterated any footprints other than their own. Mathieu also checked for horseshoe prints and scat but didn't spot any.

It took them less than ten minutes to hike up the twisting track. The hill was steep, but the switchbacks made the climb easy. And the dense brush would have provided cover for anyone coming up the path.

It may not have been the exact route the killer used, but Mathieu was confident it would have been easy for someone to bring Jensen's body up one of these trails at night and go unnoticed.

Mathieu had asked Roy Duncan, the foreman, to leave the pumpjack turned off so they could search the area again. While Fred dusted the pumpjack's walking beam for prints, Mathieu searched the ground for drag marks, cigarette butts, or other clues that might aid the investigation.

But the ground was so trampled over by their own footprints from the night before that Mathieu quickly realized it was fruitless. Fortunately, Fred found a partial palm print on the pumpjack, so it wasn't a wasted effort.

When they finished, they started back down the trail. They scanned the ground again as they descended but found nothing. When they reached the bottom, they passed the same shed they'd seen coming up. It was small, maybe six feet by six feet, with an open wall on the north side.

Mathieu peered in and saw shovels, rakes, and pipe wrenches scattered on the ground. In one corner, he spotted a coil of rope that looked similar to the type used to tie the victim.

Mathieu knelt to examine it. One end had been roughly cut and frayed. As he picked the rope up to show to Fred, he spotted a large piece of cardboard under it with writing.

He bent closer to read it. Someone had used a paintbrush to scrawl in red: "Death to the Oil Barons – Jensen is just the first!"

5

The Black Widow

Mathieu dropped Wilson off at headquarters, then drove west to Los Feliz to inform Lester Jensen's widow of his death. Jensen's house sat on a knoll south of Los Feliz Boulevard.

A circular lane ringed the top of the hill where three estates, in addition to Jensen's, dominated the landscape. Jensen's was a two-story Spanish Revival-style home with a four-car garage and a manicured lawn with a pool in the back. Mathieu pulled into the wide driveway, parked near the garage, and got out.

Jensen may have been a con man, but he'd had exquisite taste. A red Spanish tile roof and attractive windows framed in dark wood accentuated the home's thick white stucco walls. A narrow balcony ran the length of the back of the house above the garages. Directly above where Mathieu stood was a covered outdoor porch on the second story that wrapped around the house on two sides like a lookout tower.

Mathieu took the wide flagstone steps on his left past a mature cedar to the next level, where he turned right and took another set of steps to the arched, dark-timbered front door.

He knocked, and soon after, a thin, austere-looking man in his sixties opened the door. Mathieu assumed he was the butler. He showed him his badge and asked to see Mrs. Jensen. The butler informed him she was in the pool area, then stood aside so Mathieu could enter.

The butler escorted Mathieu through the tastefully appointed home, then down two flights of stairs to the back lawn to meet Jensen's widow. The widow was relaxing on a chaise lounge beside the pool, wearing a white sundress pulled up to her thighs and a wide-brimmed sun hat.

The rich seemed to love their swimming pools, Mathieu thought. They provided an impression of wealth and the good life, even more than a grand house. And the more luxuriant the pool and its setting, the more compelling the statement. Such was the case with Jensen's estate.

Mrs. Jensen made her own kind of statement with her raven hair, long, taut legs, silken skin, and curves that held the eye.

The butler stopped in front of Mrs. Jensen's chaise lounge, nodded in a deferential way, and said, "Madam, you have a visitor." Then, with a slight bow, he turned and went back to the house.

Mrs. Jensen didn't speak for a moment as she lowered her black sunglasses and appraised Mathieu with piercing blue eyes. Running her eyes the length of his tall, lean frame, she said with an ironic smile, "It's just like Lester to send a handsome young man to serve my divorce papers."

"Were you expecting divorce papers, Mrs. Jensen?"

"Why, of course," she said in a matter-of-fact tone. "I turn thirty-five next week … my time is up." Then, sighing, she added, "But I will miss this pool."

"What about your husband?" Mathieu asked with a quizzical look.

"Why would I miss that ass of a man," she said with bitterness.

Mathieu wondered if she'd be so open with her feelings if she knew he was a policeman. Testing that, he said, "I'm not here to serve you divorce papers, Mrs. Jensen. I'm Detective Mathieu from the LAPD."

A smile broke out on her face. "So, has Lester finally been arrested? Oh god, how I've secretly longed for this day."

Mrs. Jensen was so blasé Mathieu wondered if it was all an act. Attempting to shock her, he said, "No, Mrs. Jensen, your husband hasn't been arrested … he's dead."

Without a hint of sorrow or surprise, Mrs. Jensen asked, "Did someone kill him, or did he commit suicide?"

"Why do you assume it was either murder or suicide?"

"Because Lester had a lot of enemies; he was a well-known swindler."

"Why'd you marry him then?"

"Because he was a *successful* swindler, Detective, and I always follow the money."

"And your suicide remark?"

"Lester was deathly afraid of going to prison. He told me if the authorities ever got too close, he'd kill himself before going to jail."

"Your husband didn't commit suicide, Mrs. Jensen. He was murdered."

"Ah," she said, pursing her lips. "Do you know who killed him?"

"No."

"You've got your work cut out for you, Detective. There's no shortage of candidates."

"Do you stand to inherit the house?"

"Why, of course," she said with a laugh. "Why else would I sign on to marry Lester, knowing he would take my best years, then divorce me when I turned thirty-five? That was part of the deal. If he died before I turned thirty-five, I'd get the house. It was a calculated risk, but I'm a gambler like Lester was."

"May I ask where you were last night, Mrs. Jensen?"

"Certainly," she said with a confident smile. "And please call me Jacqueline. Last night, I was at a dinner party at Phillip Chandler's Tudor Manor, just below the Griffith Observatory. I assume you've heard of Phillip. He's one of Harry Chandler's sons, the publisher of the *LA Times*."

"Yes, I've heard of Phillip," Mathieu said with a noncommittal nod.

Mrs. Jensen stared at Mathieu for a few seconds, then, with a look of recognition, asked, "What did you say your last name was again?"

"Mathieu."

"Are you the son of Pierre Mathieu, who owns the famous *Mathieu's* restaurant in Frenchtown?"

"Yes."

"I thought I recognized you," Jacqueline said with a smile. "I've seen your picture in the newspapers. You're Harry Chandler's godson, the famous detective. Phillip talks about you all the time. Although I think he's jealous that his father takes more interest in you than he does in him.

"You were Lady Caroline Astor's knight in shining armor when she was almost killed in that accident on Mulholland Drive. I saw you two together at her birthday party before the accident occurred. Lady Caroline was radiant when she was with you that night," Jacqueline said. "But sadly, she married that wealthy film producer instead."

Ignoring her remark, Mathieu asked, "Were you surprised that your husband didn't come home last night?"

"No, I'm always grateful when he doesn't," Jacqueline said.

"Why is that?"

"So, I don't have to endure him pawing all over me."

"And who do you turn to for that?" Mathieu asked, assuming she must have a lover.

Jacqueline's face brightened. She put her hands around her left knee and pulled it seductively toward her chest, revealing the back of her shapely thigh as she did. She held his eyes for a moment and asked, "Is that an offer, Detective?"

"No, Mrs. Jensen," Mathieu said. "I'm just trying to understand the dynamics of your marriage."

"That's simple, Detective. I was just part of Lester's public fantasy," she said in a no-nonsense manner. "I looked good on Lester's arm. That's why he always traded up when his wives turned thirty-five. He had to keep the fantasy alive."

"How many wives has he had?"

"I'm number three," she said.

"Do you know who number four will be?"

"No ... but I assume he's been auditioning," Jacqueline said with a knowing smile.

"Do you know where these 'auditions' take place?"

"I assume at his bungalow in Laurel Canyon ... that's where I auditioned."

"What's the address?" Mathieu asked, poised to write it in his notebook.

"I don't think it has an address. It's where the old Lookout Mountain Inn used to be before it burned down. Lester bought the land cheap and built his bungalow there. It's isolated but has a great view of the city. To get there, you take Lookout Mountain Road off Laurel Canyon, and after a mile, turn left onto a dirt track that winds up to the top of the mountain.

"The bungalow is easy to spot. It's just after a wide horseshoe bend in the road. It's a spooky place if you ask me. Like a bandit's hideout, but Lester liked it for its isolation and because very few people knew he owned it."

"Did your husband have any enemies?" Mathieu asked, even though he knew the answer.

Jacqueline laughed. "As I said before, Lester was a known swindler. Everyone who lost their life savings investing in one of his failed oil wells probably hated him."

"When did you last see your husband?"

"Yesterday morning at breakfast?"

"Where was he going?"

25

"To his office, I assume," Jacqueline said with a shrug.

"And where is that?"

"In the Richfield Oil Building on Flower Street, Seventh floor, Suite 721."

"Why does he have office space in the Richfield building? Aren't they competitors?"

"Theoretically, they are," Jacqueline said with raised eyebrows, "but Jensen Oil is small change compared to Richfield. And the real reason is because Richfield needed the money.

"They went into receivership during the Depression and had to lay off a lot of people, leaving them with excess office space. Plus, they're fighting a hostile takeover from Sinclair Oil, who's trying to prevent Standard Oil of California from taking them over. So, it was a win for both of them; Richfield got some well-needed cash, and Lester got a prestigious address."

"Who is Mr. Jensen's office manager?"

A grin broke out on Jacqueline's face. "Florence Drake ... you're going to love her."

"Why is that?"

"You'll see ... she's a true believer."

6

The Office Manager

After interviewing the widow, Mathieu headed to Jensen's office in the Richfield Tower on South Flower Street in downtown Los Angeles. Mathieu parked his Buick Phaeton across from the entrance and got out.

Gazing up at the black twelve-story Art Deco office tower, Mathieu thought it looked like a secular cathedral with its gold-trimmed structural columns that rose ten stories high, topped by golden terracotta figurines that looked either like saints or gargoyles, depending on your point of view. But there was no ambiguity in the building's black and gold motif, signifying oil as black gold.

Above the tenth floor, the building's silhouette contracted into a tower. An oil-derrick-shaped spire capped it with a vertical Richfield logo and a light beacon visible for over a hundred miles at night.

Mathieu crossed the street, walked under a thirty-foot-high archway to the metal-framed glass access doors, and entered.

The lobby was easily twenty feet high, with polished green and black marble walls. Mathieu strode past a barbershop and cigar store on his left toward the bronze Art Deco elevators, where he caught the next car up to the seventh floor.

Arriving, Mathieu turned to his left and walked down a wide hallway with the same marble walls and rubber-tile flooring as the lobby. He found Suite 721 at the northwest corner of the building, where an attractive etched plaque read, "Jensen Petroleum Headquarters."

After entering, Mathieu took a moment to take in the space. It was light and airy, with diffuse sunlight from a bank of windows overlooking the building's ten-story atrium. A row of typists and salesmen at polished desks lined the length of the room. Large chalkboards displaying sales quotas hung on the wall facing them.

Mathieu approached the reception desk to his right. The receptionist was on the phone. She appeared to be in her mid-twenties with short brown hair done up in pin curls and a scowl on her otherwise attractive face. She wore metal headphones attached to a microphone harness while holding a pencil poised mid-air.

After finishing the call, the receptionist looked up at Mathieu with a strained smile and asked, "Do you have an appointment, sir?"

"No," Mathieu said, showing her his badge. "My name is Detective Mathieu. I'm from the LAPD."

Her eyes narrowed, and her guarded smile dissolved into a frown. "How can I help you?" she asked in a frosty tone.

Ignoring her attitude, Mathieu took out his notepad and asked, "May I have your name, please?" He didn't care what it was but knew the question would alarm her.

And it did, as she quickly replied, "Samantha Hathaway."

"Miss or Mrs.?"

"Miss," she said self-consciously.

Mathieu made her wait as he wrote it down, then said, "Miss Hathaway, I'd like to speak with Florence Drake."

"What is it in regard to?" she asked with a sullen expression.

"A murder investigation."

Miss Hathaway's eyes widened in what looked like either fear or shock. "Whose murder?" she asked as her voice cracked slightly.

"That's a subject I need to discuss with Miss Drake ... not you," Mathieu said evenly.

"Yes ... of course," she said, seemingly taken aback. "I'll take you to her now."

Miss Hathaway rose from her seat, removed her headphones and microphone harness, then gestured for Mathieu to follow her. They walked down the line of typists near the windows, Mathieu noting that they were all uniformly young and attractive.

When they reached the far end of the room, Mathieu saw two partially enclosed offices, with glass partitions rising halfway up to the twelve-foot-high ceiling. The offices were perpendicular to each other. The larger one on the right was empty, which Mathieu assumed was Jensen's.

They stopped in front of the office near the window. Miss Hathaway knocked, waited for a reply, then opened the door and entered.

Mathieu watched as she approached a woman sitting at the desk, partially obscured from his view by a coat rack. The receptionist bent down, whispered in the woman's ear, and pointed through the glass partition at Mathieu. The woman gestured with her left hand, after which the receptionist opened the door and said, "Miss Drake will see you now, Detective."

The receptionist stood aside as Mathieu entered, then closed the door and retreated in silence.

The office manager stood as he entered, extended her right hand, and said, "I'm Florence Drake, Detective. How may I be of assistance?"

Miss Drake was not what Mathieu had expected from the widow's description. He'd expected a woman in her late fifties with a pinched face and a tight bun of gray hair.

Instead, he was confronted with a slender woman in her early thirties with large light brown eyes, who looked like a stern but

29

beautiful schoolteacher, wearing a peach-colored linen dress with a fanciful bow tied in front, her lithe figure in stark contrast with her intense, no-nonsense gaze. She wore a chocolate-brown hat with a red band, cocked at an angle, over her mid-length brunette hair, accentuating her high cheekbones.

You only had to see her face once to burn it into your memory. It was the kind of face you'd think about before falling asleep, and you'd sleep well. Something about her stillness and the intensity of her gaze held Mathieu's attention.

Taking her delicate hand in his and shaking it, Mathieu said, "I'm Detective Mathieu from the LAPD, Miss Drake. I'm here to ask you some questions related to a murder investigation I'm conducting. May I sit down, please?"

"Of course," she said, gesturing to the lone chair in front of her desk.

When they were both seated, Miss Drake asked, "How does your investigation concern our firm, Detective?"

"The victim is someone you know."

"Who?" she asked in a business-like tone.

Mathieu hesitated for a moment as he held her gaze and then, in a quiet voice, said, "Your employer."

"Lester?" she asked, her eyes widening in shock.

"Yes … I'm sorry to inform you, Miss Drake, that Mr. Jensen has been murdered."

Miss Drake didn't react but instead became deathly still, her gaze seemingly focused inward, not at her surroundings. She stayed that way for quite a while as Mathieu observed her in silence. She didn't cry, bury her face in her hands, or show any signs of distress, just a detached stillness.

Finally, taking a deep breath, she wiped her hands across her face, sat up straight, and asked, "How was Lester killed?"

"I'm sorry," Mathieu said, "but I can't share that information with you now, Miss Drake."

"I understand," she said, nodding her head.

"But I need to ask you some questions … if you feel up to it," Mathieu said.

"Thank you for your concern, Detective, but I'm fine. Please proceed."

"When was the last time you saw Mr. Jensen?"

Miss Drake pursed her lips as if remembering and said, "Yesterday afternoon around three, we were reviewing the monthly sales figures for our Jensen Oil service stations."

"Did Mr. Jensen seem upset or worried in any way?"

"No," she said, shaking her head. "He was his usual self … upbeat and positive."

"Are you aware if Mr. Jensen received any death threats recently?"

"If he did, he didn't share them with me … Lester never showed fear … that was part of his persona."

"You seem to be implying that it was an act."

"Of course, it was an act, Detective," she said dismissively. "Lester was a master showman. That's how he got rich. That and his ability to discover successful oil drilling sites others missed."

"And what about Mrs. Jensen?" Mathieu asked. "What do you think of her?"

"Jacqueline played her part," she said with a hint of disdain. "And it appears she'll be rewarded handsomely for it by inheriting Lester's home."

"So, you knew about their arrangement?"

"Of course," she said with a shrug. "Lester and I didn't keep financial secrets from each other."

"Did Mr. Jensen have any enemies?"

Miss Drake scoffed. "I'm sure they counted in the thousands, but I doubt any of them had the courage and conviction to kill him. You have to be strong-willed to do something like that, and most of Lester's detractors are weaklings. Lester detested weaklings … and so do I."

"What was your relationship with Mr. Jensen?"

"Are you asking if I slept with him, Detective?" she asked with a knowing smile. "There's no need to be shy."

Mathieu smiled at her straightforwardness. "Yes, that's what I'm asking, Miss Drake?"

"The answer is no ... never. Our relationship was strictly business."

"What about the rest of the female staff? I noticed they all seem to be quite attractive."

Miss Drake smiled broadly. "Lester tried all of them on like socks ... and just as quickly discarded them when he was satiated."

"Did that cause any hard feelings?"

"When it did, we fired them immediately."

"Did he have any favorites?"

"Not to my knowledge."

"When did Mr. Jensen leave yesterday?"

"After our meeting."

"Do you know where he was going?"

"He told me he was going to his getaway bungalow in Laurel Canyon."

"Alone?"

"I have no idea," Miss Drake said with a shrug.

"Where were you between seven and ten yesterday evening?"

"At home."

"Can anyone verify that?"

Miss Drake smiled. "I'm sorry, Detective, but no ... only my cat."

"Where do you live?"

"In Laurel Canyon," she said simply.

"What's your address?"

"8012 Lark Lane ... but please call ahead if you plan to drop by, Detective."

"I doubt that will be necessary."

"Pity," she said, holding his eye.

"Do you live close to Mr. Jensen's bungalow?"

"Yes and no," she said cryptically.

"What do you mean?" Mathieu asked.

"I live near the Country Store. Lester's bungalow is on top of the mountain. It's a torturous drive between them. I rarely go up there. I'm afraid of the drive up … but I have a spare key if you need it."

"Yes, thank you. I might," Mathieu said with a nod. "One final question. Do you know who will be in charge of running the company in the future?"

"I assume I will, Detective, but I don't know for how long."

"What do you mean?"

"We're heavily in debt and drowning in lawsuits. I doubt we'll last six months without Lester."

"But you strike me as an accomplished businesswoman, Miss Drake."

"I am," she said, "but we need a miracle worker, and unfortunately, that's not my skill set. Lester was the magician. He could pull a rabbit out of the hat whenever he needed."

7

Lookout Mountain

It was late afternoon when Mathieu left the Richfield Building. He thought about going to headquarters to brief his boss, Chief "Bull" Braden. But instead, he decided to head to Jensen's bungalow in Laurel Canyon before the light faded. Increasingly, Mathieu suspected the bungalow might have been where Jensen had been killed or kidnapped.

Mathieu took Sunset Boulevard west to Laurel Canyon. He turned right at Haverfield Drugs, housed in an attractive stone building with Churrigueresque molding over the corner doorway, and headed north, passing the expansive Harper Ranch off to the left.

The recently graded dirt road was narrow and winding, but at least the surface was smoother than he remembered. As Mathieu entered the canyon, with its year-round spring-fed stream, he could feel the temperature drop, cooled by the willows, oaks, and sycamores shading the lane.

A mile up, he passed the one-story red brick Canyon Store. He remembered his father telling him it was originally a lodge for deer hunters who used to pay to hunt in the valley.

A few minutes later, after crossing a narrow stone bridge, Mathieu came to a tree-covered junction with Lookout Mountain

Road and turned left. Off to the right, the Bungalow Inn's rustic, wood-plank buildings sat along the stream bed. It was cool and shady here with a light breeze.

Heading west, Mathieu bounced along the dusty, rutted road for another quarter of a mile until he reached a spur on the left, where he skidded through a tight turn and entered the adjoining valley that headed due south.

He continued on the narrow track, passing the occasional isolated cabin until the end of the valley, where the road veered sharply to the right as it followed a steep ridgeline that switchbacked to the top.

The Buick Phaeton clawed its way up in first gear, the engine straining, tires slipping on the loose surface. The hillside and brush closed in from both sides, making the ride feel claustrophobic and disorienting. The only thing Mathieu could see was the next bend in the road, but no farther.

Finally, after fifteen minutes of torturous climbing, Mathieu emerged onto a narrow ridgeline where the ground cover thinned, and the vistas opened up.

The dirt path straightened here, heading southeast along the top of the ridge to a peninsula, where Mathieu spotted Jensen's bungalow perched on a knoll with a commanding view of the city. The sun was starting to set. It would be dark soon.

Mathieu parked in front of the two-story bungalow and got out. He'd seen postcards of the old Lookout Mountain Inn. Jensen had imitated the style but on a reduced scale.

The dark brown wood-plank building had a gabled roof, dormer windows on the second floor, and a covered porch that wrapped around the building at ground level.

Mathieu walked under the eaves toward the front door. The office manager had given him the spare key, but when he spotted the partially open door, he pulled out his Colt revolver instead. He pushed the door open with his left hand, hesitated, listened for movement, then entered cautiously.

No one was in the living room or den, which he could see through the bookcase colonnade between the two rooms. Off to the left, the dining room, framed by a pedestal colonnade, was also empty.

Mathieu stood in the center of the living room for a few moments and listened. The house was quiet, almost too quiet. Perhaps it was the isolation, he thought. Mathieu holstered his weapon and scanned the interior.

The craftsmen-style bungalow seemed designed for a man with rich dark wood ceiling beams, wainscotting, chair rail molding, expensive leather chairs, and a large brick fireplace on the west wall. He searched the ground floor, examining each room, including the kitchen. Everything was immaculately clean and neat, with no signs of a struggle.

Then, he headed up the stairs to the second floor. Arriving on the landing, Mathieu entered the master bedroom. As with the ground floor, the windows were large and bathed in warm light from the setting sun. Even with the gabled roof, the room was light and airy, with a great view of the city.

Mathieu assumed this was the "audition" room as he looked at the large Mission-style bed with its crumpled sheets and pillows scattered about. The room smelled of sex and perfume. A satin slip, bra, and panties lay on the floor near an overturned lamp. And a coil of rope similar to what Jensen had been tied with lay on the bed.

As Mathieu looked around the room, he was sure this was where Jensen had been kidnapped. But what happened to the woman? Was she a victim or an accomplice?

8

A Chewing Out

At headquarters the next morning, Mathieu called Fred Wilson and told him he'd found the crime scene. He asked Fred to take his forensic team up to Jensen's bungalow in Laurel Canyon and search for prints and any other evidence he could find. He emphasized the importance of looking for clues that might help identify the woman Jensen was with when he was kidnapped.

Mathieu warned Fred about the road, advising him to take two vehicles in case one got stuck. He told him he'd leave the bungalow key with Enya.

Then, he called Phillip Chandler to verify Mrs. Jensen's alibi for the night of the murder. After hanging up with Phillip, Mathieu stopped by Enya's desk to drop off the key before briefing his boss.

It was a good thing he did because before he could give her the key, Enya looked up with her freckled face and whispered, "Uncle is steaming mad."

Enya rarely referred to Bull as her uncle and then only when one of them was in trouble.

"What's he angry about?" Mathieu asked.

Enya glanced at Bull's closed door, then back at Mathieu and said, "Because you didn't brief him yesterday about Lester Jensen's murder."

"But I was busy from dawn to dusk yesterday," Mathieu said, pleading his case. "I was at the Inglewood Oil Field in the morning looking for evidence. I interviewed Jensen's widow and his office manager in the afternoon. Then, just before sunset, I drove to Jensen's bungalow in Laurel Canyon, where I discovered that's where he'd been kidnapped."

"I understand, but Chief Davis has been hounding Bull for information about the case. Apparently, the Chairman of Standard Oil called Davis into his office yesterday."

Mathieu shook his head in disgust. "Jesus, so now we're a division of Standard Oil?"

"You could have called," Enya said gently.

"You're right ... I should have," Mathieu said, conceding the point. "How angry is he on the 'red' scale?"

"Redder than my hair," Enya said with a freckled smile.

Mathieu shook his head in dismay. "I'm in so much trouble."

"Yep."

"You seem to be enjoying this."

"Not at all, but now you can understand what my childhood was like."

"By the way," Mathieu said, "this is the key to Jensen's bungalow. Please give it to Fred when he stops by."

"Okay, I'll be sure he gets it."

Mathieu let out a sigh. "I might as well get this over with."

"Good luck," Enya said with a grin. "Just remember, he'll bite your head off, but he'll never fire you."

"That's not much comfort at the moment," Mathieu said as he turned and walked to Bull's office door, where he hesitated, took a deep breath, and knocked.

"Come in!" came the quick reply.

Mathieu felt like he was ten years old, stepping into a confessional as he entered Bull's office.

"It's nice of you to stop by, Detective," Bull said, but the words belied the beet-red anger on his face. The veins on Bull's thick neck appeared on the verge of popping. Even his pomaded hair looked angry.

"I'm sorry I didn't call yesterday," Mathieu said immediately. "I was chasing down evidence and witnesses all day."

"Sit!" Bull said in response.

Mathieu sat like an obedient penitent.

"Do you know who called me yesterday asking to be briefed on the case?"

"Enya told me Chief Davis did, sir," Mathieu said.

"Correct, but do you know who else called?"

"No, sir."

"The mayor."

"Ah … that doesn't sound pleasant," Mathieu said at a loss for words.

"No, it wasn't," Bull said. "But it got worse."

"How so, sir?"

"Someone even more important called," Bull said, seemingly enjoying drawing out Mathieu's misery.

"Who was that, sir?" Mathieu asked, thinking he wouldn't get off with three Hail Marys for this.

"The governor," Bull said.

"The governor, sir?" Mathieu asked, convinced that excommunication, or worse yet, transfer to traffic duty, would be his fate.

"Yes, the Governor of California called. Do you know what progress I was able to share with the esteemed gentleman?" Bull asked, looking Mathieu in the eye.

"No, sir, I don't," Mathieu said, avoiding his gaze.

"Nothing!" Bull said as he pounded his desk. "Not a damn thing, and do you know why?" he asked rhetorically. "Because my best detective didn't call or stop by to brief me."

Mathieu couldn't think of anything to say in his own defense, so he asked, "What did you do, sir?"

"What do you think I did?" Bull asked. "I made shit up. This isn't my first rodeo, Mathieu."

"Did that work, sir?" Mathieu asked with genuine curiosity.

Bull smiled for the first time since Mathieu entered. "Yes, I think it worked quite well," he said, seemingly pleased with himself. "But now that you're here, perhaps you can enlighten me on what progress you've actually made on the case."

"Yes, of course, sir. I discovered quite a lot yesterday."

"I'm all ears," Bull said as he rocked back in his chair and stared at Mathieu.

Mathieu recounted the interview with the widow, her casual attitude, her alibi that she'd been at Phillip Chandler's house and that she stood to inherit Jensen's house because he "conveniently" died a week before he was going to divorce her.

"The widow was that cold-blooded?" Bull asked.

"Colder than a rattlesnake, sir," Mathieu said.

"Did you check her alibi?"

"Yes, I called Phillip Chandler a few minutes ago."

"What did he have to say?"

"Phillip said Jacqueline was there all evening. According to him, she was the life of the party, telling one bawdy story after another to keep everyone entertained. But he did add there was one odd thing."

"What was that?"

"Phillip told me that usually when Jacqueline came without Jensen, which was most of the time, she brought along a 'friend.' But he wasn't there that night."

"Who was it?"

"An oily type, as Phillip described him, with greased back hair and a black mustache."

"What's his name?"

"Fred Marlow."

Bull nodded in recognition. "Yeah, I've heard of him. He ran a speakeasy during Prohibition just outside the city limits on the 'County Strip.' But the Sheriff's Department never touched him because he paid them off. I've lost track of him. It might be good to check him out."

"Yes, sir. I will."

Then Mathieu told Bull about the office manager, her equally unemotional reaction, and that she would take over the firm. But she said it would probably go out of business soon without Jensen.

"So, we have at least two people with motives, the widow and the office manager," Bull said.

"Probably closer to fifteen to twenty thousand, sir."

"What do you mean?" Bull asked.

"That's a conservative estimate of how many people Jensen swindled in his phony oil drilling schemes, according to Bill Collins of the *LA Times,* who I talked to yesterday."

"So, too many suspects."

"Yes, sir," Mathieu said. "But it's usually someone close to the victim, not a stranger, as we both know."

"True," Bull said, nodding. "Concentrate on the widow and the office manager for now."

"Will do."

"What else did you learn?"

"That Jensen was most likely kidnapped from his Laurel Canyon bungalow the evening of the murder."

"Why do you think that?"

"Because I found a coil of rope in the bedroom that was similar to the rope used to tie him to the pumpjack. Furthermore, he was probably with a woman when it happened because there was the smell of sex and perfume in the room and women's lingerie lying on the floor."

"Any idea who the woman was?"

"No, sir. Not yet," Mathieu said, shaking his head. "I sent Fred up there to check for fingerprints and search for evidence."

"Do you think the woman was in on it?"

Mathieu shrugged. "It's hard to know, sir. She could have been, but she could also have been a victim. According to his wife and the office manager, Jensen slept around a lot."

"Anything else interesting?"

"Yes, sir," Mathieu said. "When Fred and I searched the oil field yesterday morning, we found another coil of rope and a hand-painted sign in a tool shed close to the pumpjack where Jensen's body was found."

"What did it say?"

"Death to the Oil Barons – Jensen is just the first!"

"Sweet, Jesus," Bull said, seemingly alarmed. "Where's the sign now?"

"Fred's team is analyzing it for prints and the type of paint used."

"You didn't mention that to Collins, did you?"

"No, of course not, Chief," Mathieu said, slightly offended. "But I wonder why the killer left it in the shed instead of hanging it on the pumpjack."

Bull looked up at the ceiling and sighed. He was silent for a moment, seemingly lost in thought, then looking at Mathieu, said, "Maybe the killer got interrupted before he could put it up, so he tossed it in the shed before leaving."

Mathieu shrugged. "It's possible, sir. But I hope he doesn't send a photo of it to the newspapers, or your phone will be ringing off the hook with calls from the governor's office."

9

A Gathering of Ravens

You don't go to an exclusive hotel to sleep. You go to escape reality. And if you're wealthy enough, you can escape for a long time. Such was the case with Edgar Mahoney.

He could have chosen the Ambassador, the Biltmore, or the Beverly Wilshire, among others, for an extended stay in Los Angeles.

But those were luxury hotels you went to if you wanted to be seen. If you didn't, you went to the Chateau Marmont, about which a studio head once said, "If you must get in trouble, do it at the Marmont."

The irony for a hotel known for its privacy is that the French Gothic-Revival chateau could be seen for miles, perched atop a steep slope rising above Sunset Boulevard, where it boomeranged southwest just past Havenhurst Drive.

This section of Sunset Boulevard was outside the city limits and a bit lawless because of it. During Prohibition, the area along the "County Strip" had been known for its speakeasies, brothels, and gambling joints.

The seven-story, L-shaped hotel with its pepperbox turret dominated the landscape at the base of the Hollywood Hills. The original owner had instructed the architects to take their inspiration from the Château d'Amboise in the Loire Valley in France.

It was a sunny afternoon as Edgar Mahoney floated along on pillowy whitewall tires in his burgundy 1933 Cadillac Series 452-C with the top down and the wind ruffling his thick salt-and-pepper gray hair.

After passing Havenhurst Drive, he glided up a narrow lane that split from Sunset Boulevard on the right. He wound up the tree-lined drive to the Chateau Marmont's main entrance, where he hopped out and tossed his key to the valet.

Tall, thin, and impeccably dressed, Edgar walked with an easy, confident gait beneath the cloister's Gothic arches toward the front door. Entering the lobby, he glanced to his left to see if there were any celebrities in the sitting room. There weren't—just a few well-coifed middle-aged women sharing tea at one of the tables.

The sitting room was cozy but not grand, with clusters of plush low seats, couches, and tables on a rust-colored carpet. The afternoon sun filtered through the arched windows, casting a warm glow on the pale yellow walls and honey-colored ceiling beams.

Without breaking stride, Edgar nodded to the young receptionist behind the front desk, who good-naturedly tossed him a green-tasseled key from the cubby behind her. It seemed like a well-choreographed routine as Edgar caught the key in one hand, spun it around on his index finger, and continued across the polished Spanish tile floor toward the bronze-clad elevators in the central tower.

Edgar pressed the UP button, then looked up at the half-moon dials. There was no movement. While he waited, he pivoted to the left and adjusted his tie in the gold-framed mirror hanging on the wall. A few moments later, hearing the ping of the elevator arrive, he pivoted back.

The elevator door nearest him slid open, and a blond vision with long, toned legs exited. She wore high heels and a cream-colored jersey dress that caressed the contours of her shapely figure. Edgar smiled in admiration, and the blond rewarded his good manners with a playful wink from her sea-blue eyes. He watched as she retreated with a seductive hip sway across the tile floor and out the front entranceway. God, how he loved this hotel!

Edgar stepped into the elevator cab with its bright red metal walls, the color of an English phone booth, and a half-length mirror that made it feel less claustrophobic. He pressed the brass button for the top floor, and the elevator began to rise. Arriving on the seventh floor, he exited and walked down the richly carpeted hallway, trimmed in royal blue, toward room 64.

Opening the door, Edgar entered the three-thousand-square-foot suite and paused in the marble-tiled foyer. The penthouse took up the entire top floor of the south wing, which looked over Sunset Boulevard. It looked like a one-story French country chateau perched atop the hotel, with a sloped roof, dormer windows, and a chimney.

The suite had a formal dining room, two bathrooms, two bedrooms, a dressing area, a kitchen, a grand piano, a wood-burning fireplace, and a fifteen-hundred-square-foot private terrace that wrapped around on three sides. Essentially, it was a French Chateau in the sky.

Edgar walked the length of the parquet hallway toward the living room, then stepped onto the terrace under the striped awning. He continued to the balcony's edge and leaned against the fleur-de-lys decorated railing to take in the view.

He could see downtown Los Angeles to his left, below him, the traffic on Sunset Boulevard, and to his right, the sun bouncing off the Pacific at the coast. He walked to the west side of the terrace and peaked over to see if Jean Harlow was sunbathing in the nude as she often did on the patio below. But alas, her chaise lounge was empty.

Edgar went back inside, made himself a dry martini, then returned to the terrace and sat in a comfortable rattan chair under the awning in front of a knee-high glass table. Five minutes later, he heard the door buzz and shouted back, "It's open!"

Moments later, his young assistant, Jeremy Daniels, stepped onto the terrace, out of breath. Jeremy looked harried, juggling three file folders in his right arm as he struggled to sit in the chair across from Edgar.

His butt hadn't hit the seat before Edgar said, "You're seven minutes late, Jeremy."

"Sorry, sir."

"Don't be sorry … be on time."

"Yes, sir," Jeremy said as perspiration glistened on his broad forehead. He brushed back a stray lock of jet-black hair on his pomaded head, took a moment to compose himself, and said, "I brought some files that need your attention."

Edgar glanced at the folders without touching them and said, "What's in them?"

"The first concerns a dairy farmer who owns the land next to one of your oil wells."

"Which field?" Edgar asked, although he already knew.

"The one west of the tar pits, sir."

"What's his complaint?"

"He claims his cows are dying and his son is getting sick because oil from our wells is running onto his property. He's threatening to sue us."

"Whose representing him?"

"Burns and Burns."

Edgar nodded in admiration. "Does he have any proof?"

"He has letters from his son's doctor that his son is developing asthma from the petroleum fumes and photos of dead cows covered in tar."

Edgar steepled his hands under his chin and asked, "Would he take a buyout?"

"Why would you want to buy his land, sir? It's worthless, with barely enough grass to feed his cows. Plus, I doubt he'll win his case in court."

"I'm feeling magnanimous," Edgar said with an enigmatic smile.

"Excuse me, sir, but you're never magnanimous. What aren't you telling me?"

Edgar smiled and said, "There's a substantial oil deposit under his pasture. I want him off before anyone else discovers it, especially Gilmore Oil."

"How do you know this?"

"I have my ways."

Jeremy hesitated for a moment, then asked, "So, it's not an accident his cows are dying?"

"It's difficult to tell," Edgar said with a shrug. "Just apologize to him and make him an offer."

"What if he doesn't accept?"

"Then perhaps all his cows *will* die," Edgar said.

Noticing Jeremy's shocked expression, Edgar added with a hint of impatience, "Just make him an offer that he'll have to accept. Understood?"

"Yes, sir."

"Good. What else do you have?" Edgar asked.

"Have you heard about Lester Jensen's murder?"

"It would be impossible not to," Edgar said. "It's been in all the newspapers."

"It's pretty spooky, sir, the way he was killed."

"I view it as an opportunity," Edgar said with hard eyes.

"What do you mean?" Jeremy asked.

"Jensen owned the rights to a few drilling plots he hid from his business partner."

"How do you know?"

"I hired a female P.I. to check Jensen out."

"Who?"

"Anita Cummings ... have you ever seen her?"

"Once at the Brown Derby," Jeremy said. "Every man in the room stared open-mouthed at her as she walked into the restaurant."

Edgar chuckled. "Anita has that effect."

"Did she sleep with him?" Jeremy asked like a naïve schoolboy.

Edgar shrugged. "A gentleman never asks, though I doubt it. Anita's a cunning tease. She usually doesn't need to."

"What did she learn?"

"That years ago, Jensen stumbled upon a field with a huge oil reserve underneath it."

"Why didn't he develop it?" Jeremy asked with a questioning look.

"Because he didn't have enough capital or expertise at the time. However, according to Anita, Jensen has recently started approaching potential partners to develop it without telling them exactly where it is. And he's been hiding all this from his office manager at Jensen Petroleum."

"What if he lied to Anita about it?" Jeremy asked. "Jensen was a notorious braggart and con artist."

"I know, but in this instance, I don't think he was lying," Edgar said.

"How can you be sure?"

"I can't," Edgar said with a shrug. "But my instinct tells me Jensen was telling the truth. Even a moron can get lucky. It happened with Edward Doheny, who discovered the first oil well in Los Angeles when he spotted a wagon wheel with tar on it and traced where it came from."

"Where is Jensen's alleged oil find?" Jeremy asked.

Edgar didn't answer at once. Instead, he reached for his martini and finished it in silence as he considered how much to reveal. "That's not relevant at the moment."

Jeremy's face showed a hint of disappointment at the answer, but he tried to recover by asking, "Did Jensen own it outright?"

"That's not clear," Edgar said. "He may have had other partners. I can't imagine he had enough money to buy the land himself."

"Who inherits Jensen's share?"

"That's not clear either," Edgar said. "But we're going to find out."

"How?" Jeremy asked.

"First, we're going to make offers to his ex-wives to purchase any oil fields he might have left them in his will. Take it off their hands in exchange for a cash buyout. Widows and ex-wives always need cash, especially Jensen's."

"But won't they get suspicious if a big oil company like ours approaches them to buy it?"

"Yes, I think they will," Edgar said with a smirk.

"But I thought you said you wanted to buy any fields they inherited."

"I do."

"Then how are we going to pull it off?"

"We'll have a small oil company approach Jensen's ex-wives to take the worthless fields off their hands."

"Which company?"

"Feldman Petroleum," Edgar said.

"I've never heard of Feldman Petroleum," Jeremy said.

"That's because it doesn't exist."

"Who's the owner of this non-existent company?"

"I am, of course," Edgar said with a self-satisfied grin. "But I hired someone to masquerade as president."

"Who?"

"Harry Fields."

"The washed-up silent film actor?"

"Yes," Edgar said, nodding his head.

"Do you think Harry can pull it off?" Jeremy asked.

"Yes, I do," Edgar said with a confident look. "Harry's a terrible actor, but he's excellent at disguises and a great liar."

"What if none of the widows inherited any of Jensen's fields?"

"Then we'll have to take other measures," Edgar said with dead eyes.

10

No One Cried

After surviving his meeting with Bull, Mathieu returned to his desk, collected his notes, and went to see Enya.

"How did it go with Bull?" she asked as he sat down.

"Not good, but at least he didn't take my badge away," Mathieu said with a sigh.

"And he never will," Enya said in a reassuring tone. "Do you need anything?"

"Yes, I need your help finding out what kind of man Jensen was."

"What do you mean?"

Mathieu rubbed his forehead and said, "No one I've talked to so far has expressed any grief about Jensen's murder. The widow seemed almost happy, and the office manager was focused only on the business. What kind of person was Jensen that those closest to him aren't distressed he's been murdered?"

"That might say more about the people around him than Jensen himself," Enya offered.

Mathieu shrugged. "Yeah, you're probably right ... but he picked them."

"How can I help?" Enya asked.

"I need you to do some research," Mathieu said. "We need to find out more about Jensen and those in his immediate circle."

"Where do you want to start?"

"Let's start with Jensen. Check whether he has an arrest record in Los Angeles or anywhere else."

"Okay," Enya said, taking notes.

"Then go to the Hall of Records and see how many lawsuits you can find against Jensen. I'm sure you'll find plenty. I'm most interested in the lawsuits that Jensen won and who the plaintiffs were.

"I want to start a list of who had an ax to grind against him. And while you're there, find out how many times he was married, who the ex-wives are, and if they still live in Los Angeles. According to his widow, she's wife number three."

"Sounds tedious but simple enough," Enya said.

Mathieu laughed. Enya didn't have a buffer between her thoughts and her mouth.

"Then see what you can find out about Jensen's background, where he was born, where he lived before coming to Los Angeles, and what kind of trouble he may have gotten into. I don't know where you can find this information, but perhaps in the *LA Times* microfiche archives. Call Francine at the *Times* if you need any help."

"Finally, something fun," Enya said with a grin. "Although I'll probably go cross-eyed scanning microfilm."

Mathieu laughed. "I'll find some way to make it up to you."

"Promises, promises, Mathieu, you haven't taken me on any adventures since we went to that Nazi bookstore in San Pedro."

"After which, I almost got fired because Bull found out the bouncer grabbed you after you left the store."

Enya shrugged. "But I wasn't hurt. You chased him away."

"But you could have been. I shouldn't have taken you there," Mathieu said. "This will have to do for now."

Enya crinkled her nose in disappointment and sighed. "Okay … what else do you need?"

Rubbing his chin, Mathieu said, "Find out as much as you can about Jensen's widow and the office manager."

"What are their names?"

"The widow's name is Jacqueline Jensen. I don't know her maiden name. She lives at 4342 Cedar Circle in Los Feliz and stands to inherit Jensen's house.

"And the office manager's name is Florence Drake, and she's in line to take over the business. But she told me it's in trouble financially and probably won't survive. Miss Drake is single and lives at 8012 Lark Lane in Laurel Canyon."

Enya raised her eyebrows. "Is Miss Drake pretty?" Enya asked. "You need someone to take your mind off Lady Caroline."

Ignoring the remark, Mathieu shrugged and said, "Yes, she's attractive but cold as an undertaker, but the same could be said of the widow, too."

"Sounds like Mr. Jensen surrounded himself with female sharks."

"That's a good way to put it," Mathieu said. "Both of these women have the most to gain from Jensen's death, so they're our prime suspects for now."

"And what will you do while I trudge through the archives?" Enya asked.

"I'm going to do some research of my own."

Back at his desk, Mathieu called Bill Collins at the *LA Times*. When Collins answered, Mathieu asked, "Can I take you to lunch today, Bill?"

"Are you buying?"

"Always."

"Is this about the Jensen murder?"

"Yes."

"What do you want to talk about?"

"His widow Jacqueline Jensen, the office manager Florence Drake, and a small-time hood named Fred Marlow."

"Okay. Where do you want to meet?" Collins asked.

"You choose," Mathieu said.

"Then let's go to the Garden of Allah Hotel and Villas."

"Why there?"

"Because it's in the heart of Sin City," Collins said with a chuckle.

"Okay," Mathieu said. "What time?"

"I'll need a couple of hours to do some research," Collins said. "How about one-thirty?"

"That'll work. See if you can find photos of Jacqueline Jensen, Florence Drake, and Fred Marlow while you're at it," Mathieu said. "That would be really helpful."

"Okay, I'll see what I can do," Collins said. "I'll meet you at the poolside tables."

11

The Garden of Allah

Mathieu felt the seductive pull of the Garden of Allah Hotel the moment he stepped onto the grounds.

There was a sensuousness to the place, as if a hot desert wind had enveloped him, while the languid sound of horns, strings, and a marimba played in the background.

He wandered down a gently sloping path toward the pool past Spanish-style bungalows hidden amongst the swaying trees and exotic plants.

It felt like a tropical paradise, a world apart, filled with intrigue and secret trysts. He heard macaws calling from the trees—or imagined he did. Reality and fantasy combined here. The rules seemed different, a place where one's sins were safe from prying eyes.

Arriving at the pool, the size of a small lake, Mathieu discovered the music wasn't a mirage after all. A quartet consisting of a violin, bass, trombone, and marimba played in the shade of a sprawling Douglas fir.

Wordlessly, Mathieu sat down across from Collins, mesmerized by the haunting melody. The trombone and marimba players were men, the bassist and violinist women, each dressed in black, each totally absorbed in the music, as was the rapt audience listening to them.

Mathieu's gaze was drawn to the violinist with her copper-red hair, delicate beauty, and high cheekbones. She was slender but with an imposing presence. And yet, there was a sadness in her eyes that intrigued him.

Time stood still as he watched her gently sway to the music as she played. He didn't notice Collins staring at him, seemingly curious about the focus of his attention.

When the song ended, the audience seated near the pool applauded in genuine admiration, as did Mathieu and Collins.

The emcee came up to the microphone soon after and said, "Ladies and gentlemen, I'd like to introduce you to the Lujon Quartet with Mike Hartman on trombone ... Carlos Mendez on marimba ... Karen Williams on bass ... and the incomparable Lillian Hennessy on violin."

When Miss Hennessy stepped forward to take her bow, Mathieu followed her with his eyes as she acknowledged the applause. The intensity of his gaze seemed to catch her attention. She glanced his way and held his eye for a moment with a timid, hesitant look, then with a shy smile, looked away.

Collins witnessed all this and said, "I've never seen you so smitten, Mathieu."

Mathieu waved away the comment with a flick of his wrist. "I just appreciate beautiful music, Bill, that's all. Their playing was enchanting."

"I agree," Collins said. "But to this reporter's eyes, you seemed enchanted by the violinist."

The waiter came at that moment with the menus and interrupted them. Collins glanced at the menu and said, "I see you have the Stuffed Tomato with Chicken today. I'll take that and an iced tea. What about you, Mathieu?"

Mathieu turned to Collins with a distracted look and said, "That'll be fine."

"What'll be fine?"

"Whatever you're having," Mathieu said with a grin.

When the waiter left, Collins handed Mathieu an envelope. "These are the photos you asked for."

Mathieu removed them and placed them on the table. "Thanks, Bill, these will be helpful."

The photos seemed to pull Mathieu's attention back to the case because he didn't notice as the violinist gathered her things, glanced his way, and then, seemingly disappointed when he didn't return her gaze, left. By the time Mathieu looked up, she was gone. He turned in his seat to search for her, but she was nowhere to be seen.

Disappointed, he turned back to Collins and asked, "Why did you pick this place?"

"Because if you want to know about the denizens of the 'County Strip,' you have to start here. Welcome to Sherman, California."

Mathieu gave Collins a quizzical look. "I don't understand."

"That's what this mile and a half strip of land between Hollywood and Beverly Hills used to be called before it was renamed 'West Hollywood' to attract the movie star set."

"It isn't an incorporated city, is it?"

Collins shook his head, "No, it's part of the county and essentially lawless because of it, especially during Prohibition."

"Did the re-branding work?"

"Yes, largely it has. After they completed Sunset Plaza, movie stars started building homes in the hills above. And hotels like this one and the Chateau Marmont across the street have become popular with Hollywood stars.

"Both hotels have become refuges for actors and actresses escaping troubled marriages or carrying on affairs in private. They're also good places for visiting actors to stay because of the proximity to the studios in Hollywood.

"Beyond that, the 'County Strip' has become LA's 'Sin City.' The rich and famous can drive a half-mile from stodgy Beverly Hills, indulge in their fantasies at a bordello, nightclub, or gambling joint, and be back in time for breakfast at their respectable manicured estates in the morning.

"And anything goes at the bordellos and clubs on the Strip: boys with girls, girls with girls, boys with boys, female impersonators, the whole lot. The sexual mores are pretty uninhibited here."

Mathieu nodded. "And what's the story with this place?" he asked as he looked around the grounds. "It's huge. I've never seen a pool this big."

"The hotel sits on two and a half acres between Crescent Height and Havenhurst. And apparently, the pool is the largest in the United States," Collins said. "Rumor has it that Tarzan has satisfied quite a few Janes in this pool late at night."

Mathieu laughed. "That seems appropriate. It feels like a tropical jungle in here. Who designed it?"

"Alla Nazimova, a Russian silent film star and a bit of a sexual libertine," Collins said. "She originally built it as her home, but as her career faded, her friends convinced her to add the villas and turn it into a hotel so she could retire. But she spent so much money upgrading it that she went bankrupt and was forced to sell. But her spirit of anything-goes sexually still pervades the place."

"It has that feeling," Mathieu said. Then, changing the subject, he asked, "What do you know about Jacqueline Jensen?"

"Ah, Jacqueline has an interesting past," Collins said with a chuckle.

"How so?"

"She used to work as a high-priced prostitute at the Hacienda Arms just down the street."

"Is that where Lester Jensen met her?"

Collins shrugged. "Who knows … it's likely."

"And the office manager, Florence Drake, what do you know about her?"

"Straight as a desert highway from what I hear," Collins said. "She graduated Summa cum Laude from Barnard College in New York City with a master's degree in economics, then made her way west to make her fortune. Lester Jensen was so impressed with her that he hired her to be his office manager after their first meeting."

"What about her private life?"

"It must be pretty private because I've never heard any rumors about her."

Mathieu nodded. "How about Fred Marlow? Phillip Chandler told me Jacqueline Jensen often brings Marlow with her to dinner parties at his house."

Collins scoffed. "Marlow's a small-time hood from Reno. He runs the downstairs gambling operation at the Café La Bohème for the owner, Joe Borgia, a retired opera singer."

"Do you think Marlow might freelance as a hired killer?" Mathieu asked.

Collins gave a sour look and shook his head. "I doubt it. Most hoods are like tradesmen. They stick to what they know. Electricians don't do carpentry, and gamblers don't do hits."

"But he might know someone who does."

"Sure," Collins said with a shrug. "But for what? So Jacqueline could inherit Jensen's house? That seems like a pretty weak motive to me."

The busboy brought their drinks at that moment. Mathieu noticed his eyes flicker when he saw the photos lying on the table.

"Have you seen them here together?" Mathieu asked, pointing to the photos of Jacqueline and Marlow.

"No habla inglés," he said with a stubborn glare.

"Los has visto aquí juntos?" Mathieu asked as he slid a buck across the glass table.

The busboy hesitated for a moment, snatched the dollar bill with his brown hand, nodded slightly, and left.

12

The Stuntman

When Mathieu got back to headquarters after his lunch with Collins, he was still thinking about the violinist. He replayed the moment he first saw her: the intensity of her concentration, her graceful bow strokes, and the swaying motion of her body as she played.

He tried to recall how she looked at him after the performance. Was her shy smile a sign of interest? Or had he simply caught her off guard, and it meant nothing? He berated himself for not approaching her, even though Collins would have never let him forget it.

Realizing there was no way he could know what she was thinking, he turned his thoughts back to the case.

He thought about Collins's remark that inheriting Jensen's house seemed like a weak motive for Jacqueline to kill her husband or have him killed. He was right it was. But maybe that wasn't the real motive.

Perhaps Jacqueline and Fred Marlow had a bigger score in mind. They both had shady pasts if Collins was right about the rumors. And it was clear from the busboy's reaction and what he'd learned from Phillip Chandler that they knew each other, perhaps intimately. He'd have to wait to see what Enya could dig up on them.

As Mathieu sat at his desk pondering this, he remembered he'd forgotten to interview a potential witness at the oil field, the retired stuntman Hank Laramie, who lived in the "haunted house" on the hill. He checked his watch. It was just past three. There was still time, so Mathieu left the office and drove to the Inglewood Oil Field.

Mathieu parked at the bottom of the cracked concrete driveway that led to the Rand house and walked up the steep slope toward the garage in the back. As he climbed, he stopped and glanced over his shoulder at the Hollywoodland sign in the distant hills to the north.

Cresting the driveway, Mathieu spotted Laramie grooming a bay horse in the corral next to the garage. Laramie looked to be in his late fifties, solidly built, perhaps five-foot-nine, with thick gray hair and a noticeable limp. He was combing the bay's haunches with a dandy brush as Mathieu approached.

Stopping a few feet away, Mathieu said, "Mr. Laramie, my name is Detective Mathieu. I'm from the LAPD. I'd like to ask you a few questions about the night of the murder here at the oil field."

Laramie turned toward the sound, saw Mathieu, then turned back and continued grooming the horse without saying a word. Mathieu walked closer until he was just behind him, close enough to see the muscles straining in his weathered forearm.

Mathieu had met taciturn men like Laramie before. They made deaf-mutes seem like chatterboxes in comparison.

"That's a nice-looking bay," Mathieu said. "How many hands?"

There was a momentary delay before Laramie responded. "Fifteen," he said, then looking over his shoulder, seemingly appraising Mathieu, asked, "You ride, Detective?"

"Yes, sir."

Laramie nodded and said, "Go fetch me that hoof pick on the hay bale, will ya?"

"Sure," Mathieu said as he went to get it. When he spotted the pick, he laughed to himself. The ones he'd used in the past were made of cast iron with straight handles and hooks at the end for cleaning the dirt out of a horse's hoof.

But this one looked like it should have been in a museum. The hook part was made of cast iron, but the handle was plated in silver with a gold bull's head ornament in the middle.

Handing it to Laramie, Mathieu said, "That's the fanciest hoof pick I've ever seen."

"Ain't it so," Laramie said. "Tom Mix gave it to me."

"Generous gift," Mathieu said.

Laramie scoffed. "Not really. Instead of paying me more for risking my life doing his stunts, he'd give me these little trinkets. At least the pick part is useful. Ever used one before, Detective?"

"Yes, sir."

"Well, then I ain't stopping you from helping out if you have a mind to," Hank said, handing it back. "My lower back is acting up today."

Mathieu smiled at Laramie, removed his suit coat, and hung it over the corral's wood railing.

Facing the rear of the horse, Mathieu sidled up to the bay's left haunch, massaged its rump with his left hand, and continued rubbing as he moved down the leg to the hock, where he lifted the leg gently, pulled it toward him, and rested the hoof on his left thigh. He kept his left arm on the front side of the horse's hipbone so if the horse kicked to the rear, it wouldn't break his arm.

Mathieu waited until he felt the horse relax, then began digging the dirt out with the pick in his right hand. He repeated the process with the right rear leg, this time using his right arm to raise the leg and the left arm to pick. Finished with the rear, he did the front hooves, which were always easier and less dangerous to clean.

When he was done, Mathieu walked back to Laramie, handed him the hoof pick, and said, "Perhaps you can answer a few of my questions now, Mr. Laramie."

Laramie rubbed his chin and said, "No need to be so formal, Detective … call me Hank. Would you rather ask your questions on horseback or here?"

"What do you think?" Mathieu asked, challenging him.

"Then saddle up the bay, and I'll ride the paint."

Laramie led the way as they trotted down a dirt path away from the brick mansion, then cut right and headed south along a ridgeline. Sitting astride the horse, Mathieu had a much better perspective of the scale of the field.

The overcast sky gave the place a dark, ominous feel. The giant wooden derricks completely covered the hillside, blocking out the horizon as Mathieu looked east toward the hills on the other side of the canyon, equally blanketed in wells. Occasionally, he'd craned his neck upward as they rode past a derrick. They looked like ancient totems to some long-forgotten god.

They rode in silence for about ten minutes, covering close to a half-mile along the ridgeline, when Mathieu asked, "Did you notice anything unusual the night of the murder, Hank?"

Laramie didn't answer at first. Mathieu thought he couldn't hear him over the clanging of the drills and pumps.

He started to ask him again when Hank said, "Well, I heard the fire alarm, of course, when they discovered the pipe leak. That always gets your attention. An oil field fire is a terrible thing, Detective. Hell's a picnic at the beach in comparison."

The way Hank said it made Mathieu think he'd experienced one or knew someone who had. But instead of interrupting, Mathieu stayed silent and let him continue.

"A friend of mine died in an oil field fire back in 1918," Hank said with a distant look. "The only thing his family had of him to bury was a badly burned body that looked like a pile of charcoal."

"I'm sorry," Mathieu said. "How did it start? Accident?"

"They claimed it was lightning ... but I think it was carelessness."

"Why?"

"Because the wildcatter running the show was known for cutting corners."

"Here in Los Angeles?"

"No, back in Desdemona, Texas, where my friend and I grew up. But I was out here by then doing rodeos and movie stunts. Desdemona was originally known as Hogtown. It was a typical oil boom town, a real hellhole. I got out of there as soon as I could, but my friend stayed. The violent crime got so bad there that they had to send in the Texas Rangers to restore order," Hank said, then fell silent.

Mathieu glanced over at Hank and saw the memory chewing on him. A few seconds later, Hank pulled on the reins, stopped, and said in obvious distress, "The hell with all of that. How about a little race, Detective?"

"Okay, but I don't think I stand much of a chance against you," Mathieu said. "Where to?"

"I'll race you to the bottom of that hill," Hank said, pointing off to his left at a steep slope that descended about thirty yards to the next plateau.

"Alright, but it looks like a damn fool thing to do," Mathieu said.

"It is, Detective ... that's the point!" Hank said as he spurred his horse and took off down the hill.

Mathieu watched in awe as Hank shed thirty years as he sped down the slope, cutting from side to side like he was on skis as he put distance between himself and Mathieu. The aches and pains of old age didn't seem to matter anymore. Hank's instincts took over. He was an equine athlete. The race was over before it began, but Mathieu urged his horse to follow despite his fears.

Mathieu leaned back in the saddle, unweighting the horse's front legs to prevent it from flipping over. After a few tentative cuts, Mathieu started to get the hang of it and gained confidence as he switchbacked down the hill and pulled up next to Hank ten seconds later.

Waiting at the bottom of the hill, Hank nodded in approval and said, "I could make a rider out of you yet, Detective."

Mathieu smiled. That was the closest to a compliment that he was going to get from Hank. "Your back seems to be okay after all," Mathieu said.

"Horses are my salvation, Detective, and my medicine."

"So, you weren't running away from answering my questions, hoping I'd break my neck coming down that hill?"

"If I was, it didn't work very well, did it, Detective?" Hank said with a bemused smile.

Mathieu laughed. "Did you notice anything else that night besides the fire alarm? Did you see any vehicles drive onto the property you didn't recognize? You must have a pretty good vantage point from the mansion."

"I do, but I'd started drinking pretty early that night," Hank said, "so I didn't notice much of anything."

Mathieu had a hard time believing Hank hadn't noticed anything, even if he had been drunk, but he let it pass. They continued riding east down the dirt track past clusters of pumps and derricks until they rounded a brush-covered knoll, and Mathieu spotted the squat pumpjack where Jensen's body had been found the night of the murder.

Mathieu pulled up short and said, "This is where we found the victim's body."

Hank turned in his saddle and looked around. "They picked a pretty good spot. It's hidden from view because of that knoll and the derricks."

Mathieu looped his reins around the saddle pommel and looked at Hank. "You know this field like the back of your hand, don't you?"

"Yeah, I ride the field almost every day. Sometimes, I spot a leak or pump that's not working, and I report it to Roy, the crew chief."

"So, if you had wanted to tie an oil baron to a pumpjack in the dead of night, how would you have done it, Hank?"

"You're the suspicious sort, aren't you, Detective?"

"That's kind of my job."

"Must be a lonely one … always suspecting the worst of people."

Mathieu nodded at the truth of that. "It can be. But everybody lies, Hank, even good people."

"I don't ride at night," Hank said. "My eyes ain't so sharp anymore … and I usually start drinking when the sun goes down. Liquor and horses don't mix well."

"Hypothetically, I mean, Hank," Mathieu said. "Because I get the feeling that whoever did this was taking a helluva of risk of getting caught unless he knew how this place ticked."

Hank spit on the ground. "Then perhaps you should be asking some of the workers … or even the night watchmen."

"My officers have already interviewed all the workers. Everyone's alibis check out. But I'd still like your opinion, Hank. How would you have done it?"

"I think I would have started a fire on that hill to the east on the other side of that dirt road."

"You mean on the other side of La Cienega?"

"Yeah."

"Why?"

"That's obvious because the firefighting crew would have been a lot farther away, and no one would have been around to see them bring up the body on this side."

"Why do you say 'them?'"

"Because it would be easier for two people to bring up a dead body than one."

"Unless the person was riding a horse."

Hank shrugged. "Sure, but that would've left tracks. Did you find any, Detective?"

"No," Mathieu said. "But a skilled rider could have tied a branch to the horse's tail and wiped them out."

"You are the suspicious type, aren't you, Detective."

"Like I said, Hank, it comes with the job. Did you ever meet the victim?"

"I don't know who the victim was," Hank said.

"Lester Jensen, the oil magnate."

Hank scratched the back of his neck and scrunched his face in thought. "Is that the guy that owns those gas stations around town that sell orange gas?"

"That's the guy. Apparently, it was some kind of marketing gimmick."

"That didn't work out so well for him, did it?"

"No, it didn't," Mathieu said without reacting to his remark. "I have one more question. Don't you think it's pretty dramatic how they tied the victim to a pumpjack? Seems like they were trying to make some kind of statement."

"Well, we do live in Hollywood, Detective. Maybe somebody in the movie business staged it," Hank said with a deadpan expression.

13

Fred Marlow

Mathieu had just sat down at his desk the next morning when Enya plopped herself in the chair beside him. "Your Mr. Marlow has an interesting past."

"Good morning to you also," Mathieu said with a bemused look.

"Oh, come on! I thought we were beyond that," Enya said, rolling her eyes. "I treat you just like I treat my brothers."

Mathieu was secretly glad she did.

Enya leaned forward in a conspiratorial way, scanning the almost empty detective's room, and whispered, "I mean, I have to behave myself with the rest of these knuckleheads … at least allow me a brief respite with you."

Mathieu bit his lower lip to keep from laughing and said, "But of course, Sis. How did it go at the *LA Times?*"

"Well, Francine was super helpful. She escorted me downstairs to the microfiche archives and introduced me to the librarian, who helped me find background information on Florence Drake and Fred Marlow."

"So, it was worthwhile?"

"Yes, their archives are great," Enya said, then, with a mischievous grin, added, "And Francine told me some embarrassing stories about when she babysat you as a child. But I'll save those for later when I need some leverage over you."

Mathieu chuckled. "Isn't there a statute of limitations on childhood behavior?"

"Not in your case, Detective," she said.

"What did you find out about Miss Drake?" Mathieu asked.

"Florence Drake is from New York. She's thirty years old and has a master's in economics from Barnard College, a private women's liberal arts college in Manhattan. According to what I read, Barnard is one of the 'seven sisters' in the northeast founded to give women the equivalent of an Ivy League education previously only available to men.

"After finishing her studies, Miss Drake came to Los Angeles and soon after got a job with Lester Jensen. She's well respected as a smart, no-nonsense office manager in the local business community. Other than that, she must live a quiet life because there's no hint of scandals in the archives."

Mathieu nodded. "That's similar to what Bill Collins at the *Times* told me about her. Besides, her motive seems weak to me. Miss Drake told me that Jensen Oil won't survive without Lester Jensen in charge. What about Fred Marlow?"

Enya laughed as she picked up her notes. "He's a totally different story. Mr. Marlow was born in Reno, Nevada. He's thirty-eight years old. He's been arrested several times in both Nevada and California for illegal gambling but never did any time. He's also a bit of a brute and did a two-month stint in Reno for assaulting a prostitute."

"Charming fellow," Mathieu said.

"Yes, but not surprising since it seems he was brought up in gambling joints and brothels since he was a child. His father, Fred Marlow Sr., was a famous faro player."

"What casino did father and son work at in Reno?" Mathieu asked.

"The Bank Club on Douglas Alley, home of illegal gambling in Reno since the 1880s until Nevada legalized it in 1931, according to the article I read."

"Who owns the Bank Club?"

"William 'Curly Bill' Graham, one of Nevada's most notorious casino owners," Enya said, then added, "By the way, all these guys seem to have nicknames."

"What's Marlow's?" Mathieu asked out of curiosity.

"'The Snake,'" Enya said. "Which fits because, from the newspaper photos I saw, he looks like a reptile with his small dark eyes and slicked-back hair."

Mathieu nodded. "What did Marlow do for Graham at the Bank Club?"

"Marlow's a man of many talents. Like his father, he's an expert faro and blackjack player. He also ran the roulette wheel for Graham. But according to the newspaper articles, gambling is only a small portion of the Bank Club's income."

"Where's the rest come from?" Mathieu asked.

"Money laundering."

"Really?" Mathieu asked. "For whom?"

"Mostly mobsters from the Midwest, like Ma Barker and her sons, who have stacks of cash from bank robberies and kidnappings they need to launder."

"Casinos are great places to launder money," Mathieu said almost to himself. "Why did Marlow leave Reno and come to LA?"

"Apparently, Graham caught him sleeping with his girlfriend and gave Marlow a choice: either leave town or he'd shoot him."

Mathieu nodded. "How long has Marlow been in LA?"

"About five years," Enya said. "During the height of Prohibition, he helped run a speakeasy on the County Strip. After that, he got a job at Café La Bohème, running the gaming tables downstairs."

"Which I'm sure the Sheriff's Department ignores because they're on the take," Mathieu said.

"Exactly," Enya said. "According to a reporter I met in the archives, there's a crap table at La Bohème nicknamed 'County Line' that the Sheriff personally shares the profits in."

Mathieu shook his head in dismay. "Who needs mobsters when you've got the LA County Sheriff's Department? What about Lester Jensen? What did you learn about him?"

"Nothing you don't already know," Enya said. "I'll have to go back tomorrow. It took all day to search the microfiche files and find out what I did about Marlow and Florence Drake."

Mathieu nodded that he understood. "Thanks, you did a great job. I guess it's time to pay Mr. Marlow a visit at La Bohème."

"Can I come along?" Enya asked. "I've never been to a nightclub before."

"Ask Bull," Mathieu said.

"You're not playing fair, Mathieu. You know Bull will never let me go with you."

"Well, you know how it is," Mathieu said with a grin, "brothers and sisters don't always play fair with each other."

Enya crinkled her nose at him. "Just wait till I tell the other detectives one of Francine's babysitting stories about you."

The Café La Bohème sat on the south side of Sunset Boulevard, across the street from Sunset Plaza, in a white, one-story, Georgian Revival-style building.

The club's lightbox sign advertised "Dining & Dancing" but failed to mention the gambling hall downstairs. Mathieu parked his Buick Phaeton in front of the club and walked to the corner entrance.

It was just past one in the afternoon. The place looked deserted. Like any other empty nightclub devoid of music, laughter, and dancing, it had all the glamour of an American Legion Hall. But at least it didn't smell of stale beer and cigarettes, Mathieu thought as he scanned the room. It looked well-kept.

Designed to look like a Parisian café in the Latin Quarter, the place had a certain charm with its dimly lit booths, plain oak tables, small dance floor, and raised stage at the east end of the room.

The room was long and narrow with dark ceiling beams, wrought-iron chandeliers, and red carpeting. Thick drapes covered the windows for privacy. Near the entrance, a hostess stand stood empty in front of a small waiting area and a polished oak bar that occupied the entire west wall.

Mathieu spotted a gangly young bartender washing glasses in the sink behind the waist-high bar. He approached him, showed his badge, and said, "My name is Detective Mathieu from the LAPD. Is Fred Marlow here?"

The bartender, who looked barely old enough to drink, gave Mathieu an innocent look, hesitated for a moment, and asked, "Are you from Vice?"

"No," Mathieu said, shaking his head. "Homicide."

"Phew, that's a relief," he said, exhaling. "The boss told me that we're all paid up."

"What's your name?" Mathieu asked.

"Sam."

"Look, Sam, I don't care what goes on here," Mathieu said. "I just need to speak with Marlow. Is he around?"

"He should be back in about thirty minutes. He went to Schwab's drugstore to get allergy medicine for his hay fever. Do you want a drink while you wait?"

"No, I'll just look around a bit. But don't worry, I won't go downstairs," Mathieu said with a knowing look.

"I appreciate that," Sam said with an embarrassed smile. "I'd probably get in a lot of trouble if you did."

Mathieu nodded, then turned and slowly ambled through the club past the plush red booths, worn oak tables, and classic bistro chairs toward the far end of the room.

He paused occasionally to look at one of the signed photos on the "celebrity wall" between the windows. Midway down, Mathieu spotted a framed photograph of Spencer Tracy and James Cagney on the wall. He stopped for a moment to study it, then continued on.

As Mathieu approached the stage at the east end of the room, he heard a saxophone begin to play. He walked toward the sound, halting beside a partially open curtain, and peered in.

Mathieu saw a tall, powerfully built man with chocolate brown skin standing with his back to him, playing the alto sax. The sound the man produced had a plaintive, haunting quality to it. He wasn't just playing; he was telling a story—a story only someone who had experienced loss could tell.

Mathieu knew who he was without seeing his face because only one man could play like that—his friend Paul Thornton.

When Thornton finished playing, Mathieu said, "That was beautiful, Paul."

Paul turned toward Mathieu with a look of surprise. "Theo! Where the hell have you been, man?"

He walked over to Mathieu, grabbed his shoulders, and said, "It's been a long time. What have you been up to?"

"I've got a day job that keeps me kind of busy, Paul," Mathieu said with a shrug.

"Yeah, I read about that Nazi shit. You're some kind of local hero."

Mathieu scoffed. "Don't believe everything you read in the newspapers," he said. "Are you playing here now?"

"Yeah, can you believe it? We've got a gig here for a month. They're very evolved here, Theo. They allow female impersonators and Negroes to perform in the same club," Paul said with a hearty laugh. "What brings you here?"

"I'm interviewing one of the staff for a case I'm working on."

"Who?"

"Fred Marlow."

"Ah! … the 'Snake,'" Paul said. "He's a piece of work."

"Do you know him?"

"Only by reputation," Paul said, shaking his head, "I try to avoid him."

"That's a good idea, from what I've heard," Mathieu said. "Did you see him here three nights ago?"

Paul took a moment, then said, "Three nights ago … that was Friday, right?"

"Yeah."

"Yeah, I saw him that night," Paul said, nodding his head. "Is he a suspect?"

"A person of interest," Mathieu said. "What time did you see him?"

"Well, he was here at six when I arrived," Paul said.

"Do you remember seeing him later in the evening?"

Paul scratched the back of his neck, seemingly in thought. "Yeah, probably, but he was in and out. Marlow spends most of his time downstairs in the gambling hall."

"If you remember anything else later on, let me know, will you?"

"Sure," Paul said. "Have you been practicing the piano, Theo?"

"Yeah, when I get a chance."

"Have you got time to play something?" Paul asked. "I'm waiting for my rehearsal partner to show up."

Mathieu glanced at his watch. "Sure, a quick one. According to the bartender, Marlow won't be back for another twenty minutes. What did you have in mind?"

"How about 'Georgia On My Mind?'"

"That'll work. I know the chords to it," Mathieu said as he walked over to the black Steinway Baby Grand and sat down on the piano bench.

"Have you been working on those spread voicings I taught you?" Paul asked.

"Yes," Mathieu said with a nod. "Root lowest in the left, melody highest in the right, spread the third, fifth, and seventh between the hands to get a full, balanced sound."

"That's it," Paul said. "Remember, your job is to listen to what I play and complement it, not compete with it. Got it?"

"Yeah, I think so," Mathieu said.

"You ready?"

"Yes."

"Then let's get started," Paul said as he counted down a slow beat. "Five, six, seven, eight."

Paul took it nice and slow as they began to play, giving Mathieu plenty of time to lock in, which he did.

Mathieu laid down a stride-style rhythm with his left hand, giving the song a nice, steady groove as he filled out the chords with right-hand voicings. At first, he was stiff and mechanical, but by the second time through the verse, he got caught up in the music and started responding to what he felt.

Soon after they began to play, a young woman entered the club carrying a violin case. Hearing the music, she strode with long, confident steps toward the stage, stopping just outside the curtain.

The violinist's gaze fell first on Thornton, his eyes closed as he blew the plaintive melody on his sax. A smile of pure bliss came over her face as she listened. She was so focused on Thornton that she didn't notice the pianist. But when she stepped forward and spotted him, she froze.

It was the young man she'd seen at the Garden of Allah with the brooding, intelligent, dark eyes. Suddenly, she felt confused and adrift, like a teenage girl with a crush.

Who was he, she wondered? What was he doing here? Her heart started to pound. She felt out of control and didn't like it. The last thing she needed now was to fall for some guy. Her career was the most important thing to her.

Trying to calm herself, the violinist watched him play. She could tell he wasn't a professional. But there was something in the intensity of his concentration that captivated her. She could see it on his face. He was fully present.

He supported Paul with beautifully voiced chords, making no attempt to call attention to himself. He played under the sax, not above it, as any good accompanist does.

Their playing had a wonderful call-and-response feel. She sensed they were friends by their easy, comfortable manner and the way Paul gently encouraged him.

When the song ended, the violinist stepped out of the shadows. Attempting to mask her anxiety, she asked in a playful voice, "Do you have a new pianist, Paul?"

Paul turned toward her, smiled, and said, "No, we were just jamming while I waited for you to arrive, Lillian."

Then, pointing to Mathieu, he said, "Lillian, this is my friend Theo Mathieu ... Theo, this is Lillian Hennessy, the best violinist on the West Coast."

Mathieu nodded and said, "It's an honor to meet you, Miss Hennessy. I had the pleasure of hearing you play recently at the Garden of Allah."

"Thank you," Lillian said with a shy smile.

There was an awkward silence between them as they looked at each other. Paul seemed to notice and said, "Theo is the famous LAPD Detective who took down Senator Barton."

At the mention that Mathieu was a detective, Lillian's smile seemed to dim, but she recovered quickly and said, "You held your own with Paul, Detective."

Mathieu colored a little and said, "Thank you, Miss Hennessy, but I should leave so you and Paul can rehearse."

Just then, Fred Marlow came up from behind Lillian and put his hand on her shapely bottom, "Hey, baby, how are you?"

Lillian turned and slapped his hand away. "I'm not your baby, Marlow ... keep your hands off me, you creep!"

"You might not be now, but your brother's my bitch, Lillian. He owes me a lot of money."

"Take it up with him!"

"If your brother doesn't pay up, I might have to take it up with you, sweetheart."

Mathieu stood, crossed the space quickly, towering over Marlow when he arrived. "Is there a problem, Miss Hennessy?

"No, Detective. Everything's fine," she said, staring into his dark brown eyes flecked with gold. "Just a little misunderstanding."

Mathieu turned toward Marlow, flashed his badge, and said, "I need a word with you."

"About what?" Marlow asked in a sullen tone.

"The murder of Lester Jensen," Mathieu said flatly.

Marlow flinched at the mention of Jensen's name. Mathieu took a step toward him. He could see fear in his eyes. "We can do it here or downtown, Mr. Marlow. You choose."

"Here is fine," Marlow said in a meek voice.

"Good," Mathieu said.

Mathieu turned to Paul and said, "Thanks for the jam, Paul. I've got to get to work. See you soon." Then, looking at Lillian, he added, "It was a pleasure to meet you, Miss Hennessy. I'm sorry for the disturbance. Here's my card. If you ever need my assistance, please don't hesitate to call."

Mathieu grabbed Marlow by the bicep and led him through the club to a secluded area, where he shoved him into a padded booth and slid into the seat across from him. Enya was right. Marlow did look like a reptile with his small darting eyes and slicked-back hair. His baby pictures probably looked like mug shots.

"How do you know Jacqueline Jensen?" Mathieu asked after they were seated.

Marlow smiled, showing his yellowing teeth. "Jacqueline and I go way back. We were friends in Reno."

"What did Jacqueline do in Reno?"

"What do you think she did with that body, Detective? Call out bingo numbers at church socials?"

"Why did she leave?"

"Reno is a hick town, Detective. Jacqueline always had ambition, always looking for the big score."

"Where did she work when she first got here?" Mathieu asked, even though he knew.

"The Hacienda Arms … just up the street. That's where she met Jensen."

"Did you and Jacqueline stay in touch?"

"Yeah, we kept in touch, and when I decided to come to LA, she helped me get a job on the Strip."

"You mean when 'Curly' Graham ran you out of Reno for sleeping with his girlfriend."

"How do you know about that?" Marlow asked with panic in his eyes.

"I know a lot about you, Marlow. I know you did time in Reno for assaulting a prostitute, for example. And that you've been arrested for illegal gambling in California and Nevada."

"Those gambling charges never stuck," Marlow said defensively.

"What a surprise," Mathieu said. "Where were you the night Jensen was murdered?"

"I was here in the club," Marlow said.

"Can anyone verify that?"

"Yeah," Marlow said with a smirk. "A couple of off-duty Sheriff's officers we hire as bouncers were here that night."

"I meant anyone reliable," Mathieu said with a dead stare.

"Why are you on my case?" Marlow asked. "I had nothing to do with Jensen's murder."

"Well, your good friend Jacqueline was the main beneficiary of Jensen's demise, and from all reports, you and her are pretty cozy," Mathieu said. "And you've been seen at the Garden of Allah together. Do you have a favorite bungalow where you get together?"

"It ain't no crime to have sex, Detective."

"No, it isn't as long as they're willing, Marlow. But it looks suspicious that a small-time hood like you is hanging out with a wealthy widow."

"I didn't have anything to do with Jensen's death."

"Then give me a better alibi."

Marlow motioned over his shoulder. "Ask Sam, the bartender. He was here that night. He'll vouch for me."

"Okay, I will."

"Can I go now?" Marlow asked.

"Sure," Mathieu said as he leaned toward Marlow with a threatening gaze. "But don't leave town, and don't bother Miss Hennessy anymore. Is that understood?"

"Yeah, sure … I hear you," Marlow said as his voice cracked slightly.

After Marlow moped away with his head down, Mathieu checked with the bartender. Sam told him that Marlow was at the club that evening.

But as Mathieu turned to leave, Sam added, "But there's an exit downstairs near the parking lot. We use it to get customers out of the casino when there's a raid. Marlow could have left that way, and I wouldn't have noticed."

When Mathieu got to the front door, he heard Paul and Lillian begin to rehearse. He paused for a moment to listen. The contrast between the soulful wail of Paul's alto sax and the ethereal sound of Lillian's violin was hypnotic.

He pictured Lillian as she played and those pensive eyes of hers. He cringed at the thought she'd heard him play. She must have thought he was a horrible amateur. Shaking off the feeling, Mathieu opened the door and stepped outside. At least he had a day job he was good at.

14

Clara Jensen

Before heading back to the *LA Times* to do more research, Enya had found the names and addresses of Jensen's first two wives at the County Courthouse. His first wife, Clara Jensen, lived in a bungalow court in Pasadena, where Mathieu headed the next morning.

Mathieu parked on South Marengo, a wide, quiet, tree-lined street three blocks east of Fair Oaks Avenue in front of the Don Carlos Court. It was an attractive Spanish Revival bungalow court with seven units nestled amongst oak-lined walking paths. The oak trees scattered about the property provided shade and a cooling breeze for the well-kept grounds.

Mathieu walked down the central flagstone path past a bubbling fountain in search of unit 378. He found it at the back of the property on the left.

The white one-story bungalow had a Spanish tile roof, dark wood framed windows, and an arched entrance. Mathieu strode across the pavers to the stone porch, stepped up, and knocked. Glancing to his right as he waited, he noticed a small table where Mrs. Jensen kept an herb garden.

A minute later, the door was opened by a tall, thin woman in her mid-forties with brown hair done in an elegant low bun. Mathieu had expected Jensen's first wife to be dowdy, but this woman looked quite sophisticated with her bright red lipstick and black chiffon dress.

"How can I help you, young man?" she asked in a calm, pleasant voice.

"My name is Detective Mathieu, Mrs. Jensen. I'm from the LAPD. I'm investigating the murder of your former husband. I'd like to ask you a few questions, if I may."

"Of course," she said with a gentle nod. "I thought someone from the police would come sooner or later. Please come in," Mrs. Jensen said as she stood aside so Mathieu could enter.

Mrs. Jensen led Mathieu to the left across the polished oak floor toward the living room. The room was spacious and airy, with a Cathedral ceiling and beige-colored walls.

A fireplace dominated the west wall, and French windows with translucent white drapes provided a diffuse light. An iron oak table with two matching chairs sat in front of the south window. Mrs. Jensen sat down in the far chair and motioned for Mathieu to sit across from her.

"Would you like some tea?" she asked, pointing to a teapot and an extra cup and saucer on the table.

"Yes, thank you," Mathieu said.

Mrs. Jensen poured the tea with a precise, steady hand, then slid the cup and saucer toward him with her slender fingers, the fingernail polish matching her lipstick.

"It's quite good," Mathieu said after taking a sip.

"It's Jasmine tea from Harney and Sons," she said. "It's one of my favorites."

Mathieu nodded, intrigued by her sophistication.

As if reading his mind, Mrs. Jensen asked, "Were you expecting Lester's first wife to be a dowdy country girl, Detective? Devastated that she had been tossed away for a younger woman?"

"I admit the thought had crossed my mind," Mathieu said with an embarrassed smile.

"I like your honesty, Detective," Mrs. Jensen said. "What would you like to know?"

"I'd like to know more about your ex-husband so I can find his killer or killers."

Mrs. Jensen nodded with a serious look. "Where would you like me to begin?"

"Perhaps at the beginning," Mathieu said.

"We met in Denver, Colorado," Mrs. Jensen began. "I was a stenographer at a real estate firm there. Lester had tried his luck selling raw land in mining towns, first in Silverton and later in Telluride. The money he made in Silverton, he quickly lost in Telluride.

"He was licking his wounds by the time he got to Denver, so he tried something safe and started selling homes. We met at the office. He wasn't arrogant then, but he was ambitious. His drive attracted me, and we started dating."

"Where was he from originally?"

"A small town in Oklahoma called Oologah. The same town Will Rogers was born in. Lester used to boast he was part Cherokee Indian like Will, but I doubt it."

"How did he get started in the oil business?"

"Lester got restless selling real estate. He'd heard about the oil boom in Texas and took off one day without warning to work as a 'roughneck' for a wildcat operation. He worked there for a couple of months when a bad oil field fire occurred, killing several field workers. After the fire, the owners shut the operation down."

"Where in Texas?" Mathieu asked.

"Desdemona," Mrs. Jensen said.

Mathieu nodded. It was the same town where Hank Laramie's friend had been killed in an oil field fire. "Where did he go next?" Mathieu asked.

"He came back to Denver discouraged. I think I represented a safe haven for him. We got married, and soon after, I got pregnant with our daughter, Melinda.

"But Lester had oil fever by then. In 1921, he heard about an opportunity at the Elk Hills Naval oil reserve in Kern County to work in the finance department for a big oil company. He applied for the job and got it. He took off, leaving Melinda and myself in Denver."

"Who did your husband work for at Elk Hills?"

"Lester reported directly to Edward Doheny, the oil tycoon who drilled the first successful oil well in Los Angeles, just south of Chavez Ravine."

"Wasn't Doheny accused in the Teapot Dome scandal of bribing Albert Fall, the Secretary of the Interior, to obtain the lease to drill at Elk Hills?"

"Yes," Mrs. Jensen said with a bemused look. "But Edward Doheny was never convicted of giving the bribe … even though Albert Fall was convicted of taking it."

Mathieu scoffed. "That defies logic, doesn't it?"

"Yes, it does, but they were never able to figure out the money trail," Mrs. Jensen said in an enigmatic tone.

"It sounds like you know."

Mrs. Jensen raised her eyebrows in a coy smile. "Perhaps, but I'm sworn to secrecy, Detective. It's why Lester was so generous when he divorced me."

"But he's dead now."

"Yes, but Lester kept his end of the bargain, and I'll keep mine," she said cryptically.

"Are you in Lester's will?"

"I assume so," she said with a shrug. "At least my daughter Melinda is."

"Why did your husband decide to start drilling his own oil wells?"

"Because he learned a lot from Edward Doheny and not in a good way," she said with a faraway look.

"What do you mean?"

"Lester changed at Elk Hills. He'd always been ambitious, but after Elk Hills, he became driven by pure greed. He learned how to play the game from Doheny. He realized that super-wealthy men always find ways to cheat the system and that you don't get wealthy playing on an even field. And most importantly, Lester learned how not to get caught from Doheny."

"What did he do next?" Mathieu asked.

"Lester got seed money from Doheny to keep quiet about what he knew about the Teapot Dome Scandal. Then he returned to Denver to get Melinda and me, and we moved to Los Angeles. Soon after we arrived, he leased his first oil field in the Rincon, where he got his first strike after a few failed attempts."

"When did your marriage fall apart?"

"Soon after his first oil strike," Mrs. Jensen said with a hint of bitterness. "Lester realized he could parlay that success into selling worthless shares in new oil drilling ventures. And even if they weren't successful, he'd still make a profit, and it was all totally legal.

"Lester knew how to manipulate people, Detective. He knew the appearance of being successful was more important than actually being successful. So, he jettisoned me for his first trophy wife."

"How did you feel about that?"

"I was hurt and angry, of course. I'd been his rock in the bad times," she said as she looked out the window, the sun revealing fine lines around her dark eyes.

"But I was secretly relieved," she said, turning back to Mathieu. "I didn't like the man Lester had become … or maybe always was. But he treated me well in the divorce because I knew his secrets. So, I bought this place. It's probably smaller than the living room in his Los Feliz mansion, but it's large enough for Melinda and me."

"Where's your daughter?"

"Melinda's at school," Mrs. Jensen said as her eyes brightened. "She goes to Mayfield Catholic School on Euclid. It's just a block away."

Mathieu stared at his hands and said, "Excuse me for having to ask this, but where were you the night of your ex-husband's murder?"

"That's easy," she said with a smile. "I was here with Melinda and one of her girlfriends from school. They were having a sleepover."

Mathieu looked straight at her and asked, "Who do you think might have killed your ex-husband?"

Mrs. Jensen sighed, glanced out the window again, and took a moment to consider the question. With a shrug, she turned back and said, "It's difficult to know because Lester swindled so many people. But I think I'd look at those who took the blame for some of his shady deals and went to jail instead of him."

Then, seemingly realizing another possibility, she added, "Or some of his competitors. They're all ruthless. They'll do anything to cheat someone else out of a big score. It's an addiction with them … like drugs or gambling."

"But would any of them kill?"

"Based on Lester's stories, I think some of them might."

"Did he mention any names in particular?"

Mrs. Jensen was quiet for a moment, seemingly trying to remember, then said, "I can't remember any specific names. But Lester did tell me how white oilmen killed Osage Indians back in the teens and twenties in Oklahoma to get ahold of the oil wells they owned. Lester implied that that kind of behavior wasn't uncommon for the most vicious."

"When was the last time you spoke with your ex-husband?"

Mrs. Jensen rubbed her forehead, sighed, and said, "About a week before he died. He called to speak to Melinda, but she was at school."

"Was it usual for him to call her?"

"No," she said, shaking her head. "He usually only called at Christmas and her birthday."

"What did he say?"

"He told me to tell Melinda he loved her deeply and was sorry he hadn't been a better father."

"How did he seem when he said it?" Mathieu asked.

"He seemed remorseful … and a little scared," Mrs. Jensen said in a reflective tone. "I'd never heard fear in his voice before."

15

A Mirage on the Plains

The dark green Chevy Eagle pickup bounced along the rutted track west of Soda Lake, heading south over the native grasslands of California's Serengeti—the Carrizo Plain.

The broad grassland plain lay between the banded slopes of the Caliente Mountains to the west and the pockmarked scar of the San Andreas Fault and Temblor Range to the east.

The young man riding shotgun glanced nervously at the driver, a lean man with gray hair and an impassive expression, seemingly focused on their quest. A quest the young man was responsible for but now felt uneasy about, wondering if they were searching for a mirage.

He stared through the dirt-smeared windshield at the vast, empty plain. It was easy to feel insignificant here. But he'd done his homework and knew its history.

The Carrizo Plain was a different world, where Tule elk, pronghorn antelope, and San Joaquin kit fox roamed free, and California condors patrolled the skies in search of carrion. It was a land sacred to the Chumash, who had lived here for over ten thousand years before the Europeans arrived.

It received less than ten inches of rain annually. But in the wet years, the plain and surrounding hills exploded with a riot of vibrant-colored wildflowers worthy of an Impressionist painting.

A mile-and-a-half before they reached the southern edge of Soda Lake, the young man pointed to a spur on the right, where they turned. Fifteen minutes later, they curved around the base of a dry slope and spotted the deserted El Saucito Ranch.

A modest two-story white clapboard ranch house sat on a knoll on the west side of the property in a cluster of oaks. To the west of it were a windmill and a small pond, and to the east, connected by a serpentine path, two outbuildings. On the far east side of the property, a large hay barn sat empty beside a barbwire-enclosed corral.

The driver parked near the ranch house and got out. He stretched his lean body after the long drive and looked around, his dark eyes watchful, missing nothing but revealing little. The place was desolate but surprisingly peaceful. They were on high ground, and he could see the grasslands stretch for miles in every direction, surrounded on three sides by mountains.

The young man led the way to the front of the house, seemingly anxious about the lean man's reticence. The windows and doors were boarded up. The house had a shaded porch on three sides with a hatch cover in one corner that led to a root cellar.

The lean man turned and surveyed the property with a critical gaze. Overgrown thigh-high grass grew wild near the house, bordered by a cluster of thick-trunked oaks and long dormant fruit trees that must have once provided apples and pears to the homestead.

Turning to the young man with an intimidating stare, the lean man asked, "What do you know about this place?"

The young man cleared his throat, then, repeating what he'd learned, said, "The last person to live here was Chester Brumley with his wife Margaret and their three youngest children. He built the house and outbuildings, and they dry-farmed and grazed sheep until he died. A few years after his death, a bank in Taft foreclosed on the property. No one has lived here since. It's just too hard to make a living out here."

Without reacting to the monologue, the lean man said, "Tell me again how you overheard Jensen talking about this place."

"I was at Musso and Frank's one night," the young man said with an eager expression, "seated at one of the small center aisle tables. Jensen was sitting directly across from me in a booth with a shapely blond whose breasts were about to spill out of her dress."

"How did you know it was Jensen?"

"I'd seen his photograph in the *Times* and on the billboards advertising stock in his oil field schemes. Anyway, the drunker he got, the louder he got. I overheard Jensen brag to the blond that he'd discover the largest oil find ever in a place no one had ever looked."

"That was probably just a ploy to get into the blond's pants," the lean man said dismissively.

"That's what I thought at first, too," the young man said. "But a few days later, I began to wonder if Jensen had been telling the truth. So, I started to piece together what he'd said to see if I could figure out where it was."

"If it was such a big find, why hadn't Jensen developed it?"

"Because he said he never had the capital to fund the drilling on a large enough scale to make it viable. After he got his first big score in the Rincon Oil Field, he put it on the back burner. But recently, he said he started playing two big oil barons off each other to find a partner, and he was getting close."

"Did he say who they were?"

"No," the young man said, shaking his head.

"When did you overhear this story?" the lean man asked.

"About a month before Jensen died."

"What led you here?"

"The hints Jensen dropped when he was bragging to the blond."

"Like what?"

"Well, first of all, he said he discovered the find when he worked at the Elk Hills Naval Oil Reserve for Edward Doheny in the mid-1920s. So, I figured it was probably somewhere in the Central Valley."

"But why on the Carrizo Plain and why this ranch?"

"Mostly from how Jensen described it," the young man said. "He said it was an old grassland ranch that sat on a rise with a pond, windmills, and a hay barn."

"There must be other ranches like this on the plains."

The young man shook his head in disagreement. "No, not really, sir. There are a few ranches on the north end of the plains, but there's a whole community up there, and there's no way Jensen could have done any wildcat drilling up there without anyone noticing. And besides, Jensen said it was remote."

"What did he use as a derrick to drill?"

The young man chuckled. "That's where Jensen got creative. He claimed he used one of the windmills on the property to support the rig."

"Where did he get the drill pipes and bits?"

"He stole some of it from Elk Hills, and the rest he scavenged from abandoned wells here on the plains."

"And he got this contraption to work?" the lean man asked with a skeptical look.

"Yes, sir, according to the story I overheard."

"What did he power it with?"

"There's a gasoline-powered generator in the powerhouse next to the bunkhouse," the young man said, pointing to the east.

"And all of this was back in the mid-20s?"

"Yes, sir."

The lean man shook his head. "It still sounds pretty far-fetched to me, kid. There's never been a big oil strike on this side of the San Andreas Fault. The Carrizo is on the Pacific Plate, not the

North American Plate. The geology here is totally different from Elk Hills."

"I know, sir, you're right," the young man said, raising his hands in concession. "But this area is so remote it hasn't been explored much. And it's difficult to explore because there's only one rutted track that runs the entire fifty-mile length of the plains."

"Did Jensen say why he chose this particular ranch to drill?"

"I overheard him say he started poking around the property and concluded that the soil composition was similar to Elk Hills. So, he decided to drill a test well."

"Where exactly?"

"I'm not sure. Jensen said he was standing next to one of the windmills when the wind suddenly picked up, and he could smell the pungent smell of tar nearby."

The lean man let out a sigh and looked around. There were three windmills on the property: one next to the water pond to the west, one next to the hay barn, and one farther out in the field to the east.

"Which one?"

"I don't know," the young man said with a shrug.

"Then let's check them out," the lean man said as he turned and marched toward the closest windmill near the pond, the young man following behind.

The two men trampled through the tall grass past the line of oaks, scanning the ground for rattlesnakes. They crossed the dirt path encircling the property and skirted around the pond's edge until they reached a forty-foot-high steel windmill. The lean man stopped to examine it. It looked like an Aermotor self-oiling windmill, probably manufactured in the late teens.

Ducking between the steel supports, the lean man walked toward the sucker rod in the center, where he knelt to inspect the water seal. It looked intact, and he could see the rod slowly turning. Straining his neck, he glanced up the rod to where an attached water line fed a twenty-foot-high steel water tank beside the windmill. The lean man stood, dusted off his pants, and walked toward the young man.

"I don't think it was this one," the lean man said, shaking his head. "It doesn't appear to have been modified, and the water seal is still intact. Let's look at the one near the hay barn. But first, I want to stop off at the powerhouse and see what kind of generator they have."

"Yes, sir, whatever you think's best," the young man said in a servile manner.

They backtracked through the grass, then walked down a curving path toward the outbuildings thirty yards east of the house. They stopped at the smallest one, the powerhouse, and peered in. A 7,500-watt Wisconsin Big Red two-cycle gasoline generator on a wheeled base with a pull handle sat in the middle of the concrete floor.

Staring at the generator, the lean man narrowed his eyes in thought and said, "It's movable. Jensen could have easily wheeled it out to one of the windmills to power the drill." Then, quickly pivoting, he strode toward the second windmill near the hay barn as the young man hurried to keep up.

Reaching it, he saw another Aermotor, the same height and type as the one near the pond. A hundred-gallon galvanized steel water trough sat beside it, partially full. He knelt to inspect the windmill's seal and water line. Both were intact and hadn't been modified.

"It's not this one either," the lean man said, seemingly discouraged. "Let's check the last one."

The third windmill was over a hundred yards east of the hay barn in the middle of the plain. It was the tallest one, over fifty feet in height. From a distance, it looked like the sucker pipe was in place, but when the lean man reached the windmill and knelt to inspect it, he could see it was all for show.

The water seal appeared to be broken, and the rod wasn't moving. Someone had disengaged the clutch. The water trough beside it was bone dry. He started digging around with his hand, clearing the deep brush near the sucker pipe, when he felt the sticky texture of tar. He bent to smell it.

The lean man stood and turned to the young man. "This is where Jensen found oil."

"So, the story I overheard was true!" the young man said with a flush of excitement.

There was a slight twitch in the lean man's dark eyes, and then, without warning, he jerked a Colt snub-nose revolver from his leather jacket and fired point-blank at the young man. A sizzling sound like meat hitting a hot pan reverberated through the air as the rattlesnake at the young man's feet did its death rattle.

The young man's mouth fell open in fright, and his gaze dropped to his torso as he frantically searched for blood. Finding none, he looked up with relief.

"Who else did you tell this story to?" the lean man asked as he kept the gun trained on the young man.

"No one," the young man said with anxiety in his voice.

The lean man's lips curled in a tight smile. "What do you want for your research?"

"Would a finder's fee be okay?" the young man asked as his voice wavered.

"Lump sum ... or percentage?"

The young man seemed unsure how to answer. "You ... choose."

"It'll be a lump sum then," the lean man said. "I'll draw up the papers." Then, narrowing his eyes, he added, "But if you renege on the deal and tell anyone else, the legal consequences will be the least of your worries. Understood?"

"Yes ... sir," the young man stammered.

16

Cinderella's Slipper

After returning to headquarters from his interview with Clara Jensen, Mathieu was about to call Jensen's second wife when Fred Wilson came to his desk. Fred stood there, restless as a puppy, changing his weight back and forth like he had to pee.

"What is it, Fred?" Mathieu asked, curious about his jitteriness.

"We got a break."

"What do you mean?"

"I found this," Fred said, bringing a red high-heeled shoe from behind his back like a kid showing off a rare marble. "It belongs to the woman who was with Jensen the night he was murdered."

"Where'd you find it?"

"At Jensen's bungalow in Laurel Canyon."

"When?"

"Yesterday."

"Why'd you go back?" Mathieu asked, confused. "I thought you searched it the day I asked you to."

"I did," Fred said as he sat down, seemingly calmer now. "The first time I went there, I dusted for prints and searched for evidence. I bagged the mystery woman's lingerie along with some other items and brought them back to the lab for analysis. But I only found one shoe, which started to bug me.

"Why was there only one shoe in the bungalow? If the woman was a victim, the shoe I found could have fallen off when they dragged her away, and that would explain it. But if the woman were one of the kidnappers, she wouldn't have walked away with just one shoe on. So, I drove back to Lookout Mountain yesterday and searched the bungalow again."

Mathieu smiled at Fred's persistence. "Where'd you find the second shoe?"

"Not where I'd expected," Fred said with an embarrassed look. "I searched the ground floor again just in case they'd dragged her down the stairs with the shoe on, and it fell off. But no luck, it wasn't there. Then I went upstairs and searched the bedroom, where we'd found the rest of her stuff. I looked everywhere, on the floor, under the bed, in the closets, and beneath the heavy furniture. But I still couldn't find it.

"Frustrated, I went into the bathroom to get a glass of water. It's a nice compact bathroom with a tub, sink, and toilet. The sink sits on top of a vanity cabinet with pull-out drawers and storage space underneath.

"As I was filling my glass, I noticed some space between the vanity cabinet and the floor. So, I knelt down, looked underneath, and there it was—the other high-heeled shoe. The woman must have been a little drunk, kicked off the shoe, and that's where it ended up."

"I'm impressed you found it, Fred," Mathieu said, rubbing his chin. "But how does that help us?"

"Because of what's on the bottom of the shoe," Fred said as he handed it to Mathieu.

Mathieu turned the shoe over. Glued to the leather shank was a small yellow tag with red lettering: "Property of Western Costume."

Mathieu looked up at Fred and smiled. "So, our mystery woman is an actress."

"Yes, or an extra working out of Central Casting. By the way, we found some female hairs on the pillow. She's a bleached blond, not natural."

Mathieu nodded. "Is Western Costume still located on South Broadway downtown?"

"No, they moved to Melrose Avenue next to Paramount Studios."

"Then I guess I'm going to have to take Cinderella's shoe over there and see if we can find out who wore it last."

"Good luck with that," Fred said. "I doubt their records are that good, especially if she was an extra. I got a tour of the old location once. Their inventory is massive."

"Well, I have to try," Mathieu said as he stood to leave.

Mathieu cruised through the intersection at Van Ness Boulevard, heading west on Melrose Avenue. Halfway down the block, after passing the four-story brick Paramount Hotel, he pulled over in front of the Western Costume Building.

The seven-story high concrete monolith had all the glamour of a warehouse despite its billboard proclaiming, "We Dress The Movie Stars."

Mathieu parked near the billboard, then walked a few steps west and entered under the arched entry, where he showed his badge to the uniformed guard and asked for directions to the shoe department.

Finding the elevator, Mathieu requested the seventh floor. The steel-framed freight elevator was at least ten feet high, with a sturdy wood plank floor and an open cage providing a view of the floors as they rose.

On the ride up, Mathieu spotted an entire wall of swords and scabbards on one floor, on another, rows of Spanish Rancho-style clothes hanging on open racks, and on a third, a vast open-columned room filled with rows of seamstresses and tailors sitting across from each other working at their sewing machines.

When the elevator stopped on the seventh floor, Mathieu got off and entered the shoe repair workshop. It looked like most factory floors, with hooded work lights hanging from the twelve-foot-high ceiling and large industrial-style windows.

But Mathieu's heart sank when he scanned the workspace. There were shoes scattered everywhere, piled on the floor, in shoe racks attached to the walls, on workbenches overflowing with cobbler's tools and metal clamps. In the midst of this chaos, Mathieu doubted anyone would remember the lone shoe he'd brought with him.

In the center of the room, two men wearing cobbler's aprons stood at their stations, one operating a chest-high Landis chain stitcher and the other repairing a dress shoe with an awl.

Mathieu approached the second man, a clean-shaven man in his early thirties with smooth olive skin and dark hair, impeccably dressed in pressed trousers, a white shirt, and a dark blue tie.

Mathieu showed him his badge, introduced himself, and asked, "What's your name, sir?"

"Ralph Linden," the man said.

"I wonder if you can help me find out who last wore this shoe, Mr. Linden?"

Linden stopped his work and, with a good-natured smile, said, "Do you see how many shoes are in here, Detective? I'd have to have a photographic memory ... which I don't."

"I realize it's asking a lot, Mr. Linden. But it's pretty important. The woman who wore this shoe may have witnessed a murder."

Linden's eyes widened at the mention of murder, and he seemed to freeze momentarily. He put down the shoe he was working on and asked, "May I look at it closer? Perhaps it will jog my memory."

Mathieu nodded and handed it to him, saying, "Even if you don't know who wore it, if you know what film it was used in, that will help me a lot."

Linden turned the shoe over and examined the heel. It was medium height but sturdy. He flipped it over again and ran his hand across the rough surface covered in glitter. He looked up at Mathieu and said, "It's sturdy but flashy. I think it probably was used in a dance number."

"Do you know which film?" Mathieu asked.

"No," Linden said, shaking his head as he handed the shoe back. "But I know someone who might."

Linden excused himself and walked toward the door to the adjoining workshop. Leaning against the doorjamb, he shouted, "Edith, can you come in here and look at something for me, please?"

A few moments later, a diminutive woman in her mid-thirties sporting a pageboy haircut came through the doorway, wearing round-rimmed dark glasses and a tape measure around her neck.

"What do you need, Ralph?" she asked on entering.

Pointing towards Mathieu, Ralph said, "This is Detective Mathieu from the LAPD. He needs our help identifying a shoe. It may have been used in a dance number, but I don't remember which film. I thought you might recognize it."

Edith marched up to Mathieu, held her hand out, and in a no-nonsense manner, said, "Let me see it."

Mathieu handed it to her.

Oblivious to his presence, Edith spent some time carefully examining it, every once in a while uttering an "Um" or "Hmm" until she finally looked up at Mathieu and said in a matter-of-fact voice, "Barroom scene in 'She Done Him Wrong.' The first movie I did for Mae West."

Mathieu's eyes widened in surprise that she recognized it. "Did Mae West wear this shoe?"

"No, no," Edith said, shaking her head. "We had three background dancers, each dressed identically and each wearing this type of shoe for a musical number. Why is it important to you?"

"Because the woman who wore it may have witnessed a murder."

"I see," Edith said, nodding with a somber expression.

"Do you know the names of the women?" Mathieu asked.

"No," Edith said, pursing her lips. "But Central Casting should. They keep track of the extras."

"That's a great help. Thank you, Miss …"

"Head," she said, "Edith Head."

"Is there anything else you remember about the women, Miss Head?" Mathieu asked.

"Well, they were all blond, similar build, nice legs, and all wore size seven shoes. Which, unfortunately, isn't going to help you identify which one wore this shoe. I never knew any of their names. I just dressed them. The dancers are supposed to return the shoes to the Assistant Director after the shoot.

"But obviously, one of the girls was naughty and kept hers," she said with a hint of frustration. "Happens all the time. The girls fall in love with the clothes we make and keep them."

"Is there someone at Central Casting I can talk to who would know their names?"

"Yes, Sally McFarland. She cast the film. She's sharp. She'll be able to help you. Here's her number," Edith said, writing it on the back of her business card and handing it to Mathieu."

"You've been very helpful, Miss Head. Thank you," Mathieu said. "If you don't mind me asking, what are your dark glasses for?"

Edith laughed. "I don't mind at all. I get asked that question all the time. The glasses are tinted blue, which helps me see how the clothes I design will look in black and white.

"And speaking of which, you look pretty good in black and white yourself, Detective," Edith said with a flirtatious smile, then peering over her glasses, added, "and quite delicious in color, too. You should have been a movie star, young man. If you ever need a new suit, give me a call. I can do much better than what you're currently wearing."

"I'm sure you can, Miss Head," Mathieu said with a warm smile. "I may take you up on your offer."

"Please do," she said with a pixyish grin, then turned and went back to her workshop.

When Mathieu got back to headquarters, he called Sally McFarland at Central Casting. The phone rang for a long time before someone picked up. "Central Casting, McFarland. What can I do for you?" came the abrupt reply over the line.

"Miss McFarland, My name is Detective Mathieu from the LAPD. Edith Head gave me your number. She thought you might be able to identify the three female dancers you cast in the barroom scene for Mae West's 'She Done Him Wrong.'"

"What do you need them for? Is one of them in trouble?"

"No," Mathieu said, "but they may have witnessed a crime."

"What kind of crime?"

"A murder."

There was a long silence on the line, and then Miss McFarland said in a more subdued tone, "I understand, Detective. Hold on a minute while I get my call sheets for that film."

"Of course," Mathieu said.

As he waited, he heard chairs scraping, file cabinets opening, and papers rustling in the background. Several minutes went by before Miss McFarland came back on the line. "You're in luck, Detective. I found the call sheet. Do you have a pen ready?"

"Yes, go ahead," Mathieu said.

"The dancer's names are Maria Ward, Pamela Marten, and Marilyn Lane. Miss Ward lives in the Fontenoy Apartments at

1811 Whitley Avenue in Hollywood. Miss Marten and Miss Lane share an apartment at the Fleur De Lis Apartment just next door at 1825 Whitley."

"Thank you, Miss McFarland. You've been extremely helpful."

"I was glad to help, Detective," she said. "There's one other thing you should know. Three days ago, I had a part I thought would be perfect for Miss Lane. I called and left a message with her answering service, but she never got back to me, which is extremely odd. That rarely happens with actresses."

17

The Roommate

The next morning, Mathieu and Fred Wilson glided to a stop in front of the Fleur de Lis Apartments at 1825 Whitley Avenue in Hollywood.

The Fontenoy Apartments were next door, separated by a parking lot. Both looked attractive and well-maintained from the street, and both provided housing for actors and actresses close to the Hollywood studios.

The five-story, brick Fleur de Lis was considerably smaller than the Fontenoy but had a distinctive charm. Cypress trees lined the front of the French chateau-style building. The façade featured gothic windows flanking a two-story-high arched entrance and a black wrought-iron gate decorated with gold fleur de lies.

Mathieu had stopped off at Central Casting before coming here to pick up headshots of the three actresses. He had a bad feeling about Marilyn Lane because she hadn't returned Miss McFarland's phone call. So, he wanted to talk to her roommate, Pamela Martin, at the Fleur de Lis first.

Mathieu and Fred walked a few steps to the entrance, opened the wrought-iron gate, and entered the lobby, a beautiful space that looked almost like a chapel.

The gothic theme continued here with arched-ceiling supports and an intricately carved, dark brown, coffered ceiling above pale-yellow walls with walnut-colored wainscotting.

There was a comfortable sitting area on the right and a concierge desk to the left. Straight ahead, an oakwood staircase led to the upper floors.

Their heels clicked on the burgundy-colored tiles as they crossed the lobby, passed under a gothic archway, and took the stairs to the third floor. Arriving, they walked down a carpeted hallway to apartment 307 and knocked.

After several seconds without an answer, Mathieu knocked again and soon after heard muffled steps inside the apartment. A sleepy-eyed blond opened the door a crack, her lace robe partially undone. "What do you want?" she asked in a throaty voice.

"Are you Pamela Martin?" Mathieu asked.

"Yes," she said. "What's it to you?"

"I'm Detective Mathieu from the LAPD," he said, showing her his badge. "We need to ask you some questions about your roommate, Marilyn Lane. May we come in?"

"Do I have a choice?"

"We could do this downtown," Mathieu said in a measured tone.

Pamela shrugged, undid the chain, turned her back on Mathieu, and padded across the hardwood floor. Mathieu and Fred followed her down the hallway and under a narrow archway to the living room. Pamela plopped down on an oversized leather couch facing the street, then crossed her long, shapely legs.

The room was long and narrow, with diffuse light coming through the floor-to-ceiling curtained windows on the east and south. The early morning light reflected off the polished wood plank floor, creating a slight glare. A ceiling fan turned lazily above the couch.

Mathieu and Fred came around the sofa and sat in leather chairs facing Pamela and the French doors behind her that opened into a kitchenette.

Pamela sat on the couch, casually dangling her legs as she stared at Mathieu. She had wavy blond hair, full lips, and arched eyebrows. She obviously knew how to pose, turning her face slightly to the right to highlight her "good side," although she didn't appear to have a bad one.

"Why do you want to ask about Marilyn?" Pamela asked with a hint of unease. "Is she in trouble?"

Ignoring the question, Mathieu asked, "When was the last time you saw Marilyn?"

Pamela scrunched her forehead, took a moment, then said, "About five days ago."

"Do you know where she is?"

"No," Pamela said, shaking her head.

"Has she called you or contacted you in any way since then?"

"No."

"Is that usual?" Mathieu asked.

Pamela shrugged. "Well, sometimes, she goes off with one of her sugar daddies and doesn't tell me … but never this long."

"Do you know who they are?"

"Not by name."

"What do you mean?"

"I mean, she's secretive about them."

"In what way?"

"She'll tell me she spent the weekend with a producer, director, or some rich guy, but she usually doesn't let on who they are."

"Why not?"

Pamela shrugged. "I don't know. She's kind of weird that way."

"Where's Marilyn's bedroom?" Mathieu asked. "We need to check her fingerprints."

"Why?" Pamela asked as her eyes widened in concern. "Is she in some kind of trouble?"

"Just routine," Mathieu said with a blank stare.

Pamela hesitated, then said, "Her bedroom is in the back."

Mathieu turned to Fred and asked, "Go check her room, will you, Fred?"

"Sure," Fred said as he rose.

Pamela called after him. "Turn to your left at the entryway and go down the hall. It's next to the bathroom."

Fred nodded and left the room.

While they waited, Mathieu asked, "Does Marilyn have any family in town?"

"If she does, she never talks about them," Pamela said, raising her eyebrows in a bored expression.

"Where did you meet Marilyn?"

"At an audition that neither of us got. We got on, and I needed some help with the rent, so Marilyn jumped at the chance when I asked her to move in."

"How long has she been living here?"

Pamela looked away, seemingly trying to remember, then said, "About eight months."

Fred returned to the room carrying a silver compact mirror in his gloved hand and nodded to Mathieu.

Pamela noticed and asked, "What's wrong? What aren't you telling me?"

Looking at his hands, Mathieu exhaled and said, "We found fingerprints matching Marilyn's at a crime scene."

"What kind of crime scene?" Pamela asked with a shocked expression.

"A kidnapping and murder," Mathieu said in a soft voice.

Pamela's face turned sheet-white in fear. "Was Marilyn murdered?"

"I don't know," Mathieu said, shaking his head, "she may have only been a witness. But I'm concerned that she hasn't contacted you since the day of the murder."

"Who was murdered?" Pamela asked with alarm.

"Lester Jensen," Mathieu said. "The oil executive."

Seemingly in a daze, Pamela nodded in recognition. "I read about that in the newspapers. How do you know Marilyn was with Jensen?"

"Because the fingerprints we found in the house where Jensen was abducted match those on the silver compact Fred just found in Marilyn's bedroom," Mathieu said. "We also retrieved some women's clothing and the red high-heeled shoes Marilyn wore in the Mae West movie."

"Did you find Marilyn's purse?"

"No," Mathieu said. "Just her fingerprints, lingerie, and the shoes. We traced her through the shoes at Western Costume. They remembered which movie they were used in."

"I told her she should have returned them," Pamela said almost to herself as she bit her nails.

"Did you know Marilyn was seeing Jensen?" Mathieu asked.

"No," Pamela said, shaking her head. "Like I said, Marilyn never mentioned names." Then, with a questioning look, she asked, "Do you think she's still alive?"

Mathieu opened his palms and said, "I don't know, Miss Martin. We haven't found her body, which is a good sign. Do you know where she might have gone to hide if she felt threatened?"

Pamela bent forward, covering her face. She stayed that way for several minutes, breathing into her hands in silence.

Then, with moist eyes, Pamela looked up and said, "One night, when Marilyn and I were feeling sorry for ourselves because we didn't get called back for an audition, we sat in this room with a cheap bottle of bourbon and got really drunk. We started talking about where we'd run off to if everything turned to shit here in Tinseltown.

"My fantasy was to head north to San Francisco and try to get a job dancing in nightclubs. But Marilyn told me she was going to run away to the mountains. She mentioned she had a friend who ran an inn in the mountains where she could stay."

"Do you remember the name of the inn?" Mathieu asked, leaning toward her.

Pamela laughed. "Yes, I do because I liked the name," she said. "Marilyn told me it was the Idyllwild Inn. Isn't that a beautiful name, Detective?"

"Yes, it is, Miss Martin ... yes it is."

18

Mountain Justice

Mathieu drove east on Florida Avenue through the small citrus town of Hemet toward the San Jacinto Mountains. East of town, at the base of the foothills, Florida Avenue became the Pines to Palms highway, rising almost 3,000 feet in twelve miles as it snaked up the ridgeline toward Mountain Center.

The first few miles on the narrow two-lane road were relatively straight before it began twisting on itself as it climbed ever higher. Three-quarters of the way up, after sliding through a horseshoe bend and straightening out, Mathieu heard the wail of a police siren behind him. He pulled off to the side of the road and stopped.

Mathieu watched in his side mirror as a sheriff wearing a tan uniform and a cowboy hat got out of the Ford Model A patrol car.

He was every cliché of a country sheriff, fat with a malevolent smile and enough chin folds to hide a card deck. Yet he was surprisingly graceful on his bird-like legs as he approached Mathieu's vehicle.

The fat man stopped just behind the driver's side door, as police are trained to. Mathieu spotted his name tag, which read Langston.

Langston rocked back on his heels, hooking his thumbs in his Sam Browne belt, then asked with a twisted smile, "You're a little out of your jurisdiction, aren't you, Officer?"

Mathieu turned his head and smiled. "No offense meant, Sheriff. I'm on my way to interview a witness in Idyllwild," he said, passing his ID to Langston. "My name is Detective Mathieu. I'm a homicide detective with the LAPD."

The fat sheriff studied Mathieu's ID for a moment, made a few throat noises, then said, "I've seen your photo in the newspapers, Detective," he said. "Aren't you the one that put Senator Barton on death row?"

"Yes, Sheriff, I am, for killing three young women."

"I voted for Senator Barton," Langston said with pride. "Twice!"

Ignoring the remark, Mathieu asked, "Why did you stop me?"

"Because this is my patch."

Mathieu nodded. "I understand, Sheriff, but as you know, there are no jurisdictional limits for murder."

"Still, it's polite to check in with the local authorities when you're in their jurisdiction, De-tec-tive," Langston said, elongating the word like an insult.

"I intended to as soon as I reached Mountain Center," Mathieu said. "But you beat me to it."

"Who are you looking for?" Langston asked.

"A beautiful blond," Mathieu said with a smile.

"Aren't we all?" the fat man said with a laugh, his heavy cologne barely covering his sour breath. "What's her name?"

"Marilyn Lane."

"Never heard of her," Langston said, but there was a flicker of recognition in his beady eyes. "Why are you looking for her?"

"Because she might be a witness to a murder."

"Whose?"

"Lester Jensen's."

"Is that the oil baron that was just killed in the LA oil field?"

"Yes, Sheriff," Mathieu said with a nod. "That's him."

"We have a few oil barons up here that own vacation homes in Idyllwild," Langston said. "I hope you're not intending to bother them."

"Farthest thing from my mind, Sheriff."

"Why do you think Miss Lane is in Idyllwild?" Langston asked.

"Because I got a tip, she might be."

"You're not planning on making any arrests without the local authorities present, are you, Detective?"

"I'm not planning on making any arrests at all, Sheriff. I'm just trying to find Miss Lane and talk to her," Mathieu said. "If you don't have any objections, that is."

The fat sheriff took a long moment to respond, then said. "Not if you leave it at that, Detective. Here's my card. Call me if anything changes."

"I will," Mathieu said as he studied the card. "If you don't have any more questions, I'd like to be on my way while it's still light."

"That's a good idea, Detective. These mountain roads can be pretty dangerous at night, especially for city folk," Langston said with a hint of malice.

"Thanks for the warning, Sheriff," Mathieu said, "I'll keep you informed if anything changes."

"See that you do," Langston said as he tipped his hat, spun on one foot, and pranced away like a movie sheriff.

Mathieu continued up the hill, checking his side mirror occasionally to see if Langston was still tailing him. He'd met country sheriffs like Langston before. They were usually bullies like he was, ruling their patch like petty dictators. Most of the locals were too scared to cross them, so they wielded their own brand of psychological terror on the populace.

After another four miles, Mathieu reached Mountain Center, turned left, and headed north along the ridgeline toward Idyllwild. It was over 4,000 feet here. The pine trees started to take over from the scrub at the lower elevations.

Mathieu looked to his left across the ridgeline. He had a clear view across the San Jacinto Valley to the west. The sun was starting to set. It would be dark soon.

Twenty minutes and five miles later, after climbing another 1,000 feet on the twisting road, Mathieu arrived in the small community of Idyllwild. He rolled down the window and inhaled the cool mountain air and the sweet scent of pine trees.

Mathieu turned right onto North Circle Drive, passing the Red Kettle Café on his left, then turned right again onto Village Center Drive. A half-block down, he turned into the dirt parking lot in front of the Idyllwild Inn.

As he got out of the car, Mathieu spotted the sunset's reddish alpenglow reflecting off the granite face of Tahquitz Peak, looming above the town at almost 9,000 feet.

His father had taken him on one of his first climbs there when he was a boy. It was a short class 3 beginner loop on the lower sloops without ropes, but it had been exhilarating, nonetheless.

The lights had just come on in the office. Mathieu walked toward the one-story country inn covered in brown shake shingles. He stepped onto the porch just as a gray squirrel scampered across the deck, then opened the door on his right to a narrow reception area and entered.

The tiny room was empty. Mathieu hit the bell on the waist-high lacquered counter and waited. A few minutes later, a young man with brown hair and a pleasant face entered.

"Sorry, I was in the back starting dinner," he said. "I wasn't expecting any more guests tonight. How can I help you?"

"I'm Detective Mathieu from the LAPD," Mathieu said as he showed the young man his badge. "What's your name?"

"Bobbie Smith," he said with concern in his eyes. "Is there a problem, Detective?"

"No, Mr. Smith," Mathieu said. "I was told that Miss Marilyn Lane might be staying here."

"Who told you that?" Bobbie asked, now seemingly evasive.

"That doesn't matter," Mathieu said. "Miss Lane isn't in any trouble. I just need to speak with her. Are you a friend of hers?"

Bobbie hesitated, seemingly unsure how to respond.

"I can assure you I mean her no harm," Mathieu said. "Here's the number for the LAPD headquarters in Los Angeles. You can call them and check on me if you'd like."

Bobbie fidgeted with his hands, trying to decide what to do, then said, "That won't be necessary. Yes, Marilyn's my friend. She was terrified when she first came up here by bus. She'd called ahead and asked if she could stay here for a while. She's helping out as a maid and sometimes at the desk to pay me back."

"Where is she staying?"

"In Cabin 10."

"Is she there now?"

"Yes ... I think so," Bobbie said. "Do you need directions to the cabin?"

"No, I think I'll be able to find it," Mathieu said. "I stayed here when I was a little boy with my parents. I know the layout of the cabins."

That seemed to reassure Bobbie as he exhaled. "You understand I'm only trying to protect her," he said.

"So am I," Mathieu said as he turned, started for the door, then stopped and said to Bobbie, "Don't call her room and warn her I'm coming. If she runs away, it will only make things worse for her ... and for you. Understood?"

Bobbie nodded, "Yes, Detective. I understand."

Mathieu left the office, got back in his police car, and drove south a few hundred feet to a gravel lane, where he turned left. The modest wood cabins were strung out along the winding drive like little hideaways, nestled amidst the pines with enough distance from each other to provide privacy and quiet.

Number 10 was the first one on the left. Mathieu parked to the right of the small cabin, with its peaked roof, shake shingles, and outdoor deck, then walked up three steps to the front porch and knocked on the dark green door. After a few moments, the porch light came on, and the door opened.

Few women have ever looked more seductive wearing a black turtleneck sweater than the woman standing in the doorway. She stared directly at Mathieu through hooded, cornflower-blue eyes with her left hand on her hip and her right leaning on the doorframe as if posing for a photo.

Her tousled blond hair suggested she'd just made love, but her bright red lipstick suggested otherwise.

She was the kind of woman who knew she was beautiful, pretended she wasn't, and used it as a test. The implied question was: "Can you look at me and still talk?" And yet, beyond that, Mathieu sensed vulnerability in her cautious blue eyes.

"What do you want, handsome?" she asked on seeing Mathieu standing there. "Are you here to turn down my bed?"

Mathieu laughed in spite of himself. "I'm Detective Mathieu from the LAPD, Miss Lane," he said, showing her his badge. "I'd like to ask you a few questions."

"About what?" Marilyn asked without taking her eyes off him.

"Lester Jensen," Mathieu said.

Her smile dimmed, but not her seductive gaze. "Ah! Then you better come in, Detective. I think I'll need to sit down for that."

Miss Lane left the door open, took a few steps in, and sat on a mission-style sofa facing the brick fireplace. The room was small but cozy, with knotty pine walls, wood plank floors, and dark green curtains.

Mathieu crossed the room and sat in a leather chair near the side window. He spotted a pair of reading glasses and an open copy of Hemingway's *A Farewell to Arms* on the end table beside the sofa.

"How did you find me here?" Marilyn asked, bringing her knees to her chest and smiling coquettishly at Mathieu.

"Your roommate told me you might be here," Mathieu said.

Marilyn pursed her lips and nodded. "I came up here about a week before Lester's death," she said, looking at the fireplace.

"I needed to get away from LA for a while and clear my head. I was shocked when I read about Lester's murder in the newspapers. I didn't know him that well. We only went out on a few dates, but there was a photo of us together in the *Times*. I guess that's why you want to talk to me."

Mathieu had suspected Marilyn would deny being with Jensen the night of his murder, and her response confirmed it. So, he decided to pretend he knew less than he did, hoping she'd trip herself up.

"I see you like Hemingway," he said, pointing to the book on the end table.

The statement seemed to throw Marilyn off. She glanced briefly at the book, and her eyes brightened. "That's not what men usually notice about me."

"That's my job, Miss Lane, to notice things."

"I may be an actress, but I can read, Detective. I'm not just a dumb blond."

"I'm sure you're not, Miss Lane."

Marilyn smiled. "I like how polite you are, Detective. Most men assume they can call me by my first name as soon as they meet me."

Ignoring her comment, Mathieu asked, "Why do you like Hemingway?"

"Because his prose is clean with a rhythm that carries you along like a gentle stream. And because he's not a showoff."

"What do you mean?"

"Hemingway doesn't call attention to himself like certain writers who want to impress you with their fancy prose. He keeps it simple. He serves the story, not himself. That's what great actors do, too. They serve the story and, in doing so, disappear into their character."

Mathieu was impressed with her analysis. "What drew you to *A Farewell to Arms?*"

A radiant smile came over Marilyn's face. "The opening paragraphs are some of the finest in all of literature," she said. "Hemingway describes a country road, not a battlefield, but in that description, he tells you everything you need to know about the futility and horror of war. Sometimes, I just read it over and over again because it's so poignant."

"That's one of the best critiques of Hemingway I've ever heard," Mathieu said.

"Really?" Marilyn asked with delight. "Do you mean that?"

"Yes," Mathieu said. "Did Mr. Jensen share your interest in literature?"

"No, but he did show great interest in my breasts," Marilyn said with a self-deprecating laugh.

"Where did you first meet?" Mathieu asked.

"At the roulette table at the Café La Bohème. Lester told me my eyes and bosom gave him good luck, but he rarely looked at my eyes," Marilyn said with a hint of sadness.

"Was the relationship serious?"

Marilyn shrugged. "Lester told me he was auditioning young women to be his next wife."

"Did you want that?"

She scrunched her face and said, "Oh, god. I don't know. Sometimes, I think it would be nice to get out of the Hollywood rat race and have somebody take care of me. Shower me with gifts and fine clothes and let me live in a big mansion instead of sharing an apartment with another starving actress."

"Where did Jensen hold these 'auditions?'" Mathieu asked innocently.

"At his bungalow on top of Lookout Mountain," she said.

"When was the last time you were there?"

Marilyn sighed, shook her head, and said, "I can't remember … at least a month ago."

Mathieu smiled at her. "You really should have given those red high-heeled shoes back to Western Costume, Miss Lane."

"What high-heeled shoes?" Marilyn asked, seemingly caught off guard.

"The ones you wore in the Mae West movie … the ones with your fingerprints on them … the ones we found in Jensen's bungalow the day after he was kidnapped and murdered."

Marilyn looked at Mathieu for a long time, then, with a resigned shake of her head, said, "You're not a dumb blond either, Detective. Is that how you found me?"

"Yes," Mathieu said with a nod. "I spoke with Edith Head. She remembered the shoes, and Central Casting remembered the three actresses who wore them."

"Am I in trouble?" Marilyn asked.

"No," Mathieu said, shaking his head. "I don't think you had anything to do with Jensen's murder. I just need you to tell me what you remember about that night."

Marilyn hesitated and said, "I'd rather not, Detective. It's a frightening memory."

"I understand, Miss Lane, but I need you to," Mathieu said. "What's the first thing you remember?"

Marilyn looked at the floor, avoiding Mathieu's eyes. "Lester and I were in bed making love when suddenly two large, masked men burst into the room. One of them grabbed Lester, and the other one grabbed me.

"The one that seized me put his hand over my mouth, yanked me out of bed naked, and threw me on the floor. He tied a blindfold around my eyes, gagged me, and wrapped me in my coat. Then he tied my hands behind my back, picked me up, and carried me downstairs to a car parked outside, where he threw me into the backseat and tied my legs together. Then he went back into the house.

"About five minutes later, he returned to the car, and we drove down the mountain, then through the city for a while. I tried to scream but couldn't. I was afraid he was going to kill me.

"We stopped somewhere off the side of the road. It was quiet, like we were in the country, but I could hear the hum of machinery in the background. I heard another car drive up and a trunk open. That must have been the car with Lester's body. I heard the two men whispering to each other, and then they walked off.

"When the man came back, he started up the car and did a quick U-turn. After what seemed like thirty minutes, the car stopped in a dark alley, and the man got out and opened the rear passenger-side door.

"He untied the rope around my legs, pulled me out, and untied my hands but left the blindfold on. Then, he handed me the flats I always keep in my purse and told me to put them on. Then he shoved me against a brick wall and had me face it. I pleaded with him not to kill me. He didn't say anything.

"He put my purse in my hand and said, 'I want you to stay here facing this wall and count to a hundred, then you can take off the blindfold. The Greyhound Bus station is two blocks from here. Take my advice, sister, get out of town for a while and keep your mouth shut.' I told him I would.

"Then he pressed some money into my hand, grabbed my ass, and said, 'Start counting.' I heard him walk back to the car. I was so grateful to be alive that I peed myself. I heard him laugh. Luckily, I was naked under the coat. Then I heard him get in and drive off. I think I counted to two hundred, just to be sure.

"When I opened my eyes and removed the blindfold, it took a while to adjust to the lights. I found a Kress Five and Dime that was open all night near the bus station and bought a cheap dress and some underwear.

"Then I called Bobbie and told him I needed a place to stay. He told me to buy a bus ticket to Riverside, and he'd pick me up there. So that's what I did. I've been up here ever since."

"And you never saw their faces?" Mathieu asked.

"No," Marilyn said, shaking her head. "Thankfully."

"How tall were they?"

"I don't know," Marilyn said. "They seemed big to me, but that was probably because I was so afraid."

"How old was the man who took you?" Mathieu asked. "Could you tell from his voice?"

Marilyn shrugged. "I guess in his late thirties."

"And you didn't see what the other man did to Jensen?"

"No, when the man dragged me out of the bedroom, the other one was still subduing Lester."

"Thanks for telling me your story, Miss Lane," Mathieu said in a soft voice. "I'm sorry I had to put you through this."

"That's okay," Marilyn said as she started to shake. "Maybe I needed to get it out."

Mathieu spotted a robe hanging from a hook on the bedroom door. He got up, fetched it, draped it around Marilyn's shoulders, then sat down again.

"Thanks," she said. "You're a kind man, Detective."

"Do you feel safe up here?" Mathieu asked.

"Mostly, except I'm still jumpy, especially when I work the reception desk alone."

"Has anyone bothered you?"

"Only that creepy fat sheriff."

"You mean Langston?"

"Yeah, that's the guy. I know he wants to sleep with me. He comes into the office sometimes and just hangs out. One time he tried to grab my ass. I screamed, and the maintenance man chased him off with a shovel. I'm afraid of him. He's a pig."

"If you want to go back to LA, I can give you a ride and try to find somewhere safe for you to stay if you're not ready to return to your apartment."

Marilyn looked at Mathieu with troubled eyes. "Can I sleep on it before I decide?"

"Sure, I'll find a room in town and come back in the morning," Mathieu said as he stood to leave.

Marilyn stopped him. "I don't want to be alone tonight, Detective," she said with pleading eyes.

Mathieu looked around the room, shrugged, and said, "Okay, I'll sleep on the sofa then."

"You can sleep in my bed, Detective," Marilyn said in a way that implied more than sleep.

"Thank you, Miss Lane," Mathieu said. "But it's best that I sleep on the couch."

"You don't know what you're missing, Detective," Marilyn said with a teasing smile.

"Unfortunately, I believe I do, Miss Lane," Mathieu said with chagrin.

The absence of sound in the mountains at night is profound. In the city, there's always background noise, but in the country, the deathly stillness is at first disconcerting.

Because of that, it took a while for Mathieu to fall asleep, but when he finally did, it was a deep sleep. In his dreams, there was a muffled crashing sound, followed by a chill breeze and heavy footsteps. He struggled to rouse himself, smelled sickly cologne, heard a whooshing sound, then felt a blow to the back of his head and blacked out.

Mathieu smelled sweet breath on his face. He struggled to open his eyes but couldn't. He started to panic, then felt soft lips on his, a warm kiss, and a plea. "Please wake up, Detective, please!"

Mathieu slowly pried his eyes open. Marilyn was sitting on the floor beside him, her face inches from his. He blinked his eyes, trying to bring her into focus.

"What happened?" Mathieu asked in a groggy voice.

"It was the fat sheriff," Marilyn said.

"He broke in, knocked you out, then came to my bedroom door. I shoved a heavy chair in front of it to block it. I heard him yelling, 'You fucked the detective, why not me, you slut?'

"I escaped through the back window, ran through the woods, and hid under Cabin 8's porch. I lay on the ground and waited. I heard a crashing sound when he broke into my bedroom, and then the lights came on as he searched the cabin.

"After that, Langston came outside with his flashlight. I think he was drunk; he was slurring his words. He called me like I was a dog. 'Here, Marilyn, here, Marilyn … I won't hurt you.'

"That went on for a while until the lights came on in one of the other cabins, and Langston ran to his car and drove off. I waited another ten minutes to make sure he wasn't coming back, then I ran back to the cabin and found you unconscious on the sofa."

"How long was I out?" Mathieu asked.

"At least fifteen minutes after I got back."

Mathieu tried to sit up, but the back of his head screamed in pain. "Help me up," he said. "Then go make some strong coffee. We have to get out of here. I'm taking you back to LA."

"Okay," Marilyn said without hesitation. "I'll brew the coffee and gather my things."

Thirty minutes later, it was precisely one in the morning when they turned right at Mountain Center and started down the Pines to Palms highway. Mathieu had asked Marilyn to lie down on the back seat until they reached Hemet in case Langston was still lurking about and saw her in the car.

About three miles down the ridge, on the most treacherous part of the road, a vehicle suddenly roared up behind them at high speed with its hi-beams on and rammed them from behind. Mathieu looked in his rearview mirror. It was Sheriff Langston with a crazed look on his face.

Mathieu sped away, trying to create distance, but Langston caught up and rammed them again just before a horseshoe bend. Mathieu struggled to control his vehicle, sliding through the curve and up onto the opposite shoulder. Then, resting control back, he accelerated on the straightaway. Langston floored it, gained on them, and fired a shot through the rear window. Mathieu ducked and yelled to Marilyn to stay down.

Langston passed on the left until he was even with Mathieu's window. Mathieu glanced over and saw Langston raise his pistol to fire. Mathieu ducked as he slammed on the brakes, his car fishtailing as he did. Langston flew by, looking back at Mathieu's car to see if it would tip over, but he didn't see the next curve coming up. By the time Langston looked forward again, it was too late.

Langston's vehicle sailed over the steep curve, twisting in mid-air, and landed halfway down the slope, where it burst into flames. When Mathieu got to the same bend, he pulled off the road, got out, and sprinted down the hill.

By the time he got to Langston's vehicle, it was engulfed in flames, and Langston's charred body lay dead a few feet away like a roasted pig. Mathieu shook his head in dismay. There was nothing he could do for him now. He ran back up the slope to check on Marilyn. She was shaken but okay. They got back in the car, this time Marilyn sitting in the passenger seat.

They drove in silence for a few miles when Marilyn said, "This is all my fault. It's always the same with men. They can't control themselves around me. I should have just slept with the creep, and none of this would have happened."

"None of this is your fault, Marilyn!" Mathieu said adamantly. "And certainly not his death. I think Langston was trying to silence us after the attack at the cabin."

Then with gallows humor, he added, "The damn fool warned me this road is dangerous at night. He should have taken his own advice."

19

The Safe House

When they reached Hemet, Mathieu found a payphone on a deserted side street. He lifted the handset with his handkerchief and dialed the local police. In a muffled voice, he told the dispatcher that a car had gone off the side of the road and burst into flames halfway down the Pines to Palm Highway, then he hung up.

Marilyn slept most of the way on the drive back to Los Angeles. At first, she curled up in a ball like a little girl and slept with her head resting against the passenger side window. Then, at some point, still half asleep, she lay down on the Buick Phaeton's bench seat with her head next to Mathieu's thigh.

It was five in the morning and pitch black out when they arrived back in LA. The only thing that had kept Mathieu awake during the long drive was the throbbing pain in his head. He needed some coffee to help him think and decide what to do with Marilyn.

He briefly considered going to the Pantry, an all-night diner at Ninth and San Francisco streets. But too many cops hung out there, and not all of them were honest.

The fewer cops that saw Marilyn with him, the better. He had a friend named Darin who worked the night desk at the Biltmore Hotel. He was sure Darin could order some coffee from room service and let them sit in the café off the lobby.

Mathieu drove to South Olive and parked in front of Pershing Square, across the street from the Biltmore. He gently pressed Marilyn's soft shoulder, trying to wake her up. She was wearing the same outfit when he first saw her: a black turtleneck and white pants.

Marilyn mumbled something, then sat up with sleep in her eyes. "Where are we?"

"In front of the Biltmore Hotel."

"Hmm, you really know how to treat a girl, Detective. Are we going to get the honeymoon suite?" she asked with a playful smile.

"No," Mathieu said. "We're going to get some coffee."

"That'll do," Marilyn said. "I'm a simple girl."

"Let's go, then."

They got out, crossed the deserted street, and entered through the revolving doors on Olive. The lobby was empty, except for a bellhop and the night desk clerk, who thankfully was his friend Darin.

The Biltmore turned out to be a good choice. They sat alone in the hotel's empty coffee shop after the night porter brought them their coffees. It felt like a cocoon after everything that had happened. Marilyn had thrown some cold water on her face in the restroom to wake up. Her makeup had faded. She looked less glamorous but no less beautiful.

"Where do you want to go next?" Mathieu asked as Marilyn sipped her coffee.

"Can't we stay here forever?" Marilyn asked wistfully.

"Not on my salary," Mathieu said with a shake of his head.

"What if we only came here once a month for coffee and lived in a cabin the rest of the time?" Marilyn asked, staring into his eyes.

"You'd get bored, Miss Lane. I think you're destined for bigger things."

"I feel safe and respected around you," Marilyn said. "I'm not sure there are bigger things."

"Thank you, but there's a reason you wanted to become an actress, Miss Lane. Don't give up on that because of what's happened. The fear will pass."

Marilyn was silent for several moments, then said, "Unfortunately, it hasn't passed yet. I don't feel safe going back to my apartment right now."

"Do you have anyone else you could stay with in town?" Mathieu asked. "Your roommate mentioned you had several gentlemen friends."

Marilyn laughed. "Is that the expression Pamela used? 'Gentlemen friends?'"

Caught out, Mathieu said, "No, I believe it was 'sugar daddies.'"

"I have a lot of those. But sugar daddies want to show me off like arm candy. It's good for their egos. I'm not ready for all that just yet."

At an impasse, they drank their coffees in silence. Marilyn occasionally glanced at Mathieu, who was considering possible places where she could stay.

After a few moments, Marilyn's face brightened in recognition. "I remember where I saw your photo now. You stopped those Nazi terrorists! And the gossip columnists printed rumors about you and Lady Caroline Astor. Is she why you're so hard to get, Detective?"

Mathieu scoffed. "You know better than to believe that stuff, Miss Lane. Besides, Lady Caroline is married and has a child."

"You're a terrible liar, Detective," Marilyn said, teasing him.

Ignoring the remark, Mathieu said, "I have an idea where you can stay. I should have thought of it earlier."

"Where?" Marilyn asked.

Mathieu checked his watch. It was almost 6 a.m. "Let me make a quick phone call first," Mathieu said as he stood and headed to the front desk. "I'll be right back."

A few minutes later, Mathieu returned and slid into the booth beside her. "Do you like animals?"

"Sure, I love them," she said, sounding like she meant it.

"Would you like to learn how to herd goats?"

Marilyn laughed. "After everything that has happened tonight, I'd love to," she said. "Where?"

"Chavez Ravine."

"Who do you know that lives in Chavez Ravine?"

"My mother," Mathieu said. "Well, at least one of them."

"You have more than one mother?" Marilyn asked, seemingly confused.

"Yes, I'll explain in the car."

On the ride to Chavez Ravine, Mathieu explained that his father had a brief affair with Julia Simpson, a beautiful woman who had worked in his restaurant.

Julia had been on the run from her husband, who had sexually abused her, and her seven-year-old daughter Irene, whom she'd given up for adoption to protect her.

When Julia got pregnant with Mathieu, she was too afraid of her abusive husband to keep him. So, his parents adopted him, and Julia went into hiding in Chavez Ravine soon after his birth.

His parents lied to him about being adopted when he was a child. But Mathieu long suspected he was, and recently he'd found Julia.

They had a tenuous relationship because of her guilt about giving him up. But Julia agreed to help because she'd spent most of her adult life in hiding and sympathized with Marilyn's plight.

Mathieu drove up a dirt track on the north slope of Radio Hill, then passed through a narrow, damp underpass beneath Figueroa Street and entered Chavez Ravine. He continued along the ravine's floor, past modest clapboard houses on the right and hillside shacks on the left.

A half-mile up, the track curved sharply to the left and snaked its way up the side of La Loma past modest cabins and cottages tucked into every crevice. After rounding a sharp bend, they reached Julia's cabin, where Mathieu pulled off to the right and parked near the porch steps.

"It's so peaceful here," Marilyn said as she got out of the car, holding her small rucksack.

"Yes, it is," Mathieu said as he looked at the quiet dwellings on the hillside. "It's hard to imagine it's only a few miles from downtown."

"Thanks for bringing me here," Marilyn said, gazing into his eyes.

"Thank Julia … come on. I'll introduce you," Mathieu said as he led Marilyn up the steps.

Julia was waiting for them when they reached the porch. Mathieu did the introductions. Then Marilyn said, "Thank you for offering to help me, Julia. You're very kind … as is your son."

"I've been in your situation," Julia said with a sympathetic voice. "As for Theo, he gets his kindness from his parents, not me."

Marilyn looked at Mathieu with surprise. "Is Theo your first name?"

Mathieu nodded.

"You mean you didn't introduce yourself to Marilyn?" Julia asked.

Mathieu shrugged. "It never came up."

"Always the policemen," Julia said, shaking her head in dismay. "Come in, Marilyn. I've just put some coffee on. You both look like you could use it."

They entered the small cabin. Julia fetched three cups of coffee from her tiny kitchen, put them on the table next to her sewing machine, and sat down. Marilyn took the stool in the corner where Mathieu usually sat. Mathieu grabbed a cup of coffee from the table and stood near the door.

Julia and Marilyn started chatting like old friends, pretty much ignoring Mathieu, except for the occasional joke at his expense. Mathieu stood there good-naturedly, smiling to himself that this odd coupling might work despite his fears.

Julia explained to Marilyn that she would be staying next door with Mrs. Rodriquez, who was getting on in years and could use some help around the house and with her goats. If that bothered Marilyn, she didn't show it. Julia asked Marilyn if she spoke any Spanish, and to Mathieu's surprise, Marilyn answered she did.

After half an hour, Mathieu excused himself and said he had to get back to headquarters. He told Julia to call him if she needed anything. She smiled at him and told him not to worry. The "gente" of Chavez Ravine would take good care of Marilyn.

When Mathieu left to walk down to his car, Marilyn followed him down the stairs to say goodbye.

"Julia is wonderful. Thank you for arranging this. Though I confess I'm not used to being the second prettiest woman in the room," Marilyn said with a self-deprecating laugh. "I can see the resemblance between you two."

Mathieu smiled and handed her his card. "I think you'll be safe here. It's a tight-knit community. They take care of their own. But if you ever need anything or feel threatened, call me at this number."

"I will," Marilyn said with gratitude in her eyes as she reached up and kissed Mathieu on the cheek.

20

A Death in Venice

Two days later, at five in the morning, Mathieu drove his police vehicle down a narrow service road paralleling the Pacific Electric trolley tracks on the Venice peninsula.

To call it a "road" was a stretch. It was an arrow-straight dirt path sandwiched between endless rows of ninety-foot-high steel oil derricks with smoke spewing from the steam engines driving them.

Any charm Venice of America had was long gone. By 1929, they filled in most of the canals. Soon after, the Ohio Oil Company discovered oil on the peninsula, creating this surreal, putrid-smelling industrial nightmare.

Steel derricks covered the sandy, marshy, pancake-flat landscape from the shoreline to the east side of the Grand Canal as far as the eye could see. The peninsula was foul-smelling and ugly. The Grand Canal had become a cesspool of oil waste, and the polluted beaches resounded with the relentless clanging of drill pipes.

Everyone seemed to be in on the action, Mathieu thought as he looked at the signs on the derricks, shoehorned into every available inch of land. Well-known names like "Mohawk" and

"Allstate" stood next to lesser-known brands like "El Camino Gasoline" and "Blueridge Oil."

The peninsula had become a gigantic Monopoly Board where you rolled the dice to drill on a quadrant of land that either turned out to be "Boardwalk" if you hit oil or "Baltic Avenue" if you didn't. Either way, it was a crap shoot.

A quarter of the way down the track, Mathieu spotted a Ford Model A squad car parked beside Derrick 15, owned by the Blueridge Oil Company. Mathieu pulled in behind the squad car and got out. His friend Sergeant Gus Lombardi was there to meet him.

"Welcome to 'Venice of America,'" Lombardi said with an ironic grin.

"It looks more like the 'Venice of Hell' to me, Gus," Mathieu replied. "What have you got?"

"Another dead oil executive. That's why I called you at home."

Mathieu nodded. "What's his name?"

"Reginald Stonebridge."

"Did he work for Blueridge?" Mathieu asked.

"Yes, according to Jimmy Thompson, the foreman, Stonebridge was the vice president of operations."

"Well-liked?"

"I didn't ask," Gus said with a shrug. "But apparently not by everyone."

"Who found him?"

"A truck driver delivering drill pipe."

"Where did he find him?"

"Hanging from a rope strung over a crossbar about fifteen feet up on this derrick," Gus said, pointing to the derrick behind them. "The driver spotted him when he was unloading his truck."

Looking at the body lying on the oil-soaked ground, Mathieu asked, "Who cut him down?"

"The truck driver did with his switchblade," Gus said. "He thought there might be a chance he was still alive."

Mathieu nodded. "Is the driver the only one that touched him?"

"Yes."

"What time did he find him?"

"The call came in around 4 a.m. I happened to be in the area, so I took it myself, then called you."

"Where did the driver call from?"

"This line shack over here in front of the derrick," Gus said, pointing to his left at a dilapidated wood shack with a tin roof.

"The shacks are open at night?" Mathieu asked with surprise.

"Yeah, the foreman told me they don't get many visitors in this hellhole. Only the occasional kids trying to climb the derricks."

"Was the foreman on duty?"

"No, but he was on call. His name is on the bulletin board inside. The driver called him after calling us."

"Did you get the truck driver's contact information?" Mathieu asked.

"Yes, he's going to come into headquarters tomorrow and sign his statement."

"Thanks. What time did Fred and Stuart get here?" Mathieu asked, spotting them near the body.

"About fifteen minutes ago."

"When's the medical examiner coming?" Mathieu asked.

Checking his watch, Gus said, "He should be here soon?"

"Who is it?"

"The Walrus," Gus replied.

Sure enough, a few minutes later, as they stood there talking, the Chief Medical Examiner pulled up in his black 1932 Hudson Series L Brougham Sedan with its swooping front fenders and running boards and got out, impeccably dressed as usual in an expensive wool suit. Marsh looked as out of place in this oil-encrusted wasteland as the Pope in a coal mine.

"Sergeant Lombardi, Detective Mathieu, good morning to you both," Doctor Marsh said with good cheer. "I hear we have another dead oil executive."

"It appears that way, Doctor," Mathieu said. "Shall we take a look?

They walked about twenty feet to where the body lay on the sandy soil, illuminated by a work-light on a nearby derrick. The pounding of the machinery was even more intense here, so they had to raise their voices to be heard over the din.

Looking at Fred, Mathieu asked, "How do you think they got the rope over the crossbar?"

"They could have climbed the service ladder or just tossed it over," Fred said as he stood up.

"I talked to the truck driver who discovered the body. He said the rope was hanging over that crossbar about fifteen feet up and tied to the service ladder down here. Either way, once the rope was over the crossbar, they could have easily hoisted the victim up and tied it off."

Mathieu nodded. "The question is whether he was already dead."

"I should be able to determine that," Marsh said, squatting beside the body, careful not to soil his pantlegs in the process.

Marsh took his time studying the ligature marks on the victim's neck and the blood spots on his face. Then he pried open the victim's mouth and examined his tongue. It was swollen. He tested for lividity by feeling the victim's skin and moving the limbs to see if they were stiff.

Marsh muttered to himself as he worked. After a few minutes, he stood, dusted off some imaginary dirt from his pants, and turned to Mathieu.

"The ligature marks on the neck are too thin to be made by that rope, Detective. I think he was strangled beforehand, probably with a belt of some kind. Plus, the swollen tongue is a sign of strangulation. You wouldn't get that from hanging."

"So, he was dead when they strung him up."

"That's my conclusion," Marsh said.

"Time of death?"

"That's a little trickier. The body is still warm, but the limbs are just beginning to stiffen. So, I'd guess he's been dead for three or four hours, which would make it between one and two in the morning," Marsh said as he looked at his watch.

Mathieu nodded and said what they were all thinking. "So, they probably strangled him somewhere else, so there wouldn't be a struggle here. Then, later, they drove down the track, stopped here, threw the rope over the derrick, hoisted him up, tied off the rope, and drove off. They could have been in and out of here in less than ten minutes."

"That's a likely scenario based on the physical evidence, Detective," Marsh said.

"What do you think, Gus?" Mathieu asked, turning to him.

"That's what I would have done," Gus said. "Get in and out of here as fast as possible."

Jimmy Thompson, the foreman, was standing close by listening. He approached the group and said, "There's almost no one here between midnight and six, Detective. We run a lean crew at night. So, it would be easy to get in and out unnoticed.

"This service road is a loop. There's a bridge at the end of the peninsula that goes over the Grand Canal and connects to the east side of the oil field. They could have driven in on this side and driven out on that one."

Mathieu studied Thompson's face as he asked, "What did you think of Mr. Stonebridge? Was he well-liked?"

Thompson stood there impassively for a moment before answering. He was a strong man with a barrel chest and arms as thick as tree limbs. He could have easily strangled Stonebridge. He seemed to realize that's what the detective and the sergeant were thinking also as they stared at him.

Mathieu was about to ask the question again when Thompson said in a measured tone, "This is dirty, dangerous work, Detective. If we get injured on the job, they fire us immediately and hire someone else. The management of Blueridge is full of heartless bastards, just like all the other oil companies. And Stonebridge was no different. But the guys I work with aren't killers, and neither am I."

Mathieu didn't respond for a moment; he just continued to look at Thompson, waiting for him to twitch or say something else, but he stood there stoically.

"I appreciate your honesty, Mr. Thompson," Mathieu said. "But we'll need a list of your crew, including whoever was on duty tonight. Please fetch it and give it to Sergeant Lombardi. But don't worry about it. It's just routine. Understood?"

"Yes, sir."

"Good," Mathieu said, nodding his head, then turning to Gus, added, "Can you go with Mr. Thompson and get that list? And then later today, detail some of your officers to take their statements."

"Sure, will do," Sergeant Lombardi said, motioning to the foreman to accompany him.

21

What Connects Them

What was the connection between Jensen and Stonebridge? That was what was on Mathieu's mind as he approached Bull's office later that morning and knocked on the open doorjamb. Bull looked up briefly, then back at the papers on his desk, and said, "Come in and shut the door."

Mathieu had barely sat down when Bull asked without looking up, "Did you get that bullet hole in your rear windshield fixed?"

"Yes, sir. I told Sam in the garage that someone threw a rock at it."

"And your bent bumper?"

"I told him I backed into a tree."

"Christ, you're a terrible liar," Bull said, shaking his head in exasperation. "Did he buy it?"

"No, sir," Mathieu said with a shrug. "But that's what he wrote in the shop log."

Bull nodded, then rubbing his chin, said, "I've decided to keep that report you wrote about the 'Idyllwild Incident' in my desk for a while."

"Why?"

"Because," Bull began, then hesitated, "it could blow up in our face."

"What do you mean?"

"Well, you did leave the scene."

"Sure, but not before checking to see if Sheriff Langston was alive. Which he wasn't. There was nothing I could do for him; Langston was already dead when I got to him. Besides, he caused the accident. He tried to shoot us and run us off the road, for god's sake. I had a civilian in the car with me. I was afraid one of his deputies might try the same thing if we hung around. I couldn't risk any more Mountain Justice. And I did call and report the accident anonymously when I got to Hemet."

Bull raised his hands in surrender. "I know, I know. I didn't say you did anything wrong, but if someone wanted to, they could twist the facts."

"The facts are Sheriff Langston broke into the cabin, sapped me, tried to rape Miss Lane, and then, to cover his tracks, tried to shoot us and run us off the road!" Mathieu said in anger. "There are no other facts! I left to avoid some kind of kangaroo court, or worse, in the mountains.

"Our lives were in danger. I'd do it again. When we got back to Los Angeles, I put Miss Lane in a safe house and wrote my report. Would you prefer I was in a jail in Hemet and his deputies were having their way with Miss Lane?"

"Calm down, Mathieu," Bull said. "I probably would have done the same thing, but we have to be smart about this, which is why I'm not going to file your report unless someone forces my hand. And you're sure no one else saw the accident?"

"Maybe a coyote did, but no humans. We were on a deserted ridgeline in the middle of nowhere. I didn't see a single car until we reached Hemet, and that was parked on the street with its lights off."

"And you think Langston's motivation was all about sleeping with Miss Lane."

"I assume so," Mathieu said with a shrug. "She has that effect on men, and besides, Langston seemed pretty twisted to me. Marilyn said he'd been hanging around the inn trying to get into her pants ever since she arrived.

"Maybe when he saw my patrol car parked next to her cabin, he assumed I was sleeping with her, and it set him off. Plus, Marilyn said he looked pretty drunk when he was outside searching for her."

Bull nodded, "Yeah, I can see that as the trigger."

"But there's another possibility," Mathieu said, unsure whether to bring it up.

"What's that?"

"Langston seemed to know a lot about Jensen's murder for a country sheriff. He warned me off bothering the oil executives who own vacation homes up there."

"Did he say who they were?"

"No," Mathieu said, shaking his head.

"Maybe you should find out," Bull said.

"Okay, but it seems too much of a coincidence. But it did get me wondering if Langston was protecting someone."

"Even a better reason to find out who those oil executives are," Bull said.

"You're right, Chief," Mathieu said. "I'll have Enya do some research."

"Are you confident Miss Lane will be safe wherever you put her?"

"Yes, sir. Do you want to know where she is?"

"No," Bull said, narrowing his eyes. "The fewer people that know, the better. What do you know about the latest victim, Reginald Stonebridge?"

"Not much," Mathieu said. "He was vice president of operations for Blueridge Oil. So, he would have had a lot of direct contact with the oil rig workers. And after talking to the foreman, there was no love lost there."

"But I get the sense you don't think it was any of the oil workers," Bull said.

"No, I don't, neither at the Venice Oil Field nor the Inglewood Field. I mean, why would they kill Jensen and Stonebridge and string them up in their own fields? That doesn't make any sense. It's way too risky.

"Plus, I've read all the interviews Sergeant Lombardi's officers did with the current and former crew members at the Inglewood Oil Field. They all have alibis that check out.

"I think whoever is killing these oil executives is trying to make a point. I just don't know what it is. Either that, or they're trying to distract us from the real reason and blame it on the oil rig workers or someone else."

"What's your gut tell you?" Bull asked.

"That there must be a connection between Jensen and Stonebridge, either something in their past, an oil deal that went bad, or something else. But I don't think this is random."

"Then get to work and find it," Bull said.

"Yes, sir," Mathieu said as he stood to leave. "And thanks for putting the report on ice."

Bull acknowledged Mathieu's comment with a grunt.

After leaving Bull's office, Mathieu went to Enya's desk and sat down beside her with a sigh.

"You look like you didn't get much sleep. Do you want some coffee?" Enya asked.

"Thanks," Mathieu said. "Maybe later, but first, I've got a list of things for you to research."

"Great," she said. "What do you need done?"

"I'd like you to find out whatever you can about Reginald Stonebridge, the latest victim. All I know is he's a white male in his mid-forties, and he was a vice president at Blueridge Oil."

"It will probably be easiest if I just call Blueridge and get most of his particulars, like address, age, marital status, etcetera, from them," Enya said.

"I agree," Mathieu said, nodding. "But if you can't find everything you need from Blueridge, try the Hall of Records or the *LA Times*.

"I'm especially interested in finding out if there's a connection between Stonebridge and Lester Jensen, our first victim. I suspect there is, but it might be obscure. So, the more you can learn about them, the better. Understood?"

"Got it," Enya said with enthusiasm. "What else?"

"The next thing is trickier," Mathieu said with an embarrassed smile. "I want you to find the names of all the oil executives who own homes in Idyllwild."

Enya looked at him, confused. "How am I going to do that?"

Mathieu smiled. "Well, I've been thinking about that, and I think one way is for you to do a little playacting … you're good at that."

"Was that a compliment?" Enya asked, seemingly unsure.

"Of course," Mathieu said with a grin. "Here's what I'd suggest. Call the operator and ask for a long-distance connection to Idyllwild. Then, ask the local operator for the names of the real estate offices in town. I can't imagine there's more than one or two."

"Okay," Enya said, nodding her head. "Then what?"

"Then call them up and tell them you're the personal secretary to some big oil executive."

"Who?"

"I don't know," Mathieu said with a shrug. "Make up a name; there are tons of oil companies in LA. Tell the real estate agent your boss is looking for a mountain home. And he's already looked at Lake Arrowhead and Big Bear but wasn't impressed. But he heard a rumor that several oil executives have vacation homes in Idyllwild, and he'd like to talk to them about how they like the town and the area.

"Lay it on thick. Say he has a lot of money to spend, and if they could help him with references, then your boss would return the favor and give them his business. Real estate agents are as cutthroat as talent agents; they'll do anything to get a client."

Enya laughed. "So, you'd like me to lie through my teeth? Is that what you're asking, Detective?"

"Yes," Mathieu said with a mischievous smile. "But only because I know you can do it so well."

Enya took a mock swipe at Mathieu. "The only thing keeping me from hitting you is that you're not actually my brother."

"That's never stopped you before," Mathieu said.

"Don't tempt me," Enya said, trying to keep a straight face. "And what are you going to do while I'm playacting?"

"Visit Lester Jensen's second wife, Gloria Harris, and see what I can learn from her. Maybe she knows something about Stonebridge."

22

Gloria

The tennis ball wasn't the only thing that bounced as Gloria Harris stretched her lithe body for a forehand on the hardcourt behind her home on South Rossmore. The two-story, brick-clad mansion with a white-columned portico was set back fifty feet from the street like all the homes in Hancock Park.

Mathieu drove onto the circular driveway and parked in front of the entrance. He got out, took the stone steps to the porch, and knocked on the mahogany-paneled front door.

Moments later, a man's eyes peeked through the stained glass porthole. Then, the door opened, and Mathieu was greeted by a uniformed butler of uncertain age, to whom he showed his badge and asked to see Mrs. Harris.

The butler stood aside so Mathieu could enter the tiled rotunda. Mathieu's first image was of a delicate chandelier hanging in front of a marble staircase leading to the second floor. Cherry-wood-framed glass doors adorned both sides of the rotunda. The door on the left opened to the dining room and the one on the right to the living room with an ornate white stone fireplace.

The butler skirted to the right of the grand staircase as he led Mathieu down a narrow corridor toward the back of the house. After passing through two open doorways, they entered a sitting room with a parquet floor overlooking the expansive lawn, tennis court, and pool. Then, through a side door on the right, down two steps to a covered wood-plank deck.

Pointing toward the tennis court, the butler nodded, then left Mathieu to his own devices to introduce himself. Mathieu went down the steps, turned to his left, and walked over a trail of stone pavers to the tennis court. He stopped near the open gate in the chain link fence and watched as Mrs. Harris rallied from the baseline with her coach at the far end.

While not an expert player, Mrs. Harris was athletic and moved to the ball with a dancer's grace. She wore a short white skirt accentuating her finely toned long legs and a lightweight form-fitting sweater highlighting her other assets.

After a few cross-court rallies, Mrs. Harris whiffed a backhand badly, and the ball clanged against the back fence. Turning to retrieve it, she spotted Mathieu and froze for a second. Then, recovering her composure, she approached him with a confident strut, stopping a few inches short and staring into his eyes.

Everything about Mrs. Harris was dark and sultry: her pageboy haircut, eyes, and arched eyebrows. "Are you my new doubles partner?" she asked with a sparkle in those sultry eyes.

Returning her playfulness, Mathieu said, "I'm sorry, Mrs. Harris, but I forgot to bring my racquet."

"I have plenty of equipment," she quipped. "You can use whatever you'd like, handsome."

Mathieu smiled. "Thank you for the offer, Mrs. Harris, but I'm here for a different reason. My name is Detective Mathieu. I'm from the LAPD. I'd like to ask you a few questions about Lester Jensen, your ex-husband," he said as she showed her his badge.

Mrs. Harris didn't respond; she just continued looking at Mathieu. Then she turned toward her coach and yelled, "That's all for today, Harrold. I'll see you next Tuesday. Thank you."

Then, turning back to Mathieu said, "I've been expecting someone from the police ... but I wasn't expecting anyone like you. Follow me. We'll talk on the porch."

She gathered her racquet and a few tennis balls, which she put in her bag, then led Mathieu across the pavers to the deck and up the steps to a blue dining table under a white portico supported by slender Ionic columns. Mrs. Harris sat with her back to the sitting room's picture window and motioned for Mathieu to sit near her at the end of the table.

Without needing to be summoned, the butler appeared. Mrs. Harris looked at Mathieu and asked, "Would iced tea suit you?"

"Yes, thank you," Mathieu said.

Mrs. Harris nodded to the butler, and he returned to the house.

When he was gone, Mrs. Harris said, "I had hoped someone from the police would have come sooner. If only for my sake. I needed to talk to someone about Lester's death and, for obvious reasons, couldn't discuss it with my current husband."

"I apologize I wasn't able to speak with you earlier, Mrs. Harris," Mathieu said. "It's a complicated case."

"I can imagine," she said with downcast eyes. "I was shocked when I heard about Lester's murder. He was a rascal, but he was one of those characters you think can outrun death and live forever. But I guess it finally caught up with him. What do you want to know?"

"How did you meet?" Mathieu asked.

"At the crap tables at the Café La Bohème," she said, smiling at the memory. "He was ogling my ass when I bent over to throw the dice. But he did it in a nice way, not like a pervert. It was like he was admiring a sculpture in an art gallery, considering whether to buy it and bring it home."

Her story was similar to what Marilyn Lane had told him. The La Bohème must have been Jensen's hunting ground. "And did he? … Bring you home?" Mathieu asked.

"Not that night, but soon after. He'd just divorced his first wife and told me quite openly he was auditioning for a younger one. He asked me if I was interested. I said I was, and after a few cold readings at his bungalow, I got the part. We married a few weeks later."

"It sounds like you were fond of him."

"I was. Lester had a lot of bad traits, and he was a crook, of course, but a charming one."

"Do you know anyone who would want to kill him?"

"Well, there was that crazy guy who threw a dud firebomb through our front window that they never caught."

"Yes, I heard about that incident," Mathieu said. "But did your ex-husband ever voice his fears about anyone in particular?"

"Lester never voiced his fears about anything, Detective, except going to jail. He told me he'd kill himself before allowing that to happen."

"Where were you the night of the murder?" Mathieu asked.

Mrs. Harris appeared offended, so Mathieu added, "It's a routine question."

"I was here at the house with my husband," she said without flinching. "We had a small dinner party for friends of his from Paramount. My husband's a producer there."

"Were you angry when Jensen divorced you?" Mathieu asked.

Mrs. Harris scoffed. "No, I'm a realist, Detective. I knew the game. I was thirty when I married him and thirty-five when he divorced me. We had five good years together and a lot of fun. And frankly, I was ready for a calmer, more secure life. Lester was always one scam away from either bankruptcy or being arrested."

"Were you worried about finding a new husband that could give you a similar lifestyle?"

Gloria laughed. "No, not at all. The good thing about being a trophy wife is you get a lot of exposure in the newspapers. You get a reputation for being desirable and presentable at parties. Trophy wives are traded like baseball cards, Detective. The offers started rolling in before the ink had dried on our divorce papers."

"If I may ask, why did you choose Mr. Harris?"

"Well, compared to the oil business, the movie business is as staid as banking. And this time, I decided to choose an older man. They're always more grateful in my experience," she said with a knowing smile.

"Did your ex-husband ever mention someone by the name of Reginald Stonebridge?" Mathieu asked.

"Stoney?" Gloria asked with a laugh. "Sure, they go way back, apparently. But that's not his real name. In the late teens, Stoney was involved in an oil field fire in Texas where Lester and he worked together as roughnecks.

"Stoney left the country soon after the accident, went to Canada, and changed his name. He stayed there for about seven years, working his way up the ladder in the oil industry. When he and Lester reconnected, Stoney had a new identity and an English accent.

"Lester got him a job at Elk Hills. They also worked together in LA and did a few deals after Stoney went to Blueridge, but I don't know any of the details."

"What was his real name?"

"Roger Stone," she said.

Mathieu hesitated for a second and said, "Mr. Stone was murdered last night."

Gloria froze, her skin turning white as her tennis skirt. "You're kidding."

"No," Mathieu said.

"How?" Mrs. Harris asked, seemingly bewildered.

"I can't share that with you."

"It can't be a coincidence they were both murdered," she said almost to herself.

"I don't think so either, Mrs. Harris," Mathieu said. "The question is why. Can you think of a reason?"

"No," Gloria said, shaking her head in confusion. "Unless it was about some shady business deal or the oil field explosion in Texas, but that was almost sixteen years ago."

23

Mrs. Stonebridge

Reginald Stonebridge and his wife Veronica owned an elegant Spanish-style home tucked into the end of a cul-de-sac at the bottom of Runyan Canyon in the Hollywood Hills. Enya got the address from Blueridge Oil, and Mathieu visited the widow the next day.

Blueridge had informed Mrs. Stonebridge of her husband's death, sparing Mathieu that grim task. Enya had given him some background on Mrs. Stonebridge. She was in her late thirties from Toronto, Canada, and had been a piano teacher before she met her husband.

By the look of the estate, Blueridge paid their executives much more than Mathieu had thought. He parked in front of the address on Hillside Avenue and got out. The white two-story T-shaped house with red roof tiles was nestled against the hillside with garage parking underneath at street level.

To the left of the garage, a white stucco wall extended the width of the compound. In the center of it, two expansive Banyan trees framed an arched passageway with a wrought iron gate. Mathieu walked to the gate, pressed the button, and stated his business to the maid, who answered and buzzed him in.

Once inside the compound, Mathieu proceeded up a set of stairs, turned to his right, and followed the brick pavers around the enclosed front lawn to a three-story hexagonal tower that joined the wings of the home together. The uniformed maid was at the door to meet Mathieu and usher him into the foyer.

The foyer had an inlaid wood floor and a stenciled ceiling adorned with a lantern-style chandelier. An arched passageway to the left led to the main salon, but the maid led Mathieu straight across the foyer to the hallway, then up a flight of stairs on the right to the second floor.

Arriving at the landing, the maid pointed to an open doorway and said, "Madam is in the music room." Then she turned and went back downstairs.

From where he stood, Mathieu could hear the sound of a piano playing. He took a few steps toward the doorway, stopped, and looked in.

Mrs. Stonebridge sat before a polished black baby grand, her back to him, wearing a black satin dress with thin straps as she played.

A scattered beam of light poured through the open window to her left, highlighting her dark brown hair and casting a warm glow on the pale green walls and drapes. The light beam seemed to provide a protective cocoon around Mrs. Stonebridge as she played one of the most evocative pieces ever composed, Debussy's "Clair de lune."

The first notes of the piece are like a plaintiff call in the night, hinting at what is to come but revealing little. The song is a shapeshifter; it can be hopeful, inspiring, exciting, contemplative, or sorrowful, depending on the emotions of the performer or the listener.

The emotions Mathieu felt as he listened to Mrs. Stonebridge play were longing and loss tinged with regret. He sensed this was her way of dealing with her husband's death.

When Mrs. Stonebridge finished playing, she bowed her head as if in prayer. Mathieu remained silent and still, not wanting to intrude.

After a few moments, seemingly sensing Mathieu's presence, Mrs. Stonebridge swiveled on the piano bench and faced him with moist eyes. "I assume you're not the piano tuner," she said with a wry smile.

Mrs. Stonebridge was unlike any piano teacher Mathieu had ever seen, with cleavage that would have stopped a Vicar mid-sermon and a string of pearls between them that made it challenging to stay focused on her hazel eyes that widened when she saw Mathieu.

"That was quite beautiful, Mrs. Stonebridge."

"Thank you," she said with a demure smile. "Are you from the police?"

"Yes. I'm Detective Mathieu from the LAPD."

She nodded. "And a lover of music, apparently."

"Yes, mam."

"Do you play?"

"A little."

"Now that Reggie is gone, I may have to go back to teaching."

"With playing like that, I don't think you'll have any trouble getting students," Mathieu said and meant it.

"Please sit down, Detective," she said, motioning to a green settee beside the window.

After Mathieu was seated, Mrs. Stonebridge sat up ramrod straight, wiped her eyes, placed her hands on her knees, and asked, "How did Reggie die?"

"I'm afraid I can't share the details with you now."

"I see," she said. "Did he suffer?"

"It was quick," Mathieu said, not really answering the question.

"Was he disfigured?"

"No," Mathieu said, shaking his head. "Not in any way."

155

"That's a blessing," she said almost to herself. "When can I see him?"

"As soon as the coroner finishes with his examination. I'll have someone call you."

"Thank you," she said. "I assume you have questions for me."

"Yes," Mathieu said. "I'd like a little history first. How did you meet your husband?"

"I was playing in a piano bar in London, Ontario, to earn some extra money. I was wearing this dress the night I met Reggie. He approached me after the set and said he admired my playing.

"But I think what he really admired were my breasts," she said with a distant smile. "He admitted as much to me later when we started dating. He used to refer to them as 'the Canadian Rockies.'"

"Did he go by Reginald Stone when you first met him?"

"No," Mrs. Stonebridge said, shaking her head. "He'd changed his name by then to Stonebridge. He told me why, about the fire in the Texas oil field, and how traumatizing it had been."

"Was Reggie responsible for the fire?" Mathieu asked.

"Absolutely not!" Mrs. Stonebridge said with conviction. "But he wanted to put all that behind him, so he left for Canada to start over. He changed his last name and began to rebuild his career. He was working in Oil Springs when I met him, which is about an hour southwest of London. We dated for about a month, then moved in together and soon after married."

"When did you move to California?" Mathieu asked.

"A few years later, Reggie got a call from Lester Jensen, who was working at Elk Hills for Edward Doheny at the time. He told Reggie he had a job for him, so we both jumped at the chance. We moved to Bakersfield, which is a cesspit, but it was better than freezing our backsides off in Ontario in the winter."

"So, Lester and Reggie had kept in touch?"

"Yes, they'd worked together as roughnecks in Desdemona, Texas. Both were traumatized by the oil field fire in different ways. So, they shared a bond."

"And how did you get to Los Angeles?"

"Lester and Reggie grew closer at Elk Hills, and when Lester left and hit his first big score in the Rincon Oil Field, he convinced Reggie to come to LA.

"Reggie worked for Lester for a few years and made a lot of money off some of his questionable deals. But when the State of California started indicting Lester for fraud, Reggie decided it was time to leave, and he got a job at Blueridge. He'd already made a lot of money, and we'd bought this house by then."

"Did they stay in touch after he left?"

"Yes, and they still plotted their next big scores, just at a distance."

"Did you socialize with Lester and his wife Jacqueline?"

"No," Mrs. Stonebridge said, shaking her head in disgust. "I liked Lester's first two wives, but Jacqueline is a little too sleazy for my tastes."

"What was your husband's reaction when Lester was murdered?"

"He was shocked," Mrs. Stonebridge said. "Reggie looked up to Lester. He thought he was invincible."

"Did your husband seem worried?" Mathieu asked.

Mrs. Stonebridge turned and looked out the window while she considered the question. After a few moments, she turned back and said with troubled eyes, "Yes, in retrospect, I think he was, even though he never said anything. But these last few weeks, he did seem increasingly jumpy and anxious."

"What happened the night of the murder?"

"Reggie got a call here around 11 p.m. Whoever called told him there was an emergency at the Venice Oil Field. So, he dressed quickly, kissed me goodnight, and told me not to wait up. He said it would probably be a late night and left."

"In his own car?"

"Yes," Mrs. Stonebridge said. "Have you found it?"

"No," Mathieu said. "What make is it?"

"A silver 1932 Packard 900 sedan with red spoked rims."

"Why do you think your husband was murdered?" Mathieu asked. "What does your instinct tell you?"

Mrs. Stonebridge was silent for a moment, then sighed as she shook her head. "I've asked myself that question repeatedly over the last two days. At first, I thought maybe Reggie hadn't told me everything about what happened in Texas with the oil field fire. But we were close. He told me the whole story before we got married. He said he didn't want any lies between us. And I believed him.

"I think his murder must be related to some scheme he and Lester were involved in. I can't think of any other reason. Reggie was the kind of guy most people liked. He didn't have any personal enemies, as far as I knew. It has to be about money."

24

The Snitch

It was late. The detective's room was empty. A muted glow from the streetlamps on Main Street illuminated the room as a stationary fan labored noisily in the corner. Mathieu sat at his desk studying his case notes under the glare of a dented gooseneck lamp.

He leaned back in his scuffed-oak chair, swiveled to the right, and gazed out the north window toward the Old Plaza.

The corner desk was an upgrade from his original one closer to Bull's office. It was quieter here, more private, easier to think. Bull assigned it to him when one of the senior detectives retired recently. Bull told him he deserved it despite his age.

Mathieu turned his attention back to the case notes just as the phone rang, breaking the stillness in the room. "Detective Mathieu, LAPD," he said, answering the phone.

He could hear nervous breathing over the line, but the caller didn't speak. Mathieu waited a few seconds, then asked, "How can I help you?"

After a long moment, the caller asked, "Are you the detective in charge of the Lester Jensen murder?" It was a male voice, probably in his early twenties, with a jumpy cadence to his speech.

"Yes, I am," Mathieu said. "What can I do for you?"

"I've got some information about the case," the caller blurted out.

"What kind of information?"

"I can't tell you over the phone."

"Who'd you get my number from?" Mathieu asked.

"A friend who knows you."

"What's their name?"

"I can't tell you that now. We need to meet."

"Okay," Mathieu said. "Where?"

Mathieu heard a sigh and a telephone cord bang against the wall of a phone booth. A few moments later, the caller said, "In the Huntington Palisades."

"Where in the Palisades?" Mathieu asked.

"On the bluffs overlooking the Long Wharf."

"The bluff is almost a half-mile long," Mathieu said. "Where exactly?"

"At the horseshoe bend at the end of Friends Street," the caller said. "There's a big eucalyptus tree there with five trunks. You can't miss it."

"Why do you want to meet there?" Mathieu asked.

"Because it's secluded," the caller said. "There's no houses there."

"Okay," Mathieu said in a level voice. "What's your name?"

"I'll tell you when we meet."

"Fair enough," Mathieu said. "What time?"

"Ten o'clock."

Mathieu glanced at his watch. It was eight-thirty. He should be able to make it.

"Okay," Mathieu said, "I'll see you on the bluff at ten."

"And come alone," the voice said, then hung up.

The offer was tempting but sketchy. The caller sounded like a druggie to Mathieu. It could be a trap. Mathieu wasn't dumb enough to walk into an ambush, so he called his friend Sergeant

Gus Lombardi before leaving. Gus was just getting off duty but agreed to go with him.

Ten minutes later, Mathieu picked up Sergeant Lombardi outside headquarters on Main Street, then made his way south to Pico Boulevard, where he turned right and headed west toward Santa Monica.

On the drive out, Mathieu told Gus about the call and the meeting place. Gus told him he was glad Mathieu called because the whole thing sounded dicey to him. Mathieu agreed but told Gus he was desperate for a lead and had to chance it.

When they passed Fairfax Avenue, the landscape started to open up. There was still farmland and ranches out here, a welcome respite from the city's grid. But even here, oil derricks dotted the landscape. To the north, the Gilmore Oil field stood out like an ugly industrial wasteland.

Ever since the case began, Mathieu had started noticing oil derricks everywhere: at major intersections, in people's backyards, even next to Beverly Hills High School. Mathieu wondered what that might do to a student's lungs after four years. Los Angeles had traded orange groves for oil fields and orange blossoms for petroleum fumes, all in the name of "progress" and greed.

While Mathieu drove, Gus checked the *Thomas Guide* for Friends Street. The Huntington Palisades was a relatively new development for the well-to-do sitting on the bluffs overlooking the bay north of Santa Monica.

A group of Methodists bought the land from the Huntington estate and started developing it in the early '20s. It did well at first, especially on the flatter "ABC" streets north of Sunset, but the Depression hit, and sales collapsed. Now, on the bluff side, it was mostly empty lots with a few expensive homes scattered over the often crumbling cliffs.

Arriving in Santa Monica, Mathieu glided down the California Incline to Roosevelt Highway, then sped north past the recently completed Sorrento Beach Club Hotel tucked into the cliffside.

Reaching Santa Monica Canyon, Mathieu turned right and snaked up Chautauqua toward Sunset.

Gus called out the turns from there. The streets in the Palisades were confusing, laid out like coiled rope, and poorly lit, making it difficult to navigate at night. The wealthy residents didn't seem to like streetlamps; they were as rare as icicles in August here.

They took Sunset north for a half-mile, then turned left onto the mostly straight Swarthmore for another half-mile until they reached Friends Street, where they turned left again as it curved out to the bluffs.

It was pitch black here with no homes nearby. Thirty yards from the cliff's edge, Mathieu slowed to a crawl. Gus hopped out, crossed the street behind the Buick, and, staying low, made his way along the northern edge of Potrero Canyon. Mathieu continued toward the point where the road made a sweeping horseshoe bend to the right.

As Mathieu's headlights swept across the clifftop, he spotted a clump of five Eucalyptus trees like the caller had described. He glided to a stop across from them, doused the lights, then, allowing a few seconds for his eyes to adjust to the darkness, scanned the scene from his vehicle.

There were no other cars in sight and no one on the bluff. Mathieu undid his shoulder holster snap, cautiously exited the car, then crossed to the cliffside.

The bluffline here was the shape of a giant thumb protruding out from the rest of the palisades toward the ocean. Mathieu walked to the edge and looked down. There were steep drop-offs on all sides. The cliff was over two hundred and fifty feet high. One false step and you'd fall to your death.

Mathieu looked across Roosevelt Highway at the abandoned Long Wharf, jutting northwest into the bay. The ocean was calm, a feeble sliver of moonlight lying on its surface. Mathieu heard a car approach and turned toward the sound.

A red 1933 Packard Eight roadster with the top down coasted to a stop behind Mathieu's police car. A young man with thickly pomaded black hair wearing a dark suit got out. He was short with a nervous gait. Mathieu had seen that kind of jerky motion before, usually with drug addicts.

Staying close to his car, the man called out in a tinny voice, "Are you Detective Mathieu?"

"Yes," Mathieu answered.

"You alone?"

"Yes."

"Let me see your hands," the man said as he nervously twitched his shoulders.

Mathieu held his arms out to the side and asked, "Satisfied?"

"Yeah, sure."

"What's your name?" Mathieu asked.

"Eddie," the man replied.

"Eddie what?" Mathieu asked.

"Just Eddie," he said.

"Are you going to stand over there all night and yell across the road, Eddie? Or are we going to talk face-to-face?"

"Just being cautious," Eddie said as he attempted to saunter across the street like he wasn't afraid, but his nervous manner betrayed him.

Eddie stopped a few feet away from Mathieu. He couldn't have been over five-foot-five with baby smooth cheeks that looked like he'd never shaved and manicured fingernails.

He looked like a spoiled rich kid, maybe a USC grad. Close up, his shifty, bloodshot eyes and nervous twitch were even more pronounced. Mathieu guessed he was either high or coming down from one. He couldn't seem to stand still longer than two seconds.

"You said on the phone you had some information about the Jensen murder," Mathieu said.

Without answering, Eddie began pacing back and forth, stopped, started up again, then, looking at the ground, said, "Sometimes I overhear things that might be worth something."

"I see," Mathieu said. "And where do you overhear these things?"

"Usually at the gambling tables downstairs at the Café La Bohème. You know how it is, Detective. Guys start drinking and gambling, and their lips get a little loose. Or there's some cute babe they want to impress, so they start bragging. You know how it is. So, I overhear things."

"Such as?"

"Slow down, Detective … we're just talking here … I ain't said nothing yet."

"That's pretty obvious, and if you don't soon, I'm leaving."

"Hey, don't get sore, Detective. We're like negotiating."

"Ah, is that what we're doing? I didn't realize that," Mathieu said. "What do you want?"

"The thing is, Detective, I'm feeling a little anxious. I ran out of Bennies."

"You've come to the wrong person for drugs," Mathieu said flatly.

"No, I mean I need some money to pay Dr. Feelgood for some Bennies," Eddie said with an innocent smile.

"Who's Dr. Feelgood?" Mathieu asked.

"How would I know, Detective? That's not a question you ask a guy who gives you drugs that make you feel invincible. You just say thank you very much, Dr. Feelgood. Have a wonderful evening, Dr. Feelgood. All the best to the little woman," Eddie said, seemingly pleased with himself.

"We're done here, pal. You got nothing … you're wasting my time," Mathieu said, turning to leave.

"Wait, wait, wait, Detective. Please!" Eddie pleaded. "What if I told you the name of the guy who kidnapped the blond the night of Jensen's murder?"

That stopped Mathieu mid-stride, and he turned back. "You're bullshitting me."

"No, I can prove I know who he is."

"How?"

"I can tell you where he dropped the blond off after he kidnapped her."

"Where?"

"A couple blocks from the Greyhound Bus Station downtown. She was naked as a jaybird under her coat and scared to death."

The hair stood up on the back of Mathieu's neck. "What's his name?"

Eddie took a few steps away, wagged his finger at Mathieu, and said, "See, I knew you'd be interested, Detective. What can you do for me in return?"

Just then, a car came screeching around the corner, and shots rang out from the rear window. Mathieu lunged at Eddie, trying to protect him. He brought him down, rolled over once, drew his revolver, and fired back at the car as it sped away. Gus came running up seconds later and returned fire at the retreating taillights, but it was too late as they receded into the distance along the bluff.

Mathieu pushed himself up and looked at Eddie's body lying on the ground. There was a bullet hole in his chest and a glazed look in his eyes. Mathieu knelt and put two fingers on Eddie's neck. There was no pulse.

He cursed himself, then started searching Eddie's clothes for an ID. He found his wallet in the breast pocket of his suit coat. Mathieu stood, opened it, and looked at Eddie's driver's license.

"Shit!" Mathieu said.

"What's wrong?" Gus asked.

"I think I know who this might be," Mathieu said.

"What do you mean?"

"His name is Edward Hennessy," Mathieu said, staring at Gus with troubled eyes. "I think he's the brother of Lillian Hennessy, a violinist I recently met at the Café La Bohème."

25

The Sister

Everything went by in a blur for Mathieu after the shooting: the wail of sirens, the crackle of flashbulbs, the victim draped in a white sheet, the ambulance leaving, and then utter silence as if nothing had happened.

If someone walked a dog here in the morning, only the dog would detect the scent of death.

On the ride back to headquarters, Gus volunteered to inform Lillian Hennessy of her brother's death. Mathieu appreciated the offer but knew he had to do it himself; anything else would be cowardly.

Mathieu called Paul Thornton in the morning and told him what had happened. Paul was shocked but confirmed that Eddie was Lillian's brother. Mathieu asked Paul if he knew where Lillian lived and if he knew anything about her relationship with her brother.

Paul told him their relationship was strained at best. Her brother was always asking Lillian for money for drugs or his gambling debts. She helped him initially, but recently, she'd given up on him and refused to give him any more money.

Paul gave him Lillian's address. Mathieu thanked him and asked him not to say anything to Lillian about her brother's death until he had a chance to inform her in person.

Lillian Hennessy lived at a stylish address on South Genesee Avenue, just off the "Miracle Mile."

But even here, it was "oil country." The La Brea tar pits were just across Wilshire Boulevard to the north, and north of them, the Gilmore Oil Field sprawled across 256 acres of Arthur Gilmore's former dairy farm.

Nevertheless, it was an expensive area, too expensive for a musician, Mathieu thought as he parked across the street. It was an attractive two-story blue and gold Art Deco building on top of a gated parking garage. The façade alternated between recessed windows and powder-blue supports that looked as soft as cake frosting.

Mathieu wondered if Lillian came from money or had a rich husband. He sincerely hoped it was the former. But whatever her situation, the coming encounter would be painful for both of them. How do you tell a woman you're interested in that her brother was shot and killed in front of you?

He crossed the street and took a set of blue concrete stairs beside the parking garage up to the entrance level, then skirted past a small, tiled pond to the front entrance. The gate was open, and he walked up a few steps to the vestibule and stopped to check the metal mailboxes on the right.

Lillian lived in apartment E on the second floor. Mathieu walked down the burnt-orange-colored tile floor to the center of the building, then took the staircase to the second floor. Arriving on the landing, he walked toward the rear of the building, where he spotted Lillian's door tucked into an alcove on the left.

Mathieu paused for a moment, gathering his courage for what was to come, then exhaling, pressed the buzzer, and waited. When there was no response after a few moments, he checked his watch. It was 8:30 a.m. He hoped she hadn't left already.

He stepped closer to the door, pressed the buzzer again, and listened as the sound echoed through the apartment. He put his ear against the door. He thought he heard a faint tumbling sound, but perhaps it was his imagination.

Frustrated, Mathieu knocked this time, calling out, "Miss Hennessy, it's the police! Open up, please!" Then he pressed his ear to the door again; there was no sound.

He tried the doorknob. It was unlocked. He unholstered his Colt, turned the knob, and burst into the room, shouting, "Police! Is anyone here?"

He entered a small, enclosed foyer with an interior wall on the right blocking his view into the apartment. With his back to the wall, Mathieu inched toward the arched opening. Reaching it, he exhaled, spun into the living room with his gun arm extended, and shouted, "Police!"

And then he saw her, sprawled face first on the floor near the faux fireplace, arms and legs bound, motionless.

Mathieu rushed to Lillian's side, knelt, undid the ropes, removed the gag from her mouth, and rolled her on her back. He brushed the hair from her face and stared into her makeup-less eyes. "Miss Hennessy, are you all right?"

Lillian looked up at him with a glazed look, seemingly disoriented. She wore a burgundy-colored bathrobe with a satin collar and cuffs; her long red hair tangled around her neck.

Mathieu gently cupped her face in his hands as he checked her eyes and asked, "Are you hurt, Miss Hennessy? I'm Detective Mathieu from the LAPD. We met once. Do you remember?"

"Yes, I remember," she said in a groggy voice, trying to sit up. "Why are you here? Did someone call the police?"

Ignoring the question, Mathieu asked, "Do you feel well enough to stand?"

Lillian nodded. Mathieu helped her up and over to a leather sofa near a large east-facing window. Then he sat in an armchair next to her.

"Tell me what happened," Mathieu said, leaning toward her.

Lillian sighed, looked down at her hands, flexing and curling her slender fingers to see if they were okay, and said, "Early this morning, there was a loud knock on the door. I thought maybe it was my brother wanting to borrow money again. I opened the door, and a man was standing there wearing a mask over his face.

"He pushed me into the room, tied my hands behind my back, and asked me where my brother kept his things. I told him my brother and I were estranged because of his drug use and that he didn't keep anything here. The man didn't believe me. He shoved me to the floor face first, tied my legs together, and gagged me.

"Then I heard him search the apartment, throwing things around. After about twenty minutes, he stormed out of the apartment and slammed the door. I tried to get up but couldn't. After that, I dozed off from the shock until I heard the doorbell ring just now. I was afraid he'd come back."

"What did he look like?" Mathieu asked.

Lillian pursed her lips, looked away, and said, "He was several inches shorter than you but stockier with a thick neck and a square head. He reminded me of a truck driver ... or a cop."

"How old?"

Lillian shrugged. "Mid-thirties, I'd guess from his voice and the way he moved." Her description was similar to Marilyn Lane's abductor.

"Do you mind if I check the apartment?" Mathieu asked.

"No, not at all, please do," she said. "I'm still a little shaken. Can you bring me a glass of water from the kitchen?"

"Of course," Mathieu said as he stood, turned to his right, then right again down the hallway off the living room. The apartment was light and spacious, with polished hardwood floors, white walls, and decorative crown molding.

As he went down the hallway, he passed an open closet on his left, its contents spilled on the floor, a small dining area with a parquet floor on the right with east-facing windows, and a galley kitchen with white cabinets in the northeast corner of the apartment that looked untouched.

To the left of the kitchen was a narrow bathroom with green tile and two small windows looking north. Next to it was the bedroom. The bedding was tossed, a lamp overturned, and a night table drawer hung open. Across from the queen-sized bed was a walk-in closet with Lillian's clothes strewn on the floor and the contents of the dresser drawers scattered about.

Mathieu returned to the kitchen, got a glass, filled it, and took it to Lillian. He found her sitting in the same spot with her head in her hands. He handed her the glass of water and said, "There are a lot of things tossed about, but nothing seems broken."

"That's a relief, at least," she said, looking up with troubled eyes. "You still haven't told me why you're here. Did someone call the police?"

Mathieu turned from her gaze, sat in the armchair, looked at the floor, and said, "I'm afraid I have some terrible news for you, Miss Hennessy."

"What is it?" Lillian asked. "Is it about my brother?"

"Yes," Mathieu said, nodding. "I'm sorry to inform you that he's been killed."

"Oh, my God!" she said as the color drained from her face. "How?"

"He was shot."

"Where did it happen?" Lillian asked, seemingly in shock.

"On a deserted bluff in the Huntington Palisades."

"When?"

"Last night around ten," Mathieu said.

"Do you know who shot him?"

"No, not yet," Mathieu said, shaking his head. "He was shot by a man in the back of a speeding car that got away."

171

"How do you know all this?" Lillian asked, seemingly trying to make sense of it. "Were there witnesses?"

"I was there," Mathieu said in a subdued voice. "I tried to save your brother but wasn't able to."

Lillian looked at Mathieu with a blank expression, then turned away. He watched her, bracing for the worst. He feared she would explode in anger—she had a right to. He steeled himself for the onslaught. But it never came.

After what seemed like forever, Lillian looked up with tears in her eyes and said in a soft voice, "I wasn't able to save Eddie, either, Detective. He was a troubled man. I always feared it would end this way. We led a privileged and pampered life. Our parents were wealthy. But then the Depression came, and everything changed.

"I'd saved some money, but Eddie burnt through his like dried kindling. Soon after, our parents died in a 'car accident.'

"Though, I suspect they committed suicide because they couldn't deal with their new station in life. I tried to help Eddie, but he just continued to mess up. It got so bad I couldn't take it anymore and gave up on him. I'm sure you tried your best, Detective."

"Unfortunately, it wasn't enough," Mathieu said.

"What I did wasn't enough either," Lillian said almost to herself.

"That's not your fault," Mathieu said.

"Perhaps," Lillian said with a shrug. "Tell me what happened. I need to know."

Mathieu told her the whole story, sparing her nothing, how Eddie contacted him promising information on Jensen's murder, their meeting on the bluff, and the attack.

He finished by saying, "I didn't know his last name until after the attack. It was then I suspected he might be your brother. Do you have any idea who might have wanted him dead? Could it be Fred Marlow? I heard him threaten you the day we met."

Lillian scoffed. "I doubt it. Marlow's a creep, but I don't think he's a killer. Marlow was at the La Bohème last night when I was playing with Paul Thornton. I saw him several times during the evening. Besides, he had no reason to kill Eddie. Eddie owed him money. He had nothing to gain from his death. I suspect Eddie was killed for the same reason you do, because of what he knew about Jensen's murder."

"I assume Eddie never mentioned anything about it to you," Mathieu said.

"No," Lillian said, shaking her head. "I haven't seen Eddie in months … and now I never will."

"How was Eddie able to afford that expensive roadster?"

"From his share of our parent's life insurance," Lillian said.

"Did you know any of Eddie's friends?" Mathieu asked.

"No," she said, shaking her head. "They were mostly gamblers and lowlifes."

"What about his girlfriends?"

"The kind of women Eddie dated you don't introduce to your sister."

Mathieu nodded that he understood. "If you think of anyone else later on who knew him, please call me," Mathieu said. "Do you still have my card?"

"Yes," she said. "I kept it in my wallet … just in case. When can I see Eddie's body?"

"I'll have someone call you after the coroner finishes his examination."

Lillian was silent for a moment and said, "I'd appreciate it if you would call instead of a stranger."

"Certainly, if that's what you'd prefer."

"Yes, I would," she said, looking into Mathieu's eyes. "And can I ask you one other favor?"

"Sure, what is it?"

"Would you go with me when I identify the body?" Lillian asked with a pleading look. "I don't want to go alone."

"Of course," Mathieu said.

"Thank you. I appreciate that," Lillian said. "You're very kind."

Then, laughing at herself, she added, "You've seen me at my worst, Detective, bloodshot eyes, disheveled hair, no makeup. I must be a sight. I don't know what you must think."

Mathieu gazed into her eyes and said, "There's no need to worry about that, Miss Hennessy. You look beautiful despite what you've been through."

"Thank you," she said as she blushed and turned away.

Mathieu stood to leave. "I don't think they're coming back, Miss Hennessy, but I'd advise getting an extra lock. And please, don't let anyone in without checking the peephole first."

"I will," Lillian said. "I promise."

Mathieu started for the door, then turned back. "I have one more question, Miss Hennessy. Do you know where Eddie lived?"

Lillian shrugged. "I don't think he had his own place. I assumed he stayed with friends. Or maybe he mooched off one of his girlfriends. Eddie had a lot of girls. He was the life of the party. He traveled pretty light, just a beat-up old satchel he kept in his car."

"A beat-up old satchel?" Mathieu repeated.

"Yes," Lillian said. "Anything that was important to him he kept in there. Have you found it?"

"No," Mathieu said, shaking his head. "But we impounded his car, and thanks to you, I know it exists now."

26

The Satchel

When Mathieu returned to headquarters, he immediately reached for the phone and called Fred Wilson, anxiously shifting his weight back and forth as he waited. When Fred answered, Mathieu blurted out, "Did you find a satchel in the victim's roadster?"

"No, sir."

"Did you search the trunk?"

"The roadster doesn't have a trunk, just that carrier on the back, but it was empty."

"What about the rumble seat?" Mathieu asked.

There was a delay. Then Fred sighed and said, "Sorry, I didn't think to check it."

"Is the roadster in the impound garage downstairs?"

"Yes."

"Good," Mathieu said, relieved. "Go to the garage and search the rumble seat and the rest of the car for a satchel. I don't know how big it is. It's even possible it's under the front seat. His sister told me Eddie always kept it in his car. It's important. And bring along any personal effects that you found on the victim."

"Yes, sir, right away," Fred said, then hung up.

While waiting for Fred to search the car, Mathieu went to Bull's office to brief him.

"Is this latest shooting related to Jensen's murder?" Bull asked as Mathieu sat down.

"I think so, Chief."

"Tell me about it."

"A snitch called me last night and asked if I was in charge of the Jensen case. When I told him I was, he said he had some information I could use. He demanded we meet on a bluff on the Huntington Palisades overlooking the Long Wharf."

"Did you know the snitch?"

"No," Mathieu said, shaking his head. "And he wouldn't tell me his name until we met in person."

"Why on the Palisades?" Bull asked with a concerned look.

"Because he said he wanted to meet somewhere remote."

"Sounds pretty dicey," Bull said.

"I thought so, too, but I thought it was worth a try," Mathieu said. "So, I asked Gus to go with me as backup."

"What happened on the bluff?"

Mathieu told Bull the whole story about getting there early, Eddie Hennessy arriving in an expensive car, and his nervous, jumpy manner."

"What did he want?" Bull asked.

"Money for drugs," Mathieu said.

"Did he have any real information?"

"Yes, sir, he knew about Marilyn Lane being kidnapped and where she was dropped off."

"How did he know about that?" Bull asked, surprised.

"He claimed he overheard a guy bragging about kidnapping her in the restroom at the Café La Bohème."

"Did he tell you the guy's name?"

"No, sir, he didn't get a chance," Mathieu said. "He started to tell me when this car came screaming around the corner and shot him."

"Did you or Gus get hurt?"

"No, sir," Mathieu said, shaking his head. "I pulled Eddie to the ground and returned fire, but the car sped away."

"So, we got nothing out of this escapade?" Bull asked, looking irritated.

"Not exactly, Chief," Mathieu said. "I went to see his sister, Lillian Hennessy, this morning after the shooting. When I got there, I found the door unlocked and Lillian lying on the floor with her hands and legs tied up. I freed her and asked what happened.

"She said a masked man had come late last night, looking for Eddie's belongings. Lillian told him she and her brother were estranged, and she didn't know where Eddie's stuff was. The man searched her apartment anyway, then left empty-handed. After she calmed down, I gave her the bad news about her brother's death."

"Do you think the sister has anything to do with this?"

"No, sir," Mathieu said. "I met her previously at the La Bohème when I went there to question Marlow. She's straight. She's a professional musician—a violinist.

"She's had nothing to do with Eddie recently because of his drug use and gambling. But she told me Eddie always kept a satchel in his car. I've got Wilson searching the car for it right now. Eddie might have kept some notes or something in it."

"Let's hope so, Mathieu," Bull said.

Mathieu returned to his desk and was fiddling with his pen when Fred showed up a few minutes later with a leather satchel and placed it on the desk. "I found it in the rumble seat, sir, just like you thought."

It was a Gladstone Bag covered in stiff chocolate-brown cowhide. It was about two feet long, a foot deep and wide, with a rigid frame and an open-mouth hinged closure that provided easy access to the contents.

The sides were scuffed and stained, but it looked like a bag that could take a beating. The closure had a stiff leather plate with a brass lock.

"Did you find the key?" Mathieu asked, looking at Fred.

"Yes, fortunately, it was on his key ring," Fred said as he handed it to Mathieu.

Mathieu stood, inserted the key, clicked it open with a flick of his wrist, undid the lanyard straps, and opened the bag. Near the top were two starched white dress shirts, gray flannel slacks, and a navy blue cable knit wool sweater.

Toward the bottom were rolled undershirts and pants, four pairs of black socks, an extra pair of shoes, and a brown calf-leather shaving case. He dumped the contents of the Gladstone Bag on the desk and scanned the items.

He'd hoped Eddie had kept a notebook or a diary, but he didn't see anything like that on the desk. Mathieu felt along the sides and bottom of the now empty satchel for anything hidden behind the lining but didn't find anything, so he searched the clothing. There was nothing of interest.

Disappointed, he sat down, reached for the chestnut-brown shaving kit, unzipped it, and laid it open on the desk. The interior had a suede lining with leather straps holding everything in place.

The lower half contained a hairbrush, chrome-plated tubes for soap, a shaving brush, and a toothbrush, along with a nail file and a brown Bakelite razor case.

Mathieu unsnapped the Bakelite case and opened it. Inside was a Gillette silver nickel safety razor and two unopened Blue Blades in their paper envelopes with King Gillette's mugshot on the front.

The top half of the leather shaving kit contained a comb and a vanity mirror held in place by two corner edge guards. Mathieu removed the mirror. Behind it was a photo of a little girl of about seven, the top edge creased from frequent handling.

In the photograph, the little girl stood beside a grand piano, her head just level with the rim, playing the violin. Mathieu's heart skipped a beat when he saw her. It was Lillian; her poise, focus, and beauty were already apparent at that young age. Her brother might have been a jerk, but he had obviously loved his sister if he'd kept this photo.

Mathieu removed the photo and stared at Lillian's face. He wondered what it would have been like if they had grown up together as kids. Would they have been boyfriend and girlfriend? Would they still be together? A smile came over his face at the thought. He remained that way for a moment until he became aware of Fred watching him.

He put the snapshot down and looked at the shaving kit again. Behind where Lillian's picture had been was a small, thin, black leather memorandum book. Mathieu's eyes widened as he reached for it.

It was about four inches high, two inches wide, and a quarter-inch thick and fit easily in the palm of his hand. The black cover was engraved: "The Prudential Insurance Company of America." It was one of those giveaways salesmen hand out to potential clients.

The first page, with Eddie's handwriting, had the heading "Loans." Mathieu spotted entries like "Feb 1 Lili $200," "Feb 15 Uncle Al $375," "Mar 7 Grandma Edna $100," and "Mar 11 Pauline $50."

Eddie had an odd scrawl. He'd penciled the dates and names in a steady hand, but the amounts looked like drunks about to topple over.

Maybe it reflected his guilt for fleecing his friends and relatives. But that was probably giving Eddie too much credit because he repeatedly hit the same people up for money.

Nevertheless, Eddie had been crafty. He rotated among his "marks," never hitting up the same person more than once a month. Mathieu doubted Eddie had repaid the "loans" because there weren't any annotations suggesting he had.

About seven pages in, the heading changed to "Gambling Debts" with only two entries on that page: "$1,000 Marlow" and "$500 Harry the Lip."

The next few pages were titled "Gossip Column Income" with entries like: "Mar 1 fifty bucks from LP for tip about Ron Reagan sleeping with two starlets at the Garden of Allah," and "Mar 7 seventy-five bucks from LP for spotting Doug Fairbanks kissing Sylvia Ashley at La Bohème."

Mathieu assumed "LP" was Louella Parsons, the famous gossip columnist who worked for Hearst's *Herald Examiner*.

After that section, the page heading changed to "Pimping." Mathieu had to laugh; at least Eddie was being honest.

One entry read, "Introduced 'Lola the redhead' to Sheriff Bradford, he slipped me a twenty in gratitude," and another said, "Took 'Sandra the body' to Edgar's penthouse at the Chateau Marmont, hung out, drank champagne, ate his caviar, left without Sandra but with a fifty in my wallet."

The final section read "Risky Business," for which there was only one entry:

"I was in a toilet stall downstairs at La Bohème Saturday night when FF and an ex-sheriff came in to take a piss. They sounded drunk by the way they were slurring their words.

"While they were standing at the urinals, FF started whispering that he'd kidnapped a blond the night of Jensen's murder and dropped her off downtown near the Greyhound Bus Station. He bragged that she had tits like the Matterhorn and was naked as a jaybird under her coat. He claimed he copped a feel on her tight little ass before he walked away."

27

The Deed

The Beverly Hills lawyer wondered how many people committed suicide driving through Bakersfield because it was so damn ugly and depressing. He'd spotted a family of Dust Bowl refugees camped outside town behind a Southern Pacific billboard, which mockingly read, "Next Time Try The Train."

He felt sorry for the Okie wretches, but the sight of the encampment made him glad he hadn't brought a knife along to slit his wrists.

Horatio Ignatius Jennings, Esq. could be forgiven his pique. He was in a foul mood. He hadn't gone to Harvard Law School to drive over a hundred and twenty tortuous miles from Los Angeles to this sweltering, godforsaken oil patch in the Central Valley to look up a goddamn property deed at the Kern County Hall of Records.

But Horatio had to take what he could get; times were tough for lawyers during the Depression, even ones from Beverly Hills. Besides, his wealthy client was paying him well for the errand.

Horatio's spirits improved somewhat when he turned off Twenty-first onto Chester Avenue in downtown Bakersfield and headed south. The locals had somehow miraculously concocted a passably attractive street. They certainly had the money for it with all the oil fields nearby.

The avenue was broad and well-paved, with angle parking on both sides. Trolley tracks ran down the center, past attractive three and four-story brick buildings flying more American flags than West Point.

Most of the vehicles parked along the avenue were black Model A Fords. In contrast, Horatio's maroon 1929 Buick Touring convertible with gold-spoked white-wall tires and a tan canvas top stood out like caviar on a saltine cracker.

Horatio didn't mind the envious stares of the locals as he cruised down Chester Avenue with the windows open to fight the oppressive heat. The sun seemed ten times brighter here, forcing him to squint through the glare coming off the tarmac.

In the distance, Horatio could see a beautiful Spanish-style clock tower in the middle of the street. He wondered how the yellow and green trolley cars got around it. As he continued, he passed a four-story building on his left with arched windows and a corner turret overhang that reminded him of San Francisco.

At Chester and 17th, he passed the sprawling El Tejon Hotel and, just past it, the clock tower in the middle of the street. Horatio noticed they'd routed the trolley lines around the tower to preserve it. He had to give the "Bakershole" City Fathers credit for that.

A block south, at the corner of Chester and Truxton, Horatio pulled over to the right and angle parked his Buick Touring car in front of the Beaux Arts style Kern County Hall of Records. It was a grand edifice with Corinthian pillars, twenty-foot-high arched windows, and a domed rotunda.

Horatio's pace was quick and assured as he strode toward the entrance stairs as if momentum alone would make him seem more important than he was.

He was a large-boned man, nearly six feet tall. And if you didn't notice the slightly frayed cuffs on his starched shirt, he looked prosperous enough in his expensive suit and cocked hat. Even though neither fit perfectly anymore because of the weight he'd lost since the Depression.

Horatio bounded up the concrete stairs hoping to get this unpleasant task over with as soon as possible and get the hell out of this hick town. He opened the heavy, dark wooden door, then walked across the polished granite tile floor to the rotunda, where he consulted the directory. The Registrar of Deeds Office was in Room 107, which was off to the left.

Entering the Registrar's office, Horatio approached a waist-high counter in the shallow vestibule. No one else was in the room, so he pressed the brass bell to his right and waited.

The counter, paneled in dark wood, held several official seals, stamp pads, and writing blotters neatly arranged on its surface.

Behind the counter was a desk, and behind it, floor-to-ceiling metal shelving with rows of leather-bound binders filled with property maps. Through an open doorway to the left, Horatio could see similar shelving units in the back room.

As Horatio's hand hovered over the bell to strike it again, a tall, fair-haired young man with wire-rimmed glasses emerged from the back and said in an Okie accent, "Keep yer pants on! I heard you the first time. What do you want?"

The young man had the peach-smooth complexion of a baby's bottom and the stern look of a Baptist preacher.

"I'm Counselor Horatio Ignatius Jennings," Horatio said, sliding his business card across the counter. "I need to look up a property deed."

The clerk studied the card for a moment, then looked at Horatio. "So, yer from Los An-jel-eeze," he said, his mouth stretching wide enough to shove a two-by-four into it as he pronounced Los Angeles like it rhymed with a foul-smelling cheese.

"Yes," Horatio said.

"Do you have a tract number or address, Counselor?"

183

"No," Horatio said. "But I have the map coordinates."

"I need a tract number or address," the clerk said with a stubborn look.

"Surely, you have a book that cross-references map coordinates to tract numbers," Horatio said.

"I do, Counselor, but that will be an extra five dollars for the service."

"That's fine," Horatio said, struggling to remain calm. "I also know the name of the property."

The clerk sighed and said, "Well, that might help, Counselor. What's it called?"

"The El Saucito Ranch. It's on the Carrizo Plain south of Soda Lake."

"Hmm," the clerk said after hearing the name. "That's curious."

"What do you mean?"

"Well, another lawyer from Los An-jel-eeze was in here two weeks ago asking about the same property."

"What was his name?" Horatio asked.

"You know I can't tell you that, Counselor," the clerk said. "That's confidential."

"How confidential?" Horatio asked, removing a twenty from his billfold and placing it on the counter.

The clerk snuck a quick look at the twenty, glanced over his shoulder, and snatched it off the counter faster than a snake's tongue.

"A lawyer by the name of Thomas Briggs," the clerk said. "Big fat guy with bad breath. I'll get that deed for you now, Counselor. I remember which binder it's in."

The clerk turned and went back into the stacks as Horatio waited, wondering who Counselor Thomas Briggs's client was. A few minutes later, the clerk emerged from the backroom with a wide grin and a leather-bound binder in his hand. He laid it on the counter, flipped through several tabbed folders, removed one, took out a deed, and placed it in front of Horatio.

The deed was from the "Southern Counties Title Insurance Company." It had a green border, with the number F3872 stamped on top. Horatio opened the deed and read the standard boilerplate on the first page.

"On this 15th day of July, in the year of our Lord One Thousand Nine Hundred and Twenty Three, Margaret Brumley appeared before me and transferred title to ... " And then the new owners were listed.

Surprised at the number of owners, Horatio narrowed his eyes and asked, "How is the title on this deed held?"

The clerk pointed to the bottom of the second page and said, "Joint tenants with the right of survivorship like it says here."

Horatio pursed his lips as he thought about the implications. After a few moments, he said, "So that means ownership passes to the surviving owners if one of them dies."

"That's correct, sir," the clerk said with a nod.

"And if all the owners die, the deed passes to the estate of the last deceased."

"That's also correct, Counselor."

Horatio looked at the names again. The deed listed three co-owners: Lester Jensen, Reginald Stonebridge ... and one more.

28

The Great Race

It didn't take Mathieu long to discover the identity of "FF" in Eddie's diary. He called the Café La Bohème in the afternoon when he assumed only a skeleton staff would be on hand. He asked to speak to Sam, the young bartender.

When Sam came on the line, Mathieu said, "This is Detective Mathieu from the LAPD. We met a few weeks ago, do you remember?"

Sam lowered his voice and said, "Yes, sir, I remember."

"Can you speak freely?"

There was a silence before Sam said, "Yes."

"Do you know anyone who hangs out at the club with the initials 'FF?'" Mathieu asked. "He's probably a tough guy, medium height, likes to brag."

There was another silence, then Sam replied in a hushed voice, "It could be Fat Freddy."

"What's his last name?"

"Fowler."

"Do you know where he lives?" Mathieu asked.

"No, but I know where he hangs out."

"Where's that?"

"At the track," Sam said. "There's a big stakes race at Santa Anita tomorrow. You'll probably find him near the paddock or in the Chandelier Room."

"Know anything else about him?"

"Rumor is he's an ex-con."

"Thanks, Sam, I appreciate it. And keep this to yourself. We never had this conversation. Understood?"

"Yes, sir," Sam replied in a nervous voice. "Understood."

After the call ended, Mathieu asked Enya to pull Freddy Fowler's arrest record and get his mug shot. Then he called Sergeant Lombardi.

"Are you doing anything special tomorrow, Gus?"

"No, why?"

"Want to go to the races at Santa Anita?"

"Sure, what's the occasion?"

"I'll explain on the ride over."

"Okay."

"And wear your best suit … no uniforms."

"Got it."

"I'll pick you up in front of headquarters at 11 a.m."

"Sounds good, see you tomorrow," Gus said and hung up.

The next morning, Mathieu and Gus drove north on Figueroa Street through the Elysian Park tunnels, then across the LA River to Highland Park, where they turned on York Boulevard, crossed over the southern section of the Arroyo Seco, and headed northeast into Arcadia.

Arriving in Arcadia, they turned off Baldwin Avenue into Gate 8 at Santa Anita Park. As they rode along the dirt entrance road, Mathieu spotted the stable area off to his left. "I can't believe how many barns they have," Mathieu said.

"Sixty-one of them," Gus said. "I was told they can house almost two thousand horses here."

Raising his eyebrows, Mathieu glanced at Gus. "I didn't know you were interested in horse racing."

"I'm not, but a buddy brought me here on opening day," Gus said. "It was quite a scene, almost 31,000 people."

Mathieu shook his head and said, "That's hard to believe in the middle of a Depression."

"People have to dream, Theo, even in a Depression."

"Yeah, I guess you're right, Gus. I didn't think about it that way," Mathieu said. "So, you know the layout of this place?"

"Mostly."

"That'll help," Mathieu said. "The bartender at La Bohème told me Fat Freddy hangs out at the paddock and someplace called the Chandelier Room."

"The paddock is where they parade the horses before each race," Gus said. "It's just north of the entrance gates. It's my favorite place because you can see those amazing thoroughbreds up close. The Chandelier Room is on the third floor of the clubhouse. That's where the track's wealthy patrons and Hollywood types gather between races. It has its own bar and lounge."

Mathieu nodded. "We'll probably half to split up then. I brought two copies of Fat Freddy's mugshot. It's in the glove box."

Gus pulled the mugshots out and looked at them. "Well, he's got a fat face, that's for sure. What about his record?"

"Freddy's been arrested for petty theft, burglary, and assault. He spent six months in prison for the last charge. But nothing else violent until this accusation."

"How do you want to play it?" Gus asked.

Mathieu sighed. "Well, all I have at the moment is hearsay evidence from a dead witness that Fat Freddy kidnapped Marilyn Lane. But obviously, that's not enough to arrest him.

"So, let's just watch him. See if he leads us to anyone he might be working for. If not, we'll follow him to his car and get his license plate number. And if we get lucky, maybe tail him home. Enya couldn't find a current address for him in the files."

"Sounds good," Gus said. "But we'll have our work cut out just finding him. The place will be packed by the looks of how many cars are already in the parking lot."

They found a parking spot about fifty yards from the entrance gate, then walked north to the ticket booth. General admission was fifteen cents, but they needed access to the entire grounds, so they paid a buck for clubhouse admission, passed through the turnstiles, and entered a different world.

The first thing Mathieu noticed was the blue-green Art Deco grandstand with its gold stripes and punched-metal friezes of galloping racehorses on the façade. To its right, the smaller Colonial Revival-style clubhouse mimicked the same color scheme. It was a classy-looking place, Mathieu thought.

Gus bought two racing forms for ten cents each and handed one to Mathieu. "What am I supposed to do with this?" Mathieu asked.

"It might come in handy while we're tailing Freddy," Gus said with a smile. "It'll make us look less like cops and more like race fans."

Mathieu nodded. It was a good idea.

Trees and waist-high hedges defined the walkway borders, guiding the crowd to the paddock, clubhouse, and grandstand. Gus had brought along a pair of binoculars. When Mathieu asked why, he said he'd learned from his first visit that they were helpful for following the races and might help them keep track of Freddy, too.

Gus pointed out the paddock area to the north. No horses were there yet. Mathieu had purposely gotten here early so they could orient themselves to the place. Tailing Freddy would be challenging enough in a crowd this size. Gus led him to the rear entrance of the grandstand, then up the stairs to the betting hall.

The betting hall had all the charm of a men's restroom but with higher ceilings. Red pari-mutuel windows with "Cash and Bet" signs lined the walls like urinals. Colorful linoleum tiles, which they probably cleaned with fire hoses, covered the concrete floor. The hall was cavernous, easily twenty feet high, with yellow-painted steel columns supporting the ceiling and the grandstand above.

But it was democratic in its own way. This is where the masses, rich and poor alike, placed their bets. The only way you could tell one from the other was by the clothing and the smell of sweat or cologne.

Staggered lines of early arrivals queued in front of the teller windows while the professionals studied their racing forms and checked the ever-changing odds on the automated tote board.

Gus and Mathieu walked through the betting hall toward the terrace. As they got close, the doorway framed the glorious backdrop of the San Gabriel Mountains to the north. It was a bright sunny day, and the ten-thousand-foot high range looked close enough to touch.

Mathieu and Gus stood in silence for a moment, admiring the view. The one-mile dirt track was wider than Mathieu had expected. It was easily twenty-five yards across, bordered on each side by white pipe railing to hold back the crowds.

A tractor passed, pulling a chain harrow to break up the soil. Some of the early arrivals were leaning on the railing, filling out their racing forms. On the inside of the track was a grass infield with trees, picnic benches, and play areas that the spectators could reach via a tunnel below the home stretch.

Mathieu turned and looked at the green Art Deco grandstand with its cantilevered roof, tiered concrete seating, and red stairs leading up from the terrace to the first-level seats.

Turning back to Gus, he asked, "How do we get to the Chandelier Room?"

Gus pointed to the east and said, "There's a footbridge over there that connects the grandstand to the clubhouse. It's above the channel where they bring the horses onto the track.

"You can also get to the Chandelier Room from the paddock by walking to the clubhouse and taking the stairs or elevator up to the third floor. That might be Fat Freddy's route if he shuttles between the paddock and the Chandelier Room."

Mathieu nodded. "In that case, let's go back to the paddock."

They backtracked to the paddock area, where Gus pointed out how to get to the clubhouse.

The paddock judge hadn't brought the horses out yet, so Mathieu told Gus, "I'd like you to stay here and be on the lookout for Freddy. I'll go check out the Chandelier Room. Then come back here before the first race."

"Okay, sounds good," Gus said.

Mathieu followed Gus's directions to the clubhouse and, arriving on the third floor, found the west entrance to the Chandelier Room. He showed his ticket to the attendant, walked through the arched doorway into the high-ceilinged room, and stopped on the landing above the main floor. The walls were pale yellow with white crown molding and wainscotting.

Directly across the room on the east wall was an identical landing, with a ten-foot-high arched mirror reflecting the tear-drop chandeliers hanging from the center of the ceiling.

On both landings, green-carpeted stairways with gold railings led up to mezzanine doors that opened onto the outdoor balcony overlooking the track.

Below Mathieu, to his right, was a grand piano. Beyond it, a polished mahogany bar that ran the width of the mirrored south wall. Two bartenders dressed in crisp white shirts, black ties, and vests served the guests seated at the captain-chair barstools.

In the center of the room, plush sofas, comfortable armchairs, and circular glass tables formed seating nooks where finely dressed early arrivals sat in animated conversation.

As Mathieu came down the stairs to the main floor, a tall, slender woman with hooded eyes and arched eyebrows approached him. She was wearing a flamboyant hat cocked at a rakish angle over a face only Michelangelo could have sculpted.

The woman stopped and gazed up at Mathieu. "You certainly know how to enter a room, young man," she said in a thick German accent. "I hope you're not an actor. That would be a terrible waste of those intelligent dark eyes of yours."

Mathieu smiled and said, "No, I'm not an actor, Miss Dietrich."

"That's a relief," she said. "So, you know who I am?"

"Doesn't everyone, Miss Dietrich?"

Marlene shrugged her finely tailored shoulders and replied, "And what may I ask, do you do?"

"I'm a public servant."

"What kind?"

"Can you keep a secret?" Mathieu asked in a whisper.

"For you, I can," she said in an equally conspiratorial tone.

"I'm a police detective."

Marlene smiled and said, "Ah, then I almost wish I had something to confess so you could handcuff me."

Mathieu laughed.

"Are you here for business or pleasure?" she asked.

"Business."

"Pity. Then I shan't detain you any longer, Detective," Marlene said, offering her hand. "Good day and happy hunting."

"Thank you, Miss Dietrich," Mathieu said, taking her hand. "It was a pleasure to meet you."

"Mine, also," Marlene said with a wink as she sashayed toward the bar, leaving a hint of expensive perfume in her wake.

When Miss Dietrich left, Mathieu scanned the room but didn't see Fat Freddy or anyone else he recognized. He continued across the center of the room, glancing at faces along the way.

Reaching the other side, he took the stairs up to the mezzanine and opened the door to the outdoor balcony.

Other than one couple at the far end of the balcony drinking champagne, no one else was on the deck. Mathieu put his elbows on the railing and gazed across the track at the mountains. He began to think this was a waste of time and Fat Freddy wouldn't show. Maybe Sam, the bartender, or his boss had tipped him off.

As Mathieu stood there frustrated, he sensed someone approaching on his right. He didn't know anyone here and wasn't in the mood for small talk, so he kept his focus straight ahead. But after a few moments, he felt the person staring at him, so he turned to meet their eyes.

A beautiful young woman with lush auburn hair smiled at him and said, "I've missed those brooding eyes of yours, Theo."

It was Lady Caroline Astor.

The surprise at seeing Caroline unnerved Mathieu. He felt off balance, confused. He stood there motionless, staring into her blue-green eyes, her lips inches from his, her sweet breath on his face. All his feelings for her came flooding back, but he knew they didn't have a future.

Mathieu took a deep breath to calm himself and said, "You look lovely, Caroline. How is your daughter?"

Lady Caroline reacted with a radiant smile and said, "She's my anchor in the storm, Theo."

"How old is she?"

"Three months," Caroline said. "Three glorious months of unconditional love, no sleep, and lots of diapers."

Mathieu laughed, took a step back, and asked, "What's her name?"

"I haven't decided yet," Caroline said with a playful grin. "I thought I'd wait and ask her."

"But she's three months old. What do you call her?"

"What do you think I should call her?" Caroline asked with arched eyebrows.

"How should I know," Mathieu said with a shrug. "She's your daughter."

Caroline hesitated, seemingly on the verge of saying something, then pulled back and said, "I was just teasing. Her name is Clarissa."

"So, she does have a name?"

"Yes, duly registered with the State of California."

"It's beautiful."

"I'm glad you approve," Caroline said in a soft voice. "What are you doing here?"

"Working. I'm tailing someone, but he hasn't shown up yet."

"What does he look like?"

"Fat face about five-foot-nine. Looks like a thug."

"I just saw someone like that come in a few moments ago."

"Really?"

"Yes, he's wearing a blue-felt hat with a pencil in the band. He's talking to Edgar Mahoney downstairs."

"Who's Edgar Mahoney?"

"Some wealthy oilman," Caroline said. "My husband spoke to him briefly in the paddock before we all walked up to the Chandelier Room."

Mathieu let out a sigh. "I'm sorry, Caroline, but I've got to go. The man with the blue hat is a key suspect."

"I understand, Theo … shall we meet here again?" she asked with a mischievous smile.

"At a racetrack?" Mathieu asked, raising his eyebrows.

"It's more respectable than a motor court, don't you think?" she said teasingly. "We can talk about your love life."

"That'll be a short conversation," Mathieu said.

"I don't believe you," Caroline said with a hint of jealousy.

They stood in silence for a moment, both seemingly reluctant to part. "Till next time, then," Mathieu said. "And all my best to Clarissa."

"Till next time," Caroline said, gazing into his eyes.

Mathieu turned and went back into the Chandelier Room. From the stairs, he spotted Fat Freddy in the center of the room, talking to a distinguished-looking man with gray hair, presumably Edgar Mahoney. Mahoney had a beautiful blond on his arm.

Mathieu knew the blond. It was Anita Cummings. Mathieu waited until Fat Freddy left the room after receiving an envelope from Mahoney, then followed him back to the paddock and met up with Gus.

At the paddock, Mathieu pointed out Fat Freddy to Gus and said, "Change of plans. I'll follow Freddy down here; you tail him in the Chandelier Room."

"Why?"

"Because a couple of people up there know me."

"Who?" Gus asked.

"Lady Caroline Astor and Anita Cummings," Mathieu said. "Looks like Freddy is handling the bets for an oilman named Edgar Mahoney—a distinguished-looking man with gray hair. You can't miss him. Anita Cummings is hanging on his arm like a Christmas ornament."

"Got it," Gus said as he handed Mathieu the binoculars. "You take these then. It'll make tracking Freddy easier in the crowd."

Horseracing has more pageantry than a Roman Catholic High Mass: the paddock parade, the silks, the jockey's colors, the bugle call to post, the starting gate, and the announcer's call. But by the third race, even Mathieu had to admit it was exciting.

Freddy had inadvertently done Mathieu and Gus a big favor by wearing his distinctive blue-felt hat. Mathieu could hang back and track him with his binoculars, especially outside, where he would remain on the terrace while Freddy went to the rail near the finish line.

Like all gamblers, Freddy was a creature of habit. After leaving the Chandelier Room with an envelope from Mahoney, he took the stairs to the paddock. He looked over the ponies, marked his racing form, then went to the betting hall to the same window each time.

He collected any winnings from the previous race, bet on the next one, then went outside to the terrace and pushed and shoved his way to the railing to watch the horses cross the finish line. Afterward, Freddy returned to the Chandelier Room, shared the winnings, and repeated the process.

Everything went well until the eighth race, the stakes race, where serious money was on the line. Freddy had gone through his whole routine, from the Chandelier Room to the paddock to the betting hall, then headed outside to the terrace, where he accidentally dropped his racing form, took a few steps, and stopped.

Freddy felt his pockets in panic, turned, and spotted his racing form on the ground. He bent down, picked it up, and clutched it to his chest like a sacred scroll. As he straightened up, Freddy caught Mathieu's eye and froze.

Maybe he recognized Mathieu from earlier that day or the newspapers. But whatever the reason, Freddy looked like a trapped animal. Mathieu casually broke eye contact as he looked down at the racing form Gus had given him. But out of the corner of his eye, he could still see Freddy.

Freddy looked to the east and then the west along the grandstand, seemingly seeking safety. Then, spotting the infield tunnel, he took it. Mathieu gave him a head start, fell in line behind two couples heading to the infield through the tunnel, and followed at a safe distance.

Once on the infield, Freddy pushed his way toward the restraining fence in front of the railing near the finish line, glancing back to see if he was still being followed. Mathieu hung back, looking through his binoculars occasionally to keep Freddy's blue hat in view.

Mathieu watched as they led the thoroughbreds onto the track, their shiny coats glistening in the late afternoon sun. Most were tranquil, a few skittish, but all were magnificent athletes, as were the jockeys riding them.

The stoic expressions on the jockeys' faces belied the courage it took for men barely five feet tall and a hundred pounds soaking wet to ride a thousand-pound animal in a bunch sprint at over forty miles an hour down the home stretch.

It was the calm before the storm as the horses trotted leisurely toward the starting gate at the far end of the straightaway.

The favorite at 2-to-1 was High Energy, a two-year-old front-runner in the post position owned by Hamilton Farms in Del Mar. His main rival, according to the morning line, was Sparky's Find, a three-year-old gray from the Bay area, a stalker who liked to run a few lengths behind the lead.

The long-shot bet was Iron Maiden, a three-year-old filly from Santa Barbara who had a reputation as a closer. It was Southern California versus Northern California for thoroughbred racing bragging rights.

It was a mile-and-a-quarter race. The starting point was in the chute to the west. The horses would pass the grandstand twice.

The starting judge and his assistants supervised the loading of the horses into the starting stall, a steel-metal frame on wheels, with padded barriers between each horse and a spring-loaded webbing that restrained the horses until the starter pressed the button, and the webbing flew up.

There was a collective hush over the field as the gate crew loaded the last horse, then retreated to the sides of the track. The starting judge's hand hovered over the start button, waiting for the horses to settle.

Then, pressing it, the webbing flew up, and the announcer intoned, "And they're off!" over the loudspeaker.

The tightly bunched horses thundered down the track for the first pass by the grandstand. Head on, you could make out individual horses and jockeys as they jostled for position.

But as they passed the infield crowd, it was a blur of whips, bobbing muzzles, streaming manes, outstretched hooves, and bright colors. Then, as they receded around the first turn toward the backstretch, they became individual horses again that the crowd could make out.

As the horses sprinted around the backstretch, the announcer's voice became more frantic. The infield crowd surged, straining the fence that held them back from the railing.

The infield crowd had become a single organism, expanding, contracting, moving, breathing, and panicking as one. It had become dangerous. It had its own smell, a mix of anxiety, excitement, cheap perfume, and sweat.

Mathieu tried to get closer to Freddy to keep him in view. But it was a mistake. Freddy glanced back and spotted him, fear showing on his face.

Moments later, as the horses flew around the stretch turn, turf flying in their wake, the crowd surged forward again; this time, the restraining fence gave way as they rushed toward the railing. Mathieu was carried forward with them, struggling to stay upright. When the crowd finally stopped, Mathieu stretched his body to full height.

He spotted Freddy's blue hat near the rail. He saw it turn toward the approaching horses, then back at him, and then, in a moment of seeming desperation, he saw Freddy duck under the rail and dash across the track.

Freddy got about a third of the way across, almost clear of the advancing horses, when Iron Maiden made a late surge on the outside. Seeing Freddy, the jockey jerked at the reins, trying to avoid a collision, but it was too late; the blinkered horse continued on in a frenzied lather.

Freddy turned toward the runaway horse, stumbling in fear as his legs gave way. A second later, Iron Maiden pounded him into the turf at full speed, crushing his back like a matchstick.

Sparky's Find won by a nose over High Energy at the wire. Iron Maiden finished third unhurt. Fat Freddy lost by two lengths, finishing out of the money.

29

An Uncommon Bond

"How did you get on to Freddy Fowler?" Bull asked the day after the tragedy at the racetrack.

"Remember that satchel I mentioned that Lillian Hennessy told me her brother always carried with him?" Mathieu asked as he leaned forward.

"Yes."

"Wilson found it in the rumble seat of Eddie's car. Inside the satchel, we found a notebook with a set of cryptic notes about Eddie's various schemes to hustle money.

"In one of the notes, he wrote that 'FF' bragged to an ex-sheriff in the Café La Bohème restroom that he'd kidnapped a blond the night of Jensen's murder and dropped her off downtown near the Greyhound Bus Station. That was the same thing Eddie told me on the bluff before he was shot, except he didn't mention 'FF.'"

"How did you make the connection between the initials 'FF' and Fowler?" Bull asked.

"I called Sam, a bartender I know at the Café La Bohème, and asked him if he knew any tough guys who hung out there with the initials 'FF.' Sam told me it was probably Fat Freddy Fowler. Sam didn't know where Freddy lived, but he told me I'd probably find him at Santa Anita the next day because there was a big stakes race.

"Enya found Freddy's mugshot in the files, and I asked Gus to go with me to Santa Anita and tail Freddy and see what we could find out."

"And did you find anything out before Freddy ran across the track and got himself killed?"

"Yes, sir," Mathieu said. "Freddy was placing bets for a wealthy oilman."

"Who?" Bull asked with alarm.

"Edgar Mahoney."

"Sweet Jesus!" Bull exclaimed. "Mahoney is one of the city's richest and most connected men. Tread lightly with him until you're sure he has anything to do with the murders. Understood?"

"Yes, sir," Mathieu said. "But I need your help with something else."

"What's that?"

"Can you contact the Arcadia Police Chief? We need to get a hold of Freddy Fowler's personal effects so we can continue investigating what role he played in Jensen's murder and who hired him."

Bull nodded and said, "I'll get on it right away. What are you going to do in the meantime?"

"I promised to escort Lillian Hennessy to the morgue today to view her brother's body."

Bull rocked back in his chair, giving Mathieu a skeptical look. "Is there anything going on between you and Miss Hennessy that I should know about, Detective?"

"No, sir," Mathieu replied a little too quickly. "But I feel I owe it to her because her brother died trying to give me information on the case."

The morgue is not a great place for a first date. At noon, Mathieu stood outside the Hall of Justice at the corner of North Spring

Street and West Temple, waiting for Lillian Hennessy to arrive. He'd called Lillian earlier that morning to tell her the coroner had released her brother's body.

The Hall of Justice occupied a fourteen-story steel-framed building clad in white granite. It stood just north of the red sandstone LA County Courthouse, making the courthouse look dour and out of place in comparison, like something from a Gothic horror movie.

When Doctor Marsh called Mathieu to inform him about releasing the body, Mathieu asked him to arrange a private viewing room for Lillian. It was going to be gruesome enough for her. He wanted to do all he could to lessen her pain.

Lillian arrived a few minutes late, dressed entirely in black: hat, sunglasses, coat, dress, and high-heeled shoes. Mathieu greeted her, extended his condolences, and then led her toward the building.

The coroner's office and morgue were in the basement. The public typically entered the building on Spring Street, checked in at the front desk, then took the elevator down to the basement, where they had to walk down a long, cold corridor toward the morgue.

But there was a side entrance on West Temple where they brought the bodies in that the police used. It was just as depressing as the other way, but it was quicker.

Mathieu opened the white metal door, showed his badge to the guard, then took Lillian's arm as they descended a concrete stairwell beside the gurney-elevator to the basement, then turned left, went through an open doorway, and walked twenty feet down a narrow corridor to a door on the right where Mathieu knocked.

The basement was cold and sterile, with bare concrete floors, white walls, exposed pipes, and huge metal exhaust fans droning away. This was not a place you lingered if you didn't have to.

Doctor Marsh was there to open the door and greet them. He was dressed in a dark gray wool suit instead of his scrubs, exuding a compassion uncommon for his profession.

Looking at Lillian with sympathetic eyes, Marsh said, "I'm sorry for your loss, Miss Hennessy. If you'll follow me, I'll take you into the next room where you can view your brother's body."

Lillian immediately turned to Mathieu and asked, "Will you go with me?"

"Of course."

Looking relieved, Lillian clutched Mathieu's hand and nodded to Doctor Marsh that she was ready. Marsh led them into a small room, where a light shaft cast a cone of natural light on the gurney, almost like a chapel. Marsh carefully drew back the white sheet covering Eddie's face, then stepped aside.

Lillian took a step forward, still clutching Mathieu's hand. She stared at Eddie's face in silence, squeezing Mathieu's hand even harder. Mathieu watched as tears began to roll down her cheek. After a few moments, Lillian looked at Doctor Marsh and said, "He looks peaceful. Did he suffer?"

Marsh shook his head and said, "No, he died almost instantly from his wound."

Lillian bit her lip, then said, "That's a relief, I guess. Is there anything else I need to do?"

"Just sign this form, Miss Hennessy," Marsh said as he handed her a clipboard and pen, "and write in the name of the funeral home at the bottom. We'll take care of the rest."

Lillian did as requested and then handed the clipboard back. "Thank you, Doctor, you've been very kind." She turned to Mathieu, almost shivering, and asked, "Can you help me back to my car?"

"Of course," he said, then turning to Marsh, added, "Thanks, Doctor. I'll talk to you later."

Outside on the sidewalk, Lillian rubbed her arms, trying to warm up as she gazed up at the sun. She looked fragile, lost, seemingly unsure what to do next.

"I don't want to be alone right now. Could we take a walk or get something to eat if you have the time?" she asked.

"Of course," Mathieu said. "Is there anywhere you'd like to go?"

Lillian looked at the ground for a moment and then said, "When I was a little girl, my mother used to take me shopping at the Broadway Department store. After we finished shopping, she'd take me for tea at the Garden Café on the top floor. It has an open roof and seating under the palms. It always felt like paradise to me. Could we go there?"

"Certainly," Mathieu said. "It's only a few blocks from here."

Lillian sighed in relief. "Thank you, and can you do me one other favor?"

"Sure, what is it?"

Looking slightly embarrassed, Lillian said, "I'm normally totally independent, but I'm feeling a bit shaky right now, especially in these heels. Would you mind if I took your arm?"

Mathieu looked at her warmly, extending his right arm, and said, "Not at all. It would be my pleasure."

They walked south on Broadway mostly in silence until they reached Fourth Street, where the elegant white nine-story Beaux Arts style Broadway Department Store stood on the corner.

They entered through the Broadway entrance and took the elevator to the ninth floor. When they arrived, Mathieu vaguely remembered being here as a child.

His mother would take him here to buy shoes and get his hair cut, and after that, they'd come up to the Garden Café for lunch.

You couldn't see the ninth floor from the street because it was set back from the edges of the building and took up only part of the roof area. They had built a rectangular two-story structure there with an interior courtyard surrounded by a restaurant.

The open courtyard was resplendent with lush ferns, palms, awnings, and a canopy suspended by wires from the roof providing shade. It was a cocoon, a respite, a place apart. Mathieu understood why Lillian had chosen to come here.

At the reception desk, a slender woman greeted them. She wore a white floor-length uniform with a starched collar and hat reminiscent of nurses' caps in the Great War. She asked if they wanted to sit inside or out. Mathieu glanced at Lillian, and she replied, "Outside, please."

The receptionist escorted them through the high-ceiling café with its sturdy columns, recessed ceiling, and patterned tile floor, past diners seated at round tables with white tablecloths and dark wood bistro chairs to the open courtyard, where she found a small table for them with two bentwood chairs in the shade of a stately palm.

Soon after they were seated, a waitress in similar garb came to the table with their menus and asked Mathieu if they knew what they wanted or if they would like time to peruse the menu first.

He nodded toward Lillian, who replied, "I'd like some Earl Grey tea." Then asked, "Do you still have blueberry scones with jam?"

"Yes, we do," the waitress said with a self-assured smile.

"Then, I would also like a scone," Lillian said.

"And for you, young man?"

"The same, please, thank you."

After the waitress left, there was an uncomfortable silence between them. Mathieu wondered what the appropriate topic of conversation might be after a visit to the morgue.

Deciding to hit the subject head-on, he asked, "Were you and your brother close as children?"

Lillian looked down at the tablecloth as she fiddled with her fork. "As kids, we were. I was two years older than Eddie. He was a sweet boy and more fun to play with than a stuffed doll. I imagined myself as a pretend mom. Everything was fine until he turned twelve. That's when the trouble started."

"What happened?"

"Being the youngest, my parents spoiled Eddie terribly. He started acting out. Little stuff at first, like shoplifting, but later more serious things like stealing cars, drugs, and hanging out with the wrong crowd. My parents always bailed him out. But I was fed up with his antics by then because he was so irresponsible.

"Fortunately, I was studying at the music academy by then. That was my refuge. I only came home to sleep. And even then, I'd lock my bedroom door to avoid Eddie's drama."

"Where did you study?"

"At the Hollywood Conservatory of Music and Arts."

"The one on Hollywood Boulevard and Serrano?" Mathieu asked.

"Yes."

"That's a prestigious school," Mathieu said with raised eyebrows.

"You know of it?" Lillian asked, seemingly surprised.

"Yes, my mother used to take me to the public concerts they held there."

"When was this?" Lillian asked, more animated now.

Mathieu looked away, trying to remember, then turned back and said, "The first time was when I was about thirteen."

"How old are you now?" Lillian asked.

"Twenty-five."

"I'm a year older than you," Lillian said, as her face colored, looking slightly embarrassed to admit it.

"That's okay," Mathieu said with a smile. "I like older women. They know what they want."

Lillian laughed. "I wonder if you heard me play there when we were kids."

"I doubt it," Mathieu said, shaking his head. "I think I would have remembered you."

"Maybe not," Lillian blushed. "I was geeky looking, then."

"That's hard to believe."

Changing the subject, Lillian asked, "How do you know Paul Thornton?"

"I met him on my first murder case when I was still a motorcycle cop," Mathieu said. "The police initially accused Paul of shooting the victim."

"Why did they suspect Paul?" Lillian asked, seemingly alarmed.

"Because she was found shot in Paul's home. But it turned out Paul was in San Francisco at the time of the murder and had nothing to do with it."

"Who was the victim?"

Mathieu hesitated for a second and said, "Irene Simpson, the personal secretary to Harry Chandler, the publisher of the *Los Angeles Times.*"

"How did you get on the case if you were a motorcycle cop?"

Mathieu looked down at the tablecloth. "Because Harry Chandler is my godfather, and he wanted me on the case."

A sudden look of recognition crossed Lillian's face, and she became very still. Shaking her head in dismay, Lillian said, "Please forgive me for being so insensitive, Detective. I should have remembered."

"There's no need to apologize, Miss Hennessy."

Lillian sighed. "But there is. I feel like a fool. I'm so caught up in my own grief that I didn't put two and two together. I didn't remember the tragedy of your story."

"It's okay," Mathieu said. "There's no way you could have put those things together."

"But I should have," Lillian said, protesting. "It was in all the newspapers. I remember now that it wasn't until after you'd solved the case that you discovered the victim was your half-sister. And all this time, while I've been feeling sorry for myself and you've been comforting me, you didn't say a word about it."

"I didn't say anything because I know how you feel," Mathieu said. "Your emotions are raw right now. Your pain is immediate. Mine has the benefit of time."

"Nonetheless, we share an uncommon bond, Detective," Lillian said as she held his gaze. "We've both lost siblings to violent death."

Just then, the waitress brought their tea and scones.

The interruption gave them both time to regroup. They were silent for a while, seemingly lost in their own thoughts.

Mathieu broke the silence first by saying, "Your brother overheard someone bragging about the Jensen murder in the men's restroom at the Café La Bohème."

"Who was it?"

"A man named Freddy Fowler."

"How did you find that out?"

"Your brother wrote some cryptic notes in the diary we found inside his satchel."

"So, you found the satchel?"

"Yes, thanks to you."

"And the man?"

"We tailed him at the Santa Anita Racetrack yesterday. He panicked and tried to escape by running across the track and was killed by a horse."

"Did he kill my brother?"

"I'm not sure, but it's possible," Mathieu said with a shrug. "He may also have been the man that attacked you in your apartment. Would you mind looking at his mugshot?"

"Okay," Lillian said tentatively.

Mathieu handed it to her. "Take your time and see if he looks familiar."

Lillian looked at the photo with a combination of dread and doubt. After a few moments, she put it down and said, "I didn't see the man's face who attacked me, but this face looks familiar to me."

"Is it possible you saw him at the La Bohème?"

Lillian shrugged. "I'm not sure, but I've seen his face before."

"If you remember anything else later on, please call me."

There followed another long silence between them. Lillian looked away, seemingly in thought, then back at Mathieu and said, "I feel comfortable being silent around you, Detective."

"I feel the same," Mathieu said in a soft voice.

There was a slight pause, then, with a wry smile, Lillian asked, "Do you always take victim's relatives to tea, Detective?"

"Not always, but occasionally."

"So, I'm not special?"

"I didn't say that," Mathieu said, holding back a grin.

Lillian hesitated a moment, then asked, "Is something happening between us, Detective?"

"Would you like there to be?" Mathieu asked, staring into her eyes.

Avoiding the question, Lillian said, "My music career is extremely important to me."

"I feel the same way about my work," Mathieu said.

"If I was away for weeks and months at a time on tour, could you handle that?" Lillian asked.

"If I was out all night on a stakeout, could you handle that?" Mathieu countered.

"Touché," Lillian said. "What are we going to do about this, Detective?"

"I'd suggest we do the same thing you do when you play the violin, Miss Hennessy," Mathieu said.

"What do you mean?" Lillian asked, gazing at him.

"That we don't get ahead of ourselves worrying about the future," Mathieu said, "and take it one measure at a time."

30

Freddy Fowler

Bull called the Arcadia Chief of Police and explained the connection between Fowler and the Jensen murder. The chief agreed to relinquish the case and transfer Fowler's body to the morgue at the LA Hall of Justice.

Bull told Mathieu privately that the chief seemed relieved to have the whole mess taken off his hands. It was bad publicity for Arcadia and the racetrack, and the sooner forgotten, the better for them.

The Arcadia police found Freddy's 1929 black six-cylinder Chevy four-door sedan in the Santa Anita parking lot and towed it to the LAPD impound garage.

When Mathieu saw the Chevy sedan later, he recognized it as the same kind of vehicle used the night Lillian's brother was gunned down. He assumed Freddy had been the driver and someone else was the shooter.

Mathieu asked Wilson to get Freddy's personal effects from the coroner and to search and dust the vehicle for fingerprints. Wilson found Freddy's wallet, driver's license, and the key to his apartment in his suit pocket.

The next morning, Mathieu and Wilson pulled up in front of the Casa Real Apartments at 1354 Harper Avenue, a half-block south of Sunset Boulevard in West Hollywood. It was a handsome four-story brick building with arched windows on the first floor complementing the rectangular ones on the upper three.

The brick and stone façade was white, with stately Queen palms on both sides of the entrance steps. It looked more like a manor house than an apartment building with its exquisitely designed façade.

Staring up at the building, Mathieu wondered how Freddy could have afforded to live here. It looked way too classy for a thug like him.

They took the stairs to the landing, walked down the arched entranceway to the front door, and entered a light-filled lobby with white walls and a sand-colored parquet floor. To the left, a stairwell led to the second-floor landing.

Mathieu glanced at Freddy's key. The apartment number was 215. They took the polished black stairs with a green runner to the second floor, where they walked down a narrow corridor toward the rear of the building. Freddy's apartment was the last one on the left.

Mathieu unlocked the door and entered a short hallway with a bathroom to the left and the living room straight ahead. The living room had exposed brick walls with gray-curtained windows on the north and east walls.

To the left of the living room, a doorway led to a tiny bedroom with a narrow steel-frame Murphy bed that was down and unmade. There was a galley kitchen off the living room on the south wall. The entire space was small, probably no more than 500 square feet.

By the look of the sparsely furnished apartment, Freddy hadn't been much of a housekeeper. It smelled of stale beer and cigarettes.

Mathieu asked Wilson to search the bedroom and bathroom while he searched the living room and kitchen. A schoolhouse ceiling fan with frosted glass turned slowly in the stuffy air. The only furnishings were a square oak table near the alley window and two wooden dining chairs beside it.

Mathieu walked over to the table. There was an ashtray overflowing with cigarette butts, two empty bottles of Zobelein's Eastside beer, an open pack of Camels, a stubby pencil, and several old racing forms from the Santa Anita racetrack.

Next, Mathieu entered the narrow galley kitchen. Dirty dishes and cutlery filled the sink on the right. A white porcelain gas stove sat in the corner; a soup pot and cast iron pan on the burners.

On the counter to the left was an aluminum Drip-O-Lator coffee maker, a two-pound can of Hills Brother's Coffee, a loaf of Wonder-Cut bread, and a half-empty jar of French's Cream Salad mustard.

Mathieu opened the white GE refrigerator. Inside were three more bottles of Eastside beer, a carton of Western Dairy eggs, a head of lettuce, and cold cuts wrapped in white butcher's paper.

He searched the kitchen cabinets next. Except for plates, cutlery, and water glasses, there was nothing else there. He wondered why there weren't any coffee cups or mugs in the living room or kitchen, even though Freddy had a coffee maker and a two-pound can of coffee on the counter.

He took the coffee maker apart and examined it. It had never been used. Then he took the lid off the Hills Brother's coffee can. It was full. Mathieu called out to Wilson, "Fred, did you find any coffee cups or mugs in the bedroom or bathroom?"

Wilson came into the kitchen a few moments later and said, "No, sir. I didn't find any coffee cups or anything else of interest in either room. Just some clothes in the closet, which I've started to search. Why did you ask about the cups?"

"Because Freddy has a two-pound can of coffee and a coffee maker he never used. But no cups. Why?"

Wilson shrugged. "I don't know, sir. It's odd."

"Hand me that waste basket, will you?"

Wilson handed him the basket. Mathieu put it on the counter, then slowly emptied the coffee beans into it. A few seconds later, two objects fell out with a clanking sound.

"What is it, sir?" Wilson asked.

Mathieu reached into the waste basket, took the objects out, and turned to Wilson. "It looks like Freddy was a budding photographer," Mathieu said, displaying a palm-sized Kodak camera and a roll of film.

"That camera must be important if he went to all that trouble to hide it, sir."

"That's what I'm thinking, too, Fred," Mathieu said with a pensive look. "Put these in an evidence bag, then finish dusting the apartment for prints while I go downstairs and talk to the manager."

"Will do, sir."

Mathieu found the manager's office off the first-floor lobby and knocked. After a few seconds, a pleasant voice said, "Come in."

Mathieu entered the narrow office and saw a woman in her late fifties with permed gray hair sitting at a small desk doing paperwork. She looked up with a pleasant smile and asked, "How can I help you, young man?"

He showed her his badge and said, "My name is Detective Mathieu from the LAPD. What is your name, please?"

"Mrs. Matilda Owens," she said, holding his gaze.

"I have a few questions about one of your tenants, Mrs. Owens."

"Which one?" she asked with a curious expression.

"Mr. Fowler in apartment 215," Mathieu replied.

"Is Freddy in any trouble?" she asked.

"No," Mathieu said as he sat down. "But I'm sorry to have to inform you that Mr. Fowler is dead."

"Oh, no," Matilda said. "How?"

"In an accident," Mathieu said. "Unfortunately, I can't share any details with you right now."

"I see," Matilda said with an understanding nod.

"Can you tell me how long Mr. Fowler has lived here?" Mathieu asked.

Matilda looked away for a moment, then said, "I think it's been at least six months."

"And have you been the manager all that time?"

"Yes," Matilda said with pride.

"This seems like a very nice apartment building, Mrs. Owens."

"It is, Detective, with no small thanks to me."

"I'm sure that's true, Mrs. Owens. I was just wondering how Mr. Fowler could afford to live here. Do you know where he worked?"

Matilda laughed. "The same place everyone else who lives here works," she said.

"What do you mean?"

"Freddy worked at the Chateau Marmont."

"Really?" Mathieu asked with a surprised look.

"Yes, this is employee housing for the staff and management of the Chateau Marmont. It's a perk for working there."

"And what did Mr. Fowler do at the Chateau?"

"He was a chauffeur and night watchman."

31

The Hidden Camera

When Mathieu got back to headquarters, he called Stuart Thomas. He asked him to come to the detective's room to look at the camera he'd found hidden in Fowler's apartment. When Stuart arrived a few minutes later and spotted the palm-sized camera on Mathieu's desk, he whistled in admiration. "Wow! That's a classic!"

"What do you mean?" Mathieu asked.

"It's a Kodak Vest Pocket camera. It was revolutionary for its time because of its size and capabilities. It was known as the 'Soldier's camera.'"

"Why?"

"Because Kodak sold a ton of them to American soldiers during the Great War."

"And the army allowed it?"

"They tried to discourage it but weren't successful. Can I see it?" Stuart asked, extending his hand.

"Sure," Mathieu said, handing him the palm-sized black metal camera.

Stuart smiled as he turned it over. "It's one of the early models, probably made around 1912."

"How can you tell?" Mathieu asked.

"Because the lens doesn't have a focusing ring. It has a fixed focus. You better hope Mr. Fowler was a good cameraman."

"There's little chance of that," Mathieu said. "Tell me about it."

"It's called the Vest Pocket Autographic camera. It's essentially a tiny bellows camera that expands when you open it. But as you can see, when closed, it can fit in your vest pocket."

"Why is it called 'Autographic?'"

"Because when the camera is loaded with a special kind of Kodak film, which this one is, you can write notes on the negative, and the note will show up on the printed photo," Stuart replied.

"Really!" Mathieu said. "How?"

Stuart turned the camera over. "See this flap on the back?"

"Yes."

"When you open it, there's a white backing paper," Stuart said. "Can you see it?"

"Yes," Mathieu said, leaning to the left to get a better view.

"To write a note, you use the metal stylus attached to the flap and write on the backing paper," Stuart said, miming writing. "A carbon tissue beneath the backing paper transfers the marks to the negative. When a print is made, the note will be visible on the border."

Mathieu nodded in recognition. "My parents must have had one. Some of our old family photos have handwritten notes on the edges. I never realized how they got there until now,"

"Kodak sold almost two million of these because of the handwriting feature and compact size," Stuart said.

"How does it work?" Mathieu asked.

"To open it, you pull on the lens assembly until the bellows are fully extended."

"And to take a photo?"

"You set the shutter speed and aperture with these levers around the lens, hold the camera about waist high, look through the glass prism, and press the red button on the back. Afterward, advance the film for the next shot."

Mathieu nodded and said, "So, a lot can go wrong. It can be out of focus, blurred, too dark, or too light depending on how you adjust the camera or how steady you hold it."

"Sure, that's always the issue in photography," Stuart said. "It's not the camera; it's how you use it."

"Well, let's hope for the best," Mathieu said with a sigh, "because Freddy didn't strike me as a genius."

"How many rolls of film did you find?" Stuart asked.

"The one in the camera and this one," Mathieu said, handing him the roll he'd found in the coffee can. "A lot is riding on this, Stuart. The images on these rolls of film might be the key to solving the case."

"Understood, sir. You can count on me," Stuart said, then added with a grin, "Besides, maybe we'll get lucky, and Freddy wrote the killer's name on one of the negatives."

Mathieu laughed. "Right, and maybe he wrote their address and phone number, too."

After Stuart left, Enya came to Mathieu's desk and sat down. "Nice of you to stop by, Detective," she said in a sarcastic tone. "I like your new desk, by the way. It's nice and cozy."

"Feel free to use it anytime," Mathieu said.

"I already have," Enya said with a deadpan expression.

Mathieu laughed.

"Somebody has to," Enya said, "you're rarely here lately."

"I've been a little busy," Mathieu said.

"Getting shot at and going to the races?" Enya asked, arching her eyebrows.

"Do you have something for me?" Mathieu asked, changing the subject.

"Yes," Enya said. "I found two oil executives who have homes in Idyllwild."

"Great," Mathieu said as his face brightened. "Who are they?"

"The first one is a man named William Boyd. He was a vice president at Signal Oil Company in Long Beach, where he was born sixty-five years ago. He retired last year, and now he spends his time up in Idyllwild in a chalet he recently purchased."

"Who's the second one?"

"Edgar Mahoney," Enya said.

"The Mahoney who lives in Los Angeles?" Mathieu asked.

"Yes," Enya said. "Do you know about him?"

"Not much," Mathieu said, shaking his head. "But he was at Santa Anita the day Freddy Fowler was killed. Freddy was placing bets for him. Where does Mahoney live?"

"According to the real estate agent, he owns several mansions, but he's currently staying at the Chateau Marmont in the penthouse suite."

"That's interesting," Mathieu said, nodding his head. "That can't be a coincidence."

"What do you mean?" Enya asked.

"Freddy worked at the Chateau as a night watchman and chauffeur. That must be how they met."

"Do you think Mahoney's involved in the murders of Jensen and Stonebridge?" Enya asked.

"I don't know," Mathieu said with a shrug. "But I'm going to find out. Did you find anything else about Mahoney?"

"No," Enya said, "do you want me to do some research on him?"

"Not right now," Mathieu said. "I'll ask Bill Collins at the *Times* about him first. But there is something else I'd like you to research."

"Sure," Enya said. "What's that?"

"About fifteen or sixteen years ago in Desdemona, Texas, there was a bad oil field fire, and several people were killed. According to what I learned, both Jensen and Stonebridge worked as roughnecks there at the time, and both left soon after the fire.

"I'd like you to call Hank Laramie. He's the caretaker of a house in the middle of the Inglewood Oil Field. He told me a friend of his died in the fire. Ask him what his friend's name was."

"Okay."

"Then, I'd like you to call the sheriff's office in Desdemona and see what you can find out about the fire. Somebody must remember what happened. Most importantly, try to discover the victims' names and anyone they suspect was responsible."

"Sure," Enya said. "I'll see what I can find out."

"Thanks," Mathieu said.

After Mathieu and Collins settled into a plush red booth at Cole's and ordered, Collins asked, "Why are you interested in Edgar Mahoney? Is he a suspect?"

"A person of interest," Mathieu said.

"Why?"

"I can't tell you right now," Mathieu said. "This is all off the record."

"What do I get out of it?" Collins asked.

"A free lunch as usual," Mathieu said with a smile.

"Okay, but promise me one other thing," Collins said.

"What?"

"If there's ever another layoff at the *Times,* you'll put in a good word for me with your godfather, Harry Chandler."

"It's a deal," Mathieu said. "Tell me what you know about Mahoney."

"Edgar owns or leases oil fields all over Los Angeles," Collins began. "He has fields adjacent to the Gilmore Oil field, some in Mid City around the tar pits, others in Venice, a big holding in the Inglewood Oil Field, and further north, an oil island off the Rincon between Ventura and Santa Barbara, and several oil derricks offshore at Summerland, just south of Montecito."

"How did Mahoney make his money initially?" Mathieu asked.

Collins scoffed. "Mahoney likes to pretend he's a self-made man, but that's bullshit. He inherited a lot of money from his father, who had an early monopoly on oil fields in Texas."

"Is he politically connected?" Mathieu asked.

"No more than any of the other oil barons in Los Angeles," Collins said, sipping his beer that just arrived. "Like the others, he's a big contributor to the mayor's re-election fund and bribes city councilmen to rezone farmland for oil exploration—the usual LA graft."

"So, there wouldn't be a huge stink if I went after him?"

Collins chuckled. "You're learning the game, Mathieu."

"Just trying to understand what the obstacles are, Bill," Mathieu said with a level gaze. "Is Mahoney married?"

"No, he likes to think of himself as a big ladies' man, though," Collins said. "He always has some beautiful starlet on his arm, though some think it's mostly for show, and he pays them to be with him."

"Is he ambitious?"

"Sure, he's ruthless," Collins said. "He pollutes farmland next to his oil fields when he thinks there might be oil on it. Then he buys the land cheap from the farmers when their crops fail, or their livestock starts dying."

"Would he kill to get what he wants?" Mathieu asked.

Collins rubbed his chin and said, "I don't know, Mathieu, there's a lot of ways to kill someone without actually using a weapon. If you bankrupt a farmer and force him to sell his land, it's a form of murder. Or if you drive him to despair and he commits suicide, it's a form of murder. But not one you're likely to go to jail for."

"Fair point," Mathieu said.

"Besides," Collins said, "the only time I ever heard of people actually being murdered over oil rights was during the reign of terror in Oklahoma between 1910 and 1926 when at least sixty Osage Indians were murdered to get their 'headrights.' And in that case, the ringleader wasn't an oil baron, but a wealthy rancher named William Hale."

"Was Hale ever brought to justice?" Mathieu asked.

"Yes, he was tried and convicted of first-degree murder in 1926. He appealed, and after several retrials that ended in hung juries, he was tried again in 1929. The jury found him guilty of first-degree murder and sentenced him to life imprisonment in Leavenworth."

Mathieu was silent for a moment, then asked, "Do you know if Mahoney ever worked with Edward Doheny during the Teapot Dome Scandal?"

Collin sighed, looked away, then said, "Yeah, I think I remember he did. Why?"

"Because Jensen's first wife intimated to me that Jensen knew something damning about where the payoff money came from, and Doheny paid him to keep silent."

"So, what are you thinking?" Collins asked.

"That maybe Jensen and Stonebridge were blackmailing Mahoney also, and he had them eliminated."

Collins smiled. "You're becoming as cynical as I am, Mathieu."

"I'm just considering all the possibilities, Bill. That's all."

32

The Voyeur

The fourteen 3x5 black-and-white prints lying on Mathieu's desk told a story. But what the story was about was difficult to determine. Arrayed next to each other, they looked like a storyboard for a film—but one without names, dialog, or an obvious plot.

"The prints look great, Stuart," Mathieu said. "They're sharp and clear."

"Thanks, Freddy turned out to have a pretty steady hand. But the subject matter suggests he was a bit of a voyeur if not a downright pervert."

"Yeah," Mathieu scoffed. "He seems to be hiding in the shadows for most of them."

"Freddy took most of them at the Chateau Marmont," Stuart said.

"How can you tell?" Mathieu asked, surprised.

"I've shot some weddings there."

"Are you doing some moonlighting on the side, Stuart?"

"I have to take what I can get these days," Stuart said with a shrug.

Mathieu nodded that he understood. "Is this the sequence Freddy took the photos?"

"Yes, sir. The first eight came from the freestanding roll. And the last six from the roll that was in the camera."

"Let's start at the beginning, then," Mathieu said, picking up the first print.

Like most of the fourteen photos, Freddy took it at night. The view was of a long covered outdoor walkway framed by gothic arches resembling a cloister in a monastery. At the far end, a man and woman stood with their backs to the camera in front of a fountain.

"Was this taken at the Chateau Marmont?" Mathieu asked, turning to Stuart.

"Yes," Stuart said. "It's called the cloisters. It's the entrance colonnade to the hotel. Freddy probably took the photo near the driveway on the west side of the property. The lobby door is to the left of where the couple is standing."

The second photo was from the same vantage point, but the couple had turned to enter the lobby, and Freddy caught them in profile.

"I recognize the woman," Mathieu said immediately.

"Really, who is she?" Stuart asked.

"Jacqueline Jensen—Lester Jensen's widow. I've only seen Mahoney once at Santa Anita, but I'm guessing he's the man in the photo," Mathieu said as he shuffled through some press clippings Enya had found of Mahoney.

Picking one up, he compared it to the man's profile in the photo, and it seemed to match. "That's interesting," Mathieu said, resting his chin in his hand. "Mahoney and Jensen's wife together. I suppose we can't tell when Freddy shot this."

"No," Stuart said, shaking his head. "Freddy didn't write anything on the negatives, but we can probably narrow it down by studying the rest of the photos."

Mathieu nodded. "Okay, let's keep going then."

Presumably, Freddy took the next few photos the same evening because Edgar and Jacqueline were wearing the same outfits. The first showed the couple sitting in the lobby, enjoying a cocktail.

"Where do you think Freddy was standing when he took this?" Mathieu asked.

Stuart studied it for a moment and said, "Given the angle, I'd say he was standing just past the reception desk."

The next photo showed Edgar and Jacqueline entering a room at the far end of a carpeted hallway, presumably Edgar's penthouse suite.

Freddy shot the final photo in the sequence in daylight. It showed Jacqueline getting into her car in the parking garage. "Freddy must have taken this the following morning," Mathieu said to himself. "Jacqueline is still wearing the same dress."

"The elevators go down to the garage from the upper floors," Stuart said with a sly smile. "So, overnight guests don't have to endure a 'perp' walk through the lobby with wrinkled clothes and mussed-up hair."

Mathieu laughed. "Well, the Chateau Marmont is known for its discretion."

Stuart pointed to the last four photos on the roll and said, "These were all shot at night by the pool at the Chateau Marmont."

Mathieu picked up the first photo in the poolside sequence. Freddy must have taken it behind some thick foliage at the east side of the oval-shaped pool because a cluster of fern fronds obscured part of the image.

Nevertheless, the object of Freddy's attention was clear enough: a naked woman pushing herself out of the pool, her alluring backside illuminated by the pool lights. A chaise lounge in the background held some discarded women's clothes.

"Do you think that's Jacqueline Jensen?" Stuart asked.

"I don't know," Mathieu said with a shrug. "The only time I ever met her, she was wearing a sundress ... but she has a similar build and hair length to the woman in the photo."

The next photo showed the same naked woman strutting proudly toward a chaise lounge at the far left edge of the pool. The only thing visible on the chaise was a man's bare feet and legs, but nothing else.

"We can't see the woman's face in this one either," Mathieu said with a sigh. "It's always in the shadows, and the man is out of the frame, too."

The final two photos were essentially duplicates of each other. The woman was kneeling naked at the end of the chaise lounge, her head between the man's legs.

"Maybe Mrs. Jensen was helping Edgar find his room key," Stuart quipped.

"Yeah, that seems likely, Stuart," Mathieu said with a deadpan expression. "Nevertheless, if this is Edgar and Jacqueline in the photos, they certainly were getting cozy, weren't they?"

"Yes, sir, they were."

"Is this the last photo on the first roll?" Mathieu asked.

"Yes," Stuart said. "There's six more to go on the second one."

Mathieu picked up the first print of the last six. His stomach sank when he saw it. He knew precisely when Freddy had taken it—the night of Lester Jensen's murder.

The photo showed Marilyn Lane lying in the fetal position in the backseat of a car with a black cloth tied around her head and her coat pushed up so high that the top of her thighs showed. Freddy had staged it like a trophy photo as he did with the next one, where he'd pushed the coat up even higher, revealing Marilyn's bare bottom.

"Freddy was a real creep, wasn't he," Mathieu said in disgust.

"Yes, he was," Stuart said, shaking his head. "I can't believe he was stupid enough to document his own crime."

Mathieu scoffed. "I have a feeling this was for Freddy's private collection, Stuart."

If the photos of Marilyn Lane were voyeuristic, the next one was chilling. Freddy took it the night Reginald Stonebridge was hanged in the Venice Oil Field. It looked like he shot it hastily behind a vehicle because it was a little out of focus.

The print showed a burly man in profile, tying off the rope he'd used to haul Reginald Stonebridge's body up the side of an oil derrick about twenty feet away. The profile of his face was in the shadows, but his height and build were evident in the photo.

Turning to Stuart, Mathieu said, "See if you can blow this up a little so we can get a better look at his face."

"Yes, sir," Stuart said. "Freddy took a helluva chance taking this photo."

Mathieu nodded. "I agree, but he probably wanted some insurance if he ever got arrested. It looks like he hid himself pretty well behind the car. I'm assuming he was the driver and lookout that night."

"Most likely from the looks of things," Stuart said, nodding in agreement.

The location for the next two photos was in the same hallway at the Chateau Marmont as the ones with Jacqueline Jensen and Edgar Mahoney. But these showed Eddie Hennessy, Lillian's brother.

In the first one, Eddie was with a statuesque blond as he knocked on an apartment door, presumably Mahoney's. The following photo showed Eddie leaving the same apartment without the blond but with a large envelope in his hand.

The final photo so angered Mathieu that he picked it up, tore it to pieces, and put the scraps in his suit pocket. "There's no need for anyone else to see this photo, Stuart," Mathieu said with an intense gaze. "Is that clear?"

"Yes, sir," Stuart said. "What should I do with the negative?"

"Leave it be," Mathieu said. "I'm not asking you to destroy evidence. But I know this young woman, and I don't want any prints of her lying around the station house that would embarrass her. The same thing goes for the photos of Miss Lane; keep them locked up. Is that clear?"

"Understood, sir."

The photo that Mathieu tore up was of Lillian Hennessy, laying on her stomach in her apartment with her hands tied behind her back and her bathrobe pushed up to her thighs.

33

The Sunbather

After studying the photos, Mathieu felt like the proverbial blind man touching an elephant. Were the images part of one story or several? It was tempting to conclude that Jacqueline Jensen and Edgar Mahoney were involved in the murders, but if so, why?

The only obvious thing Jacqueline got out of her husband's murder was the house. And as far as Mathieu knew, Jacqueline didn't benefit from Stonebridge's murder at all. And what did Mahoney get out of either murder, unless it was related to some oil rights Mathieu wasn't aware of?

The more likely explanation was that Jacqueline knew her husband was going to divorce her, so she decided to jump ship early and snag Edgar Mahoney to continue the lifestyle she'd become accustomed to. It was clear she didn't have any scruples about using her body to manipulate men.

The only way Mathieu was going to find out was by questioning them. But which one first? If he started with Jacqueline, she'd immediately be on the phone and warn Mahoney. Then Edgar would have time to prepare, lawyer up, or apply pressure through the mayor's office. No, he'd talk to Edgar first, but before he did, he'd question the manager of the Chateau Marmont about Freddy Fowler.

While Mathieu was thinking about this, Stuart came to his desk and handed him a photo. "This is the blowup of the stocky man at the Venice Oil Field," Stuart said to Mathieu. "Unfortunately, his face isn't any clearer in the blowup. It's fuzzy. The photo was out of focus, so blowing it up just made it worse."

Mathieu rubbed his chin as he examined the photo. "I agree, it's not very useful for identification," Mathieu sighed, "but it does show his body type. Let's put out an APB and see if we get lucky and some patrolman recognizes him. Can you handle that?"

"Sure, should we try to get it printed in the *Times* or the *Examiner*, too?"

"No," Mathieu said, shaking his head. "It's too risky. I've made that mistake before. If we publish it, either he goes into hiding, or his masters kill him. I need him alive so he can lead us to who's calling the shots."

"Okay, I'll get on that APB now," Stuart said as he walked away.

Mathieu knew from experience that wealthy, powerful men were difficult to interrogate. Most are excellent liars and even better at rationalizing their actions as being beneficial to society. He needed some leverage against Mahoney, so he made a quick call to Bill Collins before heading to the Chateau Marmont.

When Collins came on the line, Mathieu asked, "Do you know anything that Edgar Mahoney is sensitive about?"

There was a brief silence, then Collins said, "I hear he's a little sensitive about his age."

"Why?"

"Because he parades around town with young starlets thirty years younger than him. The gossip columns have pillared him for robbing the cradle."

"How old is he?"

"Early fifties, I think," Collins said. "Although he thinks he looks much younger."

Mathieu scoffed. "Don't all men that age? But probing that might help throw him off, which is all I need. Thanks, Bill. I'll let you know how it goes."

Arriving at the Chateau Marmont, Mathieu handed his car key to the valet, then walked up five steps to the cloister's walkway. The midday sun streamed in from the south, casting long shadows on the chateau's stonewalls.

It looked like a great place to stay if your last name was Rockefeller. Smartly dressed guests sat at wicker tables on the outdoor patio, enjoying a late lunch. The air was fragrant with money and delicate perfume. Even the cigarette butts in the ashtrays looked expensive. Mathieu felt as out of place here as a janitor at a debutante's ball.

He made a quick stop at the front desk to get directions to the manager's office, then turned right at the first hallway, walked to the end, and knocked.

The person who answered the door looked more like a physics professor than a hotelier, with his wiry gray hair, spectacles, and a navy blue V-neck pullover with a name tag that read "Martin Stroud – Manager."

"How can I help you, young man?" Stroud asked as he squinted through his thick fingerprint-smudged glasses.

"I'm Detective Mathieu from the LAPD, Mr. Stroud," Mathieu said, displaying his badge.

Stroud nodded. "I've been expecting you, Detective. Mrs. Owens called me the other day and told me of your visit. I assume you want to discuss Mr. Fowler."

"Yes, sir."

"Please come in and have a seat," Stroud said, standing aside so Mathieu could enter.

It was a small, narrow room with a lone French window on the east wall overlooking the pool area. What the office lacked in space, it made up in elegance.

A Regency-style mahogany desk with light wood veneer faced the window. A green felt writing pad on its surface, flanked by a nickel-plated rotary telephone and a brass table lamp.

Mr. Stroud angled his desk chair toward an armchair to his right, where Mathieu sat.

"How long did Mr. Fowler work here?" Mathieu asked after they were seated.

"A little over six months," Stroud said. "I checked his employment file yesterday."

"And he worked as a chauffeur and night watchman. Is that correct?"

"Yes," Stroud nodded. "We try to hire staff who can perform multiple duties when we can."

"How did Mr. Fowler come to you?"

"One of our most important guests recommended him," Stroud replied.

"And who was that?"

"Do I have to answer?" Stroud asked. "We have a reputation for confidentiality here."

"I understand that, Mr. Stroud," Mathieu said. "But this is a murder investigation, so I'd appreciate an answer. In return, I will assure you of my discretion."

Stroud steepled his hands in front of his mouth, nodded, and said, "Edgar Mahoney, a long-time guest, recommended Mr. Fowler."

"I see," Mathieu said as he took notes. "And was Mr. Fowler a good employee?"

"Yes," Stroud said. "Freddy was eager and always fulfilled his assignments."

Mathieu pulled out the blowup of the stocky man and handed it to Stroud. "Have you ever seen this man at the hotel alone or in the company of Mr. Fowler or Mr. Mahoney?"

Stroud took a while to examine the photo, then, shaking his head, returned it to Mathieu. "No, I don't recall seeing this man at the chateau," Stroud said, then added, "Why are you interested in him and Mr. Fowler?"

"Because they both may have been involved in a double homicide," Mathieu said with a direct gaze.

Stroud's face turned pale. "Oh, dear," he said, muttering to himself. "I hope it won't get out that Mr. Fowler worked at the Chateau Marmont."

"I'll do my best to ensure it doesn't, Mr. Stroud, as long as you cooperate fully with the police," Mathieu said. "Is that clear?"

"Yes, of course, Detective," Stroud said, rushing to get his words out.

"That's all the questions I have for now, Mr. Stroud," Mathieu said as he stood. "I'd appreciate it if you could direct me to Mr. Mahoney's room."

"Certainly," Stroud said. "It's the penthouse suite on the top floor. Turn left after you get off the elevator."

Mathieu checked with the front desk to make sure Mahoney was in, then took the elevator up to the top floor. Arriving, he followed Stroud's directions to the suite, took a deep breath to calm himself, and knocked.

The man who answered was tall, thin, and fit for his age but perhaps an inch shorter than him. Mathieu would take any advantage he could get as he calmly displayed his badge and said, "Mr. Mahoney, my name is Detective Mathieu from the LAPD. I need a word with you."

"About what?" Mahoney asked, not budging an inch from the doorway.

"Mr. Fowler," Mathieu said.

"I've never heard of him," Mahoney said in a belligerent tone.

Mathieu repressed his instinct to react and said calmly, "That's odd because the hotel manager just told me you recommended Mr. Fowler for a job here. And I have several witnesses, including myself, who saw Mr. Fowler placing bets for you at Santa Anita the day he died."

Mahoney hesitated, then backpedaling, said, "Oh, you must mean Fat Freddy. I didn't know his last name. Everyone called him by his nickname. Why are you interested in him? I thought his death was a damn fool accident."

"It was," Mathieu said, thinking it was unlikely he didn't know Freddy's last name.

"Then why are you bothering me?" Mahoney asked.

"Because I have some questions about Freddy that I need your help with. May I come in? If this is an inconvenient time, we can do the interview downtown at LAPD headquarters tomorrow instead."

Seemingly deciding he didn't want the hassle of going to police headquarters, Mahoney relented, stood aside, and said, "As long as you make it quick, Detective. I have a guest."

"Of course, it will only take a few minutes, and I'll be on my way."

Mahoney led Mathieu across the parquet floor toward a spacious living room, then through an open French door to the deck, where Mahoney sat down under a striped awning with his back to the sun, forcing Mathieu to take the chair facing it.

Instead, Mathieu casually dragged the chair next to Mahoney's.

"Nice deck," Mathieu said with a smile as he sat down beside him. He noticed an unoccupied chaise lounge with a beach towel near the railing and wondered who Edgar's "guest" was.

"How did you first meet Mr. Fowler?" Mathieu asked.

Edgar showed annoyance that the young detective had outflanked him but replied in a casual tone, "I met Freddy at the Café La Bohème. He was an amusing guy. He told me he had some experience as a chauffeur and night watchman, so I did him a favor and recommended him to the hotel manager. And since Freddy worked here, it was convenient for me to have him do odd jobs for me occasionally."

"What kind of odd jobs?"

"Picking up friends or running errands. That kind of thing."

"I see," Mathieu said, nodding. "Did you ever meet any of Freddy's friends?"

"No, of course not," Edgar said in an irritated tone.

"What about this man?" Mathieu asked, handing him the blowup of the burly man at the Venice Oil field.

Edgar looked at the photo for a moment with a neutral expression, then shook his head and said, "I've never seen him before."

"What about at the Café La Bohème?"

"No, not there either. Who is he?"

"A man involved in the deaths of Lester Jensen and Reginald Stonebridge," Mathieu said in an even tone. "It seems that he and Freddy had a thing about killing oil executives. I wonder if they intended to kill you next."

Mahoney's smug expression dropped faster than a French guillotine while his tanned face turned white as a pillowcase. "What are you saying?"

Edgar's fear looked genuine enough, which made Mathieu question his involvement in the murders. "Mr. Fowler was stalking you."

"Stalking me!" Edgar said. "Why?"

"I don't know for sure," Mathieu said with a shrug, "but he was taking photos of you at the hotel."

"What kind of photos?" Edgar asked, clearly shocked.

"Photos of you with various women," Mathieu said.

Sensing Mahoney was off balance, Mathieu added, "By the way, how is it you know Jacqueline Jensen, Lester Jensen's widow?"

"Who says I know Jacqueline Jensen?" Edgar asked.

"Because I've seen some rather intimate photos of you with Jacqueline that Freddy took. So, I'd advise you to start telling me the truth, Mr. Mahoney."

Edgar scoffed, attempting to brush it off. "So, what if I know Jacqueline? She knew Lester was going to divorce her and wanted to change teams."

"That's a curious phrase," Mathieu said. "'Change teams,' given that Lester ended up dead soon after Freddy took the photos of you and Jacqueline together. Did you help Jacqueline 'change teams' by ordering Jensen's death?"

"I had nothing to do with Jensen's murder," Edgar said adamantly.

"Perhaps," Mathieu said with a shrug, "but you can understand why I might think you did, given the photos I saw and the fact that you keep lying to me."

"I demand to see those photos!" Mahoney said.

"All in good time, Mr. Mahoney," Mathieu said with a smile. "But for now, they're locked up in the evidence room until the investigation is complete."

Just then, they heard the padding of bare feet on the living room floor as a statuesque blond, totally naked, stepped out onto the deck; a patch of hair confirmed she was a natural blond, and her beautiful face confirmed she was Anita Cummings—not that anyone was looking at her face at that moment.

"Excuse me, Edgar, I didn't realize you had a guest," Anita said non-plussed.

"Not exactly a guest, Anita," Edgar said with chagrin. "This is Detective Mathieu from the LAPD."

"I know who it is," Anita said as she sat down across from Mathieu, glaring at him as she crossed her shapely legs.

"Perhaps you should cover up, Anita," Edgar said.

"Why? He's seen it before," Anita said, dismissing Edgar with a wave of her hand. "I saw you at Santa Anita, Detective. Why didn't you say hello?" Anita asked like a spurned lover.

"I was working," Mathieu replied.

"That didn't stop you from talking to Lady Caroline Astor, your former girlfriend."

"Lady Caroline approached me, and she was never my girlfriend."

"That's not what Lord Crossley told me."

"Lord Crossley is misinformed," Mathieu said flatly.

Edgar was undoubtedly the wealthiest person on the deck and perhaps in the entire city. But at that moment, he looked like the kid neither team had picked to play sandlot baseball after school.

Turning to Edgar, Mathieu said, "Thank you for your time, Mr. Mahoney. Those are all the questions I have for now. I'll leave you to your guest." Then, standing, Mathieu handed Edgar his card and added, "Please, don't leave town without informing me."

"Am I a suspect, Detective?"

"No, sir, but you're a person of interest," Mathieu said. "Good day."

Edgar rose to escort him out, but Anita stopped him and said, "I'll do it."

At the door, still totally naked, Anita pressed her luscious body against Mathieu. He could feel her heat on his thighs. "It's not what you think," Anita said.

"What do I think?" Mathieu asked.

"That I'm sleeping with him."

"What are you doing then, cleaning his penthouse?"

"Very funny," Anita said. "Edgar hires me to investigate his potential male business partners."

"In the nude?" Mathieu grinned. "That must be distracting."

"No. But Edgar lets me sunbathe nude on his deck sometimes. It's hard to find a place this private in the city."

"So, nude sunbathing is a perk of the job."

"Yes," Anita said with a sly smile. "And for your information, the only part of my body Edgar has ever touched is my back, to put suntan lotion on it … Edgar likes to watch, Detective, if you get my drift."

"I see."

"Why are you interested in Edgar?" Anita asked.

"The Lester Jensen murder."

"Is he a suspect?"

"I don't know," Mathieu said with a shrug. "You seem to know him better than I do. Should he be?"

"Well, he's a ruthless businessman, but it's hard to see him as a murderer. Especially given what I just told you about him."

"People can be surprising, Anita."

"Maybe we could talk about it sometime," Anita said, pressing closer.

"I look forward to it."

"Where?" Anita asked, her eyes glistening in anticipation.

"Somewhere where you'd have to keep your clothes on."

"What fun would that be?"

"I'll call you soon, Miss Cummings," Mathieu said as he opened the door and left.

When Edgar heard the door close, he went into his bedroom and made a call. "I'm worried I might be next," he said over the line.

34

Travis

It was a desolate cesspit of a place in the middle of a searing desert with a few scattered ranches and more tumbleweed than people. But it had a natural spring. And in 1905, the cesspit got lucky.

A railroad came through and built a station. Not because anyone wanted to get off in the godforsaken place but because the nearby wells provided the water needed for the steam engines of the Los Angeles and Salt Lake Railroad.

In 1931, with a population of 5,000, the cesspit got lucky again. The federal government began construction of the Boulder Dam on the Colorado River in a nearby canyon. Building a dam requires workers, lots of them, and the population exploded to almost 25,000.

Most were young men marooned in the middle of nowhere with nothing to do. The city fathers of Las Vegas, who'd already dedicated an entire city block to saloons and brothels, rose to the challenge and legalized gambling.

Travis had come years earlier, in 1919, to escape his past. The remoteness and smallness of the place suited him just fine. He didn't work. Mostly, he stayed to himself in his tiny hotel room, where he'd taken down all the mirrors. He bought a gun and tried to commit suicide a few times but couldn't go through with it.

When he was on the streets, Travis wore a large drooping cowboy hat that covered the right side of his face. Occasionally, he'd visit one of the brothels in Block 16 on Ogden Street, but always with the lights out. But most nights, he just drank himself to sleep.

On the fifteenth of each month, a cashier's check would arrive from Los Angeles. It was his payoff for keeping quiet. But this month's check hadn't arrived yet, and he was worried. Travis was breathing, but he wasn't alive. He'd died a long time ago in an oil field fire that killed his father and older brother.

35

Bunker Hill

Bunker Hill was an area known for loose skirts and looser morals. So, it wasn't a surprise when a call came in the dead of night that a man had been shot through the chest in a rooming house next to the Angel's Flight funicular railway.

What was a surprise was that the patrolman dispatched to the scene recognized the victim as the burly man from the APB.

The once exquisite Victorian mansions on Bunker Hill had long since been torn down or converted into rooming houses after the wealthy abandoned the area at the turn of the century.

The same was true for the more modest buildings like the Sunshine Apartments halfway up the hill on the north side of Angel's Flight, where the body was found.

The four-story faded green clapboard structure looked like a misplaced farmhouse with its dilapidated open-air wood balconies, squatting atop a ten-foot-high retaining wall above the Clay Street alley.

The apartment's address was 421 Third Street, but there was no "street" here. The slope between Hill and Olive was too steep for a road, which is why they'd built the funicular and why Third

Street ran through a narrow, claustrophobic tunnel at the base of the hill.

The only other way up the hill was to labor up one hundred forty-three steep steps on the north side of Angel's Flight, which had probably claimed its share of heart attack victims over the years.

The inhabitants of this section of Bunker Hill were a mixed lot: thugs, con artists, thieves, day laborers, secretaries, and prostitutes.

It was easy to tell the prostitutes from the secretaries by how tightly their skirts clung to their thighs and the sway of their hips. Lucy Simmons, who saw the assailant run away, definitely wasn't a secretary.

She stood on the seventh-floor fire escape balcony of the adjoining Hillcrest Apartments in a clinging light brown satin dress, her hands on her hips, smelling of sweat and cheap perfume; it was a pleasant smell.

But the vertigo-inducing view from the rickety balcony as she pointed down the slope at the Sunshine Apartments wasn't for the faint of heart.

"I was in the bedroom with a 'guest' when I heard the gunshot," Lucy said as she turned back to Mathieu, gliding her emerald-green eyes up and down his lean body.

"What time did you hear the shot?" Mathieu asked.

"Around 3 a.m."

"Are you the one that called the police?"

"Yes."

"Did you get a good look at the shooter?"

"No," Lucy said, shaking her head. "With all these rooming houses on the hill, the sound echoes through here like a canyon. By the time I got out on the balcony and figured out where the shot had come from, I only caught a fleeting glimpse of them rounding the corner at the bottom of the steps on Hill Street and running north toward the Hotel Belmont."

"Man or woman?" Mathieu asked.

Lucy shrugged. "Hard to tell it was too dark. They were in the shadows."

"Do you remember anything else about the assailant?"

"No, sorry, I don't, Detective," Lucy said, shaking her head.

"What apartment are you in?" Mathieu asked.

"703," Lucy answered with a hopeful smile.

"I'll have an officer come up and take your statement, Miss Simmons."

Lucy's smile faded. "Can't you take it?" she asked.

"I have to get back to the crime scene," Mathieu said as he handed her his card. "But if you remember anything else later, even the smallest detail, please call me."

"I will," she said, looking into his dark, brooding eyes.

Mathieu took the outdoor fire escape to the first floor, then walked down the steep concrete steps to the Sunshine Apartment building. The victim's room was on the first-floor landing facing Angel's Flight.

Fred Wilson and Stuart Thomas were already in the room. It was a dingy squat in the southeast corner of the building. The room was narrower than a train car, with a ceramic wash basin, spindly chair, and a toilet crammed into a water closet. The victim lay sprawled face up on the bed wearing white boxer shorts and an undershirt soaked in blood.

Turning to Wilson, Mathieu said, "Take all the time you need, Fred. We have to find a fingerprint or some other evidence tying the killer to the scene."

"Understood, sir."

"Was the door jimmied?"

"No," Fred said.

"So, it was either unlocked or the killer had a key," Mathieu said.

"Yes, sir. From the looks of things, the killer snuck in and shot the victim in the chest while he was sleeping. There's no sign of a struggle."

"Do we know the victim's name?"

"Yes, sir. We found his driver's license. His name is Harry Doyle. We also found a handgun in the night cabinet beside the bed. I'll compare the gun with the cartridges we found at the Eddie Hennessy killing. My guess is they'll match."

Mathieu nodded. "So, whoever killed Doyle used their own weapon. That might help us in the end."

"Yes, sir," Fred said. "That's what I was thinking, too."

"I'll wait outside. I don't want to get in your way," Mathieu said. "When you finish, come get me, and I'll start searching the place."

"Will do," Fred said. "By the way, Officer Franklin, who responded to the call, is canvasing the other residents. He called headquarters to request some more officers to take statements in the adjoining rooming houses."

"Great," Mathieu said, always grateful for an officer who took the initiative; they were rare. "What about the time of death?"

"The medical examiner already came and went," Fred said. "His estimate was around 3 a.m."

"That was quick. Was it the Walrus?"

"No, sir," Fred said, shaking his head. "Some new guy, Doctor Rollins is his name."

"Three matches the time Lucy Simmons, a witness in the Hillcrest Apartments, told me she heard the shot," Mathieu said as he turned and went out on the porch.

He paused at the weathered railing speckled with green paint, deciding what to do. Then, he took the steps down to Hill Street to talk to the night manager at the Hotel Belmont.

The Hotel Belmont occupied a mammoth nine-story mustard-yellow brick building at the base of Bunker Hill, that used to be a YWCA headquarters. A faded sign painted on the wall advertised rooms with private baths for $1.50 a day and free parking. Not that it was likely many of the residents of this fleabag hotel had cars.

Mathieu took the steps to the arched entrance and entered. With its two-story-high lobby, mezzanine, chandeliers, marble floor, and spectacular open-air light well in the middle of the building, Mathieu could see it had once been an elegant address when it was the YWCA headquarters.

There was a long wooden bench on the left that you'd expect to see in a train station and a threadbare rug in the center of the floor. Mathieu approached the check-in desk on the right and showed his badge to the night manager.

"Were you on duty this morning?" Mathieu asked the middle-aged man after introducing himself.

"Yes, Detective."

"Did you see anyone run past the hotel around 3 a.m.?"

"No, sir," he said, shaking his head. "But I did hear a car tear out of here around that time."

"What kind?"

The night manager took a moment and said, "Late model, fancy car, a Studebaker maybe."

"Color?"

The manager shrugged. "Hard to tell, a dark color, maybe blue or black."

"Did you see the driver?"

"No, by the time I glanced toward the street, all I saw were the taillights speeding away, heading south on Hill Street."

"Thanks, you've been a big help," Mathieu said. "If you remember anything else later, please call me. Here's my card."

By the time Mathieu got back to the Sunshine Apartments, the coroner's van had taken the body away, Stuart had left, and Fred was finishing up. The room was so small there weren't many places to hide anything.

"Did you already search the nightstand, Fred?"

"Yes, sir. All I found was the revolver, a pack of cigarettes, matches, and a packet of Blondtex condoms in the drawer."

Mathieu nodded and said, "Pack up the few clothes he has, and we'll search them at headquarters."

"Yes, sir."

Mathieu went into the water closet and searched the water tank. Finding nothing, he came back to the room and stripped the bed. He shook out the sheets, turned over the thin mattress, and propped it against the wall. A small card was tucked into the bedframe springs.

Picking it up, Mathieu examined it and said, "I found something, Fred."

"What is it?"

"It's a Requiem Mass card from the Plaza Church."

"Really," Fred said, looking surprised. "I didn't take Mr. Doyle for a religious man."

"Neither did I," Mathieu said.

"What does it say?"

"It's handwritten and says, 'The Holy Sacrifice of Mass will be offered for the repose of the souls of Arnold Hays and his son Arlo Hays.'"

"Who are they?"

"I don't know," Mathieu said, shaking his head. "But we need to find out."

36

Doyle

"Why do you think they killed Doyle?" Bull asked Mathieu later that day at headquarters.

"To silence him," Mathieu said.

"But why now?"

"Maybe we're getting too close, and they're starting to panic."

"What makes you think that?" Bull asked.

"Because I don't think it's a coincidence that Doyle was killed right after I visited Mahoney."

"Fair point," Bull said with a nod. "Do you think Mahoney ordered the hit?"

"I don't know," Mathieu said with a shrug. "But Mahoney did seem genuinely scared when I told him Fowler had been stalking him and taking photos of him with Jacqueline."

Bull was silent for a moment as he rubbed his chin. "There's another possibility."

"What's that, sir?"

"That after you met with Mahoney, he became afraid Doyle was either going to kill him or double-cross him. So, he had him bumped off before he could."

"That's also possible, Chief," Mathieu said, nodding. "Either way, I don't think it's a coincidence. I think it's related to my visit."

"What's your best guess on the motive for the Jensen-Stonebridge murders?" Bull asked.

"Revenge or greed," Mathieu said, "or possibly both."

"Why revenge?" Bull asked with a level gaze.

"Because of the dramatic way Jensen and Stonebridge were killed."

"Why greed?"

"Because from what I've learned so far, the oil business is full of greedy, cutthroat men like Jensen and Mahoney," Mathieu said. "Who seem capable of doing almost anything to get their next big score."

"Including murder?" Bull asked with a skeptical look.

"I don't know, Chief, that's the big question," Mathieu said, raising his hands in frustration. "But let's suppose Jensen discovered oil on a piece of land that no one else knew about, and he bragged about it. And somebody killed him to get ahold of it."

"But Jensen was a known conman and huckster," Bull said. "Why would anyone believe him?"

"Maybe he got lucky this time and really did find a big score."

"Are Mahoney and Jacqueline Jensen still your top suspects?"

"Yes," Mathieu said. "And possibly the office manager, Florence Drake, who controls Jensen Petroleum now."

"But I thought you told me Jensen Petroleum is fighting a mountain of lawsuits and is almost bankrupt."

"It is, Chief."

"Then gaining control of a worthless company seems like a weak motive for murder."

Mathieu shrugged. "That's true, sir. That's why Mahoney and Jacqueline are still at the top of the list.

"Mahoney's the only one I know who had a direct connection to Fowler. Mahoney got Freddy the job at the Chateau Marmont, and he used him for personal errands. Freddy was a known thug, so he probably recruited Harry Doyle to help with the killings. And from the photos Freddy took, it's clear something was going on between Mahoney and Jacqueline before Jensen was murdered."

"But you don't have any evidence that Mahoney paid Fowler and Doyle to do the killings."

"No, I don't. But it's clear from the photos that Freddy kidnapped Marilyn Lane the night of Jensen's murder and that Doyle strung up Stonebridge. It's hard for me to believe that either of them had a personal motive for killing Jensen or Stonebridge. Someone must have hired them to do the job."

"Did you find any money on either of them?"

"Not a fortune, but a lot for thugs like Freddy and Doyle," Mathieu said. "Freddy had around seven hundred dollars, and we found about a grand in Doyle's clothes. And they could have squirreled away the rest somewhere or even put it in the bank.

"I asked Enya to check with the local banks to see if they had any accounts in town. Plus, you know how thugs are, sir. They spend money on booze, gambling, and prostitutes as fast as they make it."

Bull nodded. "And if the motive is revenge … revenge for what?" Bull asked.

"Possibly the oil field fire back in Texas," Mathieu said. "Allegedly, both Jensen and Stonebridge worked there and left soon after."

"But that was almost sixteen years ago, wasn't it?" Bull asked. "That seems like a long time to wait to get revenge. Why now?"

"I don't know, sir," Mathieu said with a shrug. "Maybe it took that long for the killer to find them. It's the only thing that explains the dramatic deaths. But there's another possible motive."

"What's that?" Bull asked.

"That Jensen and Stonebridge were blackmailing someone related to Elk Hills and the Teapot Dome scandal."

"But that was Edward Doheny's scandal, wasn't it?" Bull asked. "And he's an old man now."

"I know, but according to Bill Collins at the *Times*, Mahoney worked closely with Doheny at Elk Hills in the early '20s when Jensen and Stonebridge were there. And Jensen's first wife intimated that Lester knew something about the Teapot Dome scandal and had something on Doheny."

"Maybe Jensen had something on Mahoney also, and he and Stonebridge were blackmailing him. When Mahoney got tired of it, he hired Freddy and Harry Doyle to bump them off."

"But why do it so dramatically?" Bull asked. "Mahoney could have had them both shot in a back alley, and that would have been the end of

"I don't know, sir," Mathieu said, arching his eyebrows. "That's what I don't understand. Perhaps to throw us off."

"What are you going to do next?" Bull asked.

"Have another chat with Jacqueline Jensen," Mathieu said. "After that, talk to Anita Cummings. She's done some investigating for Mahoney. She might be able to fill me in on some angle I'm not aware of."

Mathieu didn't call ahead to Jacqueline's home. He'd found surprise visits to be much more effective. Even if it sometimes meant a wasted trip.

Mathieu parked in the driveway of Jacqueline's Los Feliz mansion. The same austere butler greeted him at the front door and escorted him to the pool area where Jacqueline was swimming. The butler announced Mathieu's arrival with a slight bow and left.

Jacqueline swam to the side of the pool, where Mathieu stood. She looked at him like an ice cream cone she wanted to lick and asked, "To what do I owe this pleasure, Detective?"

"I have a few more questions for you, Mrs. Jensen."

"I'm not Mrs. Jensen anymore," Jacqueline grinned. "I'm a free woman, and it feels wonderful."

Jacqueline pushed herself out of the pool like the woman in Freddy's photo at the Chateau Marmont. Stretching her back, she stood dripping wet like the goddess Aphrodite in a form-fitting one-piece bathing suit, staring at Mathieu.

She bent over seductively to wring out her dark hair, then led Mathieu to a table and chairs at the far end of the pool under an umbrella.

After they were seated, Jacqueline took a sip of iced tea from her glass and asked, "Would you like something to drink, Detective?"

"No, thank you," Mathieu said.

"What questions did you want to ask me?"

"What's your relationship with Edgar Mahoney?" Mathieu asked, holding her gaze.

Jacqueline stared at Mathieu a moment and then laughed. "Are you asking if I'm sleeping with him, Detective?"

"No, I assume you are, and I assume Edgar called you after I visited him recently," Mathieu said. "I'm more interested in why you're sleeping with him and if it has anything to do with your husband's death."

Jacqueline paused a moment to formulate her answer, seemingly thrown off by Mathieu's brusqueness. "Let's say I'm planning for my future, Detective," Jacqueline said in a cryptic way.

"Does that planning include killing off your ex-husband? Because the photos I have of you and Edgar were taken before Lester was murdered."

"No," Jacqueline said with a wave of the hand, seemingly amused. "Edgar told me about the photos. How exciting to be spied on! What would killing Lester achieve anyway, except getting to keep this house? I'm looking for a much bigger score than that."

"Such as what?"

"I want to trade up for someone with real wealth while I still can, not a conman like Lester."

"Such as Edgar."

"Yes."

"How's that going?"

"Let's just say I've had several 'undressed' rehearsals that went well," Jacqueline said with a self-satisfied smirk.

"Have you had any rehearsals with anyone besides Edgar?"

"Yes, Detective," Jacqueline said. "I'm casting a wide net."

"Anyone who would want your ex-husband dead?"

"No, as you've rightfully noted, I started auditioning while Lester was still alive. My suitors were as shocked as I at his untimely demise."

Changing tact, Mathieu asked, "Did Lester mention anything to you about a new oil discovery before his death?"

Jacqueline chortled. "Lester always claimed he had a new oil find, Detective, but they rarely panned out. I long since stopped listening to those boasts."

"One other question, Mrs. Jensen. Did Lester ever talk to you about the oil field fire in Texas in 1918 where he worked?"

"That was well before my time, Detective," Jacqueline said. "You'd have to talk to the first Mrs. Jensen about that."

"I have," Mathieu said. "I just wondered if Lester ever discussed it with you."

Jacqueline's face turned serious for the first time. "I brought it up once early in our marriage because I'd overheard a rumor about it. Lester turned on me in a violent rage and warned me if I ever mentioned it again, he'd kick me out of the house and divorce me immediately. That's the last time we ever discussed it."

37

Anita

It was late when they met in the coffee shop off the lobby at the Biltmore Hotel. And almost deserted, as Mathieu hoped it would be.

Mathieu arrived first. Anita glided into the room fifteen minutes later, transforming it into a stage. She looked radiant in her light brown dress and smelled even better as she slid into the booth beside him.

"I'm not wearing anything under this," Anita said with a wink as she leaned close to him. "If you'd like to get a room."

"The Biltmore is way above my pay grade, Anita. You'll have to settle for coffee."

"Is that all I get?" Anita asked, pouting.

"I'll throw in a slice of pie," Mathieu said with a smile.

Anita laughed. "Okay, if you share it with me."

"Deal."

They ordered two coffees and a slice of key lime pie. When the waitress left, Mathieu said, "You told me Edgar hired you to investigate potential business partners. Who were they?"

"Lester Jensen was the first," Anita said, seemingly unfazed by the revelation.

"Really!" Mathieu said, raising his eyebrows in surprise. "When?"

"A couple of months before he was killed," Anita said as she twirled her long blond hair around her fingertip.

"Why did Edgar want you to meet with Jensen?" Mathieu asked.

"Edgar told me he heard a rumor that Jensen had a potentially huge oil find that he was shopping around to local oil barons. And Jensen was hiding it from his business manager."

"Where did Edgar hear the rumor?"

Anita shrugged. "I don't know, he didn't say."

"So, what did you do?"

"I heard Jensen liked to hang out at the bar at Musso and Frank's on Tuesday nights after work. So, the following Tuesday, I sat at the bar in a revealing gown and waited for the prey to show up."

Mathieu laughed. "I assume Jensen fell into your trap."

"Yes," Anita said with a self-satisfied smile. "Like a rat in a spring trap. It was child's play."

"Then what happened?" Mathieu asked.

The waitress came with their coffee and pie at that moment. Anita waited until she left and said, "We had a few more drinks at the bar, then moved to a booth for dinner.

"We kept drinking at the table, and Jensen kept staring at my breasts like he'd seen the face of god. At one point, Jensen leaned in to get a better view, and in a stage whisper you could hear on Hollywood Boulevard, started bragging about this big oil find he was shopping around."

"Did Jensen say where it was?"

"No," Anita said, seductively tossing her long blond hair back. "He wasn't that stupid."

"Did you learn anything else that night?" Mathieu asked.

"Not really," Anita said. "A little later, Jensen got so drunk he lunged at my breasts with his hands and tried to grab them. I shoved him away, and he did a face-plant on the tablecloth and passed out. After which, I grabbed my purse and left."

"Charming fellow," Mathieu said. "Did you ever see Jensen again?"

Anita arched her eyebrows. "What do you think, Mathieu?"

"Apparently not," Mathieu said with a laugh. "What happened afterward?"

"I reported back to Edgar what Jensen told me, which confirmed the rumor he'd heard."

"And that was the end of it?" Mathieu asked.

"I thought so," Anita said, "but Edgar contacted me a few weeks later. He said a young man called him and claimed he'd overheard Jensen bragging the same story to another blond. The young man did some research on his own and discovered where the oil field might be."

"Where?" Mathieu asked.

"On an abandoned ranch in the Central Valley."

"Did Edgar believe him?"

"Not at first," Anita said, shaking her head, "but Edgar drove out to the ranch with the young man. When they got there, he walked the property and discovered where Jensen had dug a test well. The land was still seeping oil."

"Do you know where the ranch is exactly?"

"No, of course not," Anita said with a sour look. "Edgar would never tell me that."

"Who owns the ranch?" Mathieu asked.

"That's where it gets interesting. Edgar sent a lawyer named Horatio Jennings to Bakersfield to get a copy of the deed. Who do you think was on it?"

"Jensen and Stonebridge," Mathieu said, making a guess.

"Exactly, and one other person."

"Who?" Mathieu asked, surprised.

"Travis Hays."

"Who's Travis Hays?" Mathieu asked, remembering the mass card with the names Arnold and Arlo Hays on it.

"I don't know," Anita said, finishing the last bite of pie. "That's what Edgar asked me to find out. But I haven't had any luck. I can't find him. He's a ghost."

"A ghost?"

"Yes, but a potentially wealthy one if he's alive," Anita said, "because as the last surviving person on the deed, he's the sole owner."

"And if he's dead?" Mathieu asked.

"Then the widow of the last deceased will inherit the land."

"You mean Mrs. Stonebridge," Mathieu said, wondering if he'd underestimated Mrs. Stonebridge's cunning.

"Yes," Anita said with a nod.

"Does anyone else know about the deed?" Mathieu asked.

"At least one other person."

"Who?"

"Jennings told Edgar that another Los Angeles lawyer obtained a copy of the deed several months before."

"What's the other lawyer's name?"

"Thomas Briggs."

"Did you meet with Counselor Briggs?"

"No," Anita said, shaking her head. "Edgar decided to have Horatio check him out."

"What did he learn?"

"You'll have to ask him yourself, Detective," Anita said, resting her chin in her palm with a sleepy smile. "You only get so much for a cup of coffee and a slice of pie."

38

The Lawyers

Taking Anita's advice, Mathieu started with Edgar Mahoney's lawyer, Horatio Jennings. He didn't expect to learn anything new about the deed, but he might learn something about the other lawyer, Thomas Briggs, who was his real interest.

Jennings's law office was on the ground floor of the Writers and Artists building at the corner of Rodeo and "little" Santa Monica Boulevard in Beverly Hills.

Mathieu parked behind a flashy red Buick Touring convertible in front of a sign advertising "Horatio Ignatius Jennings Esquire Law Offices." It was a mouthful of a sign that was almost as wide as the office frontage.

Mathieu hadn't called ahead. He didn't want to give Jennings an opportunity to refuse to see him. Instead, he decided to arrive before regular office hours. It was twenty-past-seven when he stepped out of his Buick Phaeton and approached the building.

It was an attractive white three-story stucco building with brown piping designed in an indeterminate faux Spanish style. Its long, narrow shape was a result of being hemmed in by Santa Monica Boulevard and the Red Car tracks. Two requisite palm trees towered lazily over the building in front, completing the look of casual Beverly Hills elegance.

The front door was unlocked, and the anteroom was empty when Mathieu entered. Despite its Beverly Hills address, the place smelled moldy and needed a good cleaning.

He skirted to the right of the empty receptionist's desk, then went down a short hallway to a door marked "Horatio Jennings Esquire" and knocked.

Mathieu heard a rustling of hurried movement behind the door. Soon after, a large-boned man opened the door a crack. His rumpled hair and clothes gave the impression he'd slept in the office.

The man stared at Mathieu through glazed eyes. "Who are you?" he asked in a surly voice.

"I'm Detective Mathieu from the LAPD," Mathieu said as he showed him his badge. "I assume you're Counselor Jennings."

"I am," Jennings said. "What do you want with me?"

"I'm a homicide detective," Mathieu said. "I'd like to ask you a few questions."

"About what?" Jennings asked, still surly and still hiding behind the partially opened door.

"Some work you did for Edgar Mahoney."

"Any work I do for a client is protected by attorney-client privilege, Detective."

"I'm aware of that, Counselor," Mathieu said. "However, I already know you went to Bakersfield on Mr. Mahoney's behalf to obtain a copy of a deed to a ranch in the Central Valley. I also know the names of the three men on that deed. Two of them, Lester Jensen and Reginald Stonebridge, have been murdered, and I'm in charge of their case.

"I'm certain a man of your standing wouldn't want to hinder a murder investigation. In return for your cooperation, I can assure you I won't ask anything that would violate attorney-client privilege."

Jennings hesitated for a moment, then said. "Give me a moment to straighten up, and I'll be right with you, Detective." Then, Jennings shut the door in his face.

Mathieu could hear furniture being moved around, drawers closing, and hurried footsteps in the room. After several minutes, Jennings opened the door and said, "Please come in, Detective, and have a seat."

It had probably been an impressive office once, with its solid mahogany desk, brass lamps, and dark wood bookcases filled with bound volumes on civil, commercial, and criminal law.

But now it looked unkempt, with case notes piled on every available surface, a pillow and blanket stuffed in one corner of the room, and Jennings's "Harvard Law Diploma" hanging askew behind his desk, not to mention his clothing, which hung loosely on his large frame.

Jennings cleared his throat, straightened his tie, and said, "How can I help you, Detective?"

"It's my understanding that when you went to Bakersfield to get a copy of the Parker Ranch deed …"

Jennings interrupted him. "Let me correct you, Detective. It was the El Saucito Ranch," he blurted out before catching himself.

Looking embarrassed, Mathieu checked his notes and said, "Of course, excuse me, Counselor, I misspoke. I was thinking of a different aspect of the investigation. I have a lot to juggle here."

"It's perfectly understandable," Jennings said with a magnanimous smile.

Mathieu had no idea what the ranch's name was, but by pretending to, he'd forced Jennings to correct him.

Continuing, Mathieu said, "When you obtained a copy of the deed to the El Saucito Ranch, you discovered that another lawyer had been there a few months earlier to get a copy of the same deed. Is that correct?"

"Yes," Jennings said, now sitting confidently with his hands folded in his lap.

"And that lawyer's name is Thomas Briggs."

"That's correct," Jennings said with a smile.

Mathieu took a moment to formulate his next question. "When you reported this to Mr. Mahoney, he requested that you look into Counselor Briggs. Is that correct?"

"May I ask how you know all this, Detective?" Jennings asked.

"Certainly," Mathieu said quickly, "I've already spoken to Mr. Mahoney on this matter." Which was almost true but not quite. "I'd just like to get your impression of Counselor Briggs. I promise to keep it in confidence, but it might be important to the case."

"Why?" Jennings asked with a critical gaze.

"Because it's possible, most likely unknowingly, that Counselor Briggs has had contact with the killer."

Mathieu let that hang in the air for a moment, then added. "I'm not asking you to betray any confidences. I'd just like to get your opinion of Counselor Briggs. I don't want him to become a victim. Two other people associated with the case have already been murdered to silence them."

"I see," Jennings said, looking alarmed as he sat back in his chair. "Well, he's not one of us."

"What do you mean?" Mathieu asked, looking confused.

"He's not a Beverly Hills lawyer."

"Ah, I understand," Mathieu said. "Where are his law offices?"

"On Bunker Hill."

"Where exactly?"

"I don't remember the exact address," Jennings said, shifting in his chair uncomfortably, "but it's on Second and Olive next to a liquor store a few blocks from Angel's Flight."

"Did you visit Counselor Briggs there?" Mathieu asked.

Jennings hesitated, then said, "Yes ... about a week ago. It's a depressing area."

"What was your impression of Counselor Briggs?"

Jennings hesitated again, seemingly conflicted, then said, "I found him rather crude."

"In what way?" Mathieu asked. "Did you ask him who he was representing for the El Saucito Ranch property?"

"Yes, but he refused to tell me," Jennings said as his face turned red.

Mathieu sensed there was more to the story, so he remained silent.

After a tense delay, Jennings added, "He threatened to throw me out of his office if I didn't leave. I've never been treated that way before by a member of the bar."

"I can see how that would be upsetting, Counselor," Mathieu said. "Did you find out anything else about him?"

Jennings cleared his throat and said, "Not from him. But I called around to some of my associates, who told me they had similar experiences with Briggs. I discovered the bar has reprimanded him several times and that he has a reputation for representing petty thieves and thugs."

Mathieu nodded and said, "Thank you for your candor, Counselor. You've been very helpful. That's all the questions I have for you now."

An hour later, Mathieu pulled up in front of Briggs's law office on Second Street near the corner of Olive, a block below the crest of Bunker Hill. He locked his car after getting out. This wasn't an area to leave your vehicle unlocked, even if it was a police car.

Brigg's office was in a dilapidated two-story clapboard building with peeling paint next to a corner liquor store. Two men in work pants, cloth coats, and soiled hats stood outside Grant's Liquor, sharing a smoke. A sign behind them proclaimed, "This is the place."

The place for despair, Mathieu thought. Because while Hope Street was only a few blocks away, there was no hope here, only desperation as thick as the sidewalk grime.

Briggs's law office was to the left of a warped wooden staircase in the middle of the clapboard building. A window placard read, "Your Prosperity is my Business."

Mathieu took the stairs to the landing. He noticed a waist-high shelf to the left of the door, stacked with small manilla envelopes typically used to hold coins. Opening the door, he entered a cramped waiting room with chairs along the front window, several of which were occupied by waiting clients.

Straight ahead behind the reception desk sat a secretary in her mid-thirties with short, curly red hair, smoking a cigarette. Her head bent to one side, holding a telephone receiver in place as she extended her hand to take several coin envelopes from a small boy wearing a newsboy hat.

"Don't forget to take some more envelopes when you leave, Jimmy."

"I won't, Dorothy," the little boy said as he dashed out the door.

While the building's exterior looked derelict, the waiting room was bright, clean, and well-furnished. The busy secretary looked harried, talking on the phone while taking notes and depositing the coin envelopes she'd just received into a metal box on her desk beside a black Underwood typewriter.

Mathieu wondered if Briggs was running a numbers game out of his office, which was common in poor neighborhoods in New York but less so here. If he was, it might explain the fine furnishings and the slogan, "Your prosperity is my business."

Finishing the call, Dorothy smiled at Mathieu through hooded eyes and asked, "What can I do for you, handsome?"

"I'm Detective Mathieu from the LAPD," he said, displaying his badge. "I'd like a brief word with Counselor Briggs."

At the mention of the LAPD, Dorothy's smile melted like ice cream on a hot summer day. "What is it regarding?" she asked.

"Tell the Counselor it's about the copy of the deed to the El Saucito Ranch he obtained a few months ago in Bakersfield," Mathieu said in a neutral voice.

He had purposely provided as much detail as possible to avoid the inevitable subterfuge that would follow if he hadn't.

"Just a moment," Dorothy said as she rose and opened an unmarked door to her left that led toward the rear of the building. She returned a few minutes later with a flushed face. "Counselor Briggs can see you now," she said, pointing toward the door where she just exited.

Mathieu opened the door and went down a long, narrow corridor to a second door marked "Counselor Thomas Briggs," where he knocked, then entered after a booming voice said, "Come in!"

It was a spacious, beautifully appointed room that would have made the Beverly Hills lawyer jealous—and probably had.

Briggs himself was no less impressive, a large man in his sixties with jowls like a bulldog, a bulging waistline the size of a wine barrel, and a receding hairline. He had a jolly smile that started at his lips but didn't quite make it to his intelligent, hazel eyes that held a hint of menace.

"Please have a seat, Detective," Briggs said without rising to shake hands. "You're rather young to be a detective, aren't you?"

"You're rather old to be running a numbers game, aren't you, Counselor?"

Briggs let out a hearty laugh. "I like you, Detective. You're observant. What was the tell?"

"The stack of coin envelopes outside your door and the young newsies making drop-offs," Mathieu said. "How do you pay them—in bubble gum?"

Briggs chuckled again. "I view my little sideline as a service to the community, Detective. I'm doing my part to bring hope to the inhabitants of Bunker Hill in these troubled times."

"I'm sure the city fathers will reward you handsomely for your service, Counselor," Mathieu said as he took a seat in front of Briggs's desk. "But that's not why I'm here. My interest is the deed to the El Saucito Ranch you obtained."

Briggs steepled his hands in front of his face. "You're rather direct, Detective; you robbed me of the opportunity to dance around the subject with you."

"I figured we'd both want to lead, Counselor, which would be tedious and time-consuming. I'm sure you're a busy man and have better things to do."

"Fair enough," Briggs said. "What do you want to know?"

"Who hired you to get a copy of the deed?"

"You know I don't have to tell you that, Detective," Briggs said.

"And you know, Counselor, if I decided to have a squad car park in front of your offices for a few weeks, it would cut into your 'community service' activities."

"Point taken," Briggs said with a reluctant nod. "Would you believe me if I told you I don't know the client?"

"Try me," Mathieu said.

"About two months ago, one of the newsies dropped off an envelope," Briggs began. "Inside were three one hundred dollar bills and a note."

"What did the note say?" Mathieu asked.

"It said, 'I want to hire you to go to Bakersfield to obtain a copy of the deed to the El Saucito Ranch on the Carrizo Plain. Upon successful completion of the task, you will receive an additional five hundred dollars.'"

"Where were you instructed to deliver the deed once you obtained it?" Mathieu asked.

"To a P.O. box written on the note," Briggs said as he took a puff off his cigar.

"What happened after you got a copy of the deed in Bakersfield and sent it to the P.O. box?"

"Someone delivered my five hundred dollars in an envelope the next evening."

"Do you know who delivered it?"

"No," Briggs said, shaking his head. "They dropped it in the overnight mail slot in the front door."

"Do you remember the P.O. box number?"

"No, I thought it best to destroy the note," Briggs said. "Why are you so interested in the deed, Detective?"

"Because it's related to the Lester Jensen and Reginald Stonebridge murders I'm in charge of."

"Ah, I see," Briggs said with a hefty sigh as he rocked back in his chair and stared at Mathieu. "Let me level with you, Detective. I admit that I peck around the margins of the law, sometimes crossing over for petty stuff, but regardless of what you may have heard about me, murder is way beyond my remit."

"For your sake, Counselor, I hope you're telling the truth."

"What do you mean?" Briggs asked, narrowing his eyes in concern.

"Two people involved in the case have already been killed to silence them. I don't want you to be the third."

Briggs tensed for a moment, then replied, "I've had no direct contact with the person that hired me to get the deed, Detective. I couldn't pick them out of a lineup if I were threatened at gunpoint."

Ignoring the protestation, Mathieu handed Briggs a photo of Harry Doyle from the police archives. "Have you ever seen this man?"

Briggs took his time looking at the photo. Mathieu watched him closely for any telltale sign of recognition. Briggs handed it back, shaking his head. "No. Who is he?"

Mathieu didn't answer. Instead, he handed Briggs Freddy Fowler's mugshot. "What about this man?"

Briggs scratched the back of his head as he studied the photo, then looking up, asked, "Isn't this the guy who got killed by a horse at Santa Anita? I saw his photo in the *Times*."

"Yes, that's the same man," Mathieu said. "You've never seen him before?"

Briggs pursed his lips and said, "No, aside from his photo in the *Times*. I've never seen the man."

39

The Ghost

Mathieu decided to pay another visit to the widows to see if either of them had a connection to 'the ghost'—Travis Hays. But this time, he brought the photos Freddy Fowler had taken at the Chateau Marmont.

Mathieu arrived unannounced at Jacqueline Jensen's Los Feliz mansion. He was greeted again by her ghoulish butler. But for once, Jacqueline wasn't by the pool.

The butler led Mathieu up the red Spanish tiled staircase with its finely decorated wrought iron balustrade to the second floor. Mathieu was again taken by the exquisite details in the home, like a terracotta vase in a wall alcove and the kiva-style fireplace in the living room that he could see from the stairs.

Arriving on the landing, they walked toward the southwest corner of the house. Then, entered the master bedroom, a light-filled room with dark hardwood plank floors, exposed ceiling beams, and a large low-slung bed with beige bedding.

The butler motioned toward the outdoor deck, then left. Jacqueline sat in a rattan chair wearing a white blouse and shorts that showed off her taut, tanned legs, her bare feet propped on the railing.

She gave a come-hither glance at Mathieu as he sat down next to her. "You visit so often I should give you a key, Detective," she said in a playful tone.

"You have a nice view here, Mrs. Jensen," Mathieu said as he looked southeast toward downtown LA.

"Thank you. There's an even better view from the bed," Jacqueline said with a glint in her eye. "To what do I owe the pleasure of your visit, Detective?"

"I have a few more questions for you, Mrs. Jensen."

"Like what?" she asked in a wary tone.

"Do you have any friends or family in Texas?"

"No," she said. "I'm sure you've done your research on me, Detective. As you know, I grew up in Reno, Nevada."

"Do you know a Travis Hays?"

"No," Jacqueline said, shaking her head. "I've never heard of him."

"Did your husband ever mention him to you?"

"No, why are you asking about him? Who is he?"

"If he's still alive, he'll inherit a ranch your husband thought had oil on it."

"And you think that's why Lester and Reggie were murdered?"

"Possibly," Mathieu said.

Jacqueline looked away and shivered. She was silent for a moment, seemingly lost in thought, then said, "That would be ironic with all of Lester's schemes."

Mathieu nodded. "Yes, it would be."

Mathieu had been watching Jacqueline all this time. She seemed genuinely shocked. He changed the subject and asked, "Do you mind looking at a few photos Freddy Fowler took of you and Edgar at the Chateau Marmont?"

"No, if you think it will help."

Mathieu handed her the tame photos first. Jacqueline audibly gasped as she studied them. "When Edgar told me about the photos, I initially thought it was exciting. But looking at them gives me the creeps. Knowing that someone was spying on us, even in the hotel corridors. Is this all of them?"

"No, this last one is a little more explicit," he said, handing her the photo of the naked woman emerging from the pool at night at the Chateau Marmont.

Jacqueline studied the photo carefully, then let out a huge sigh of relief and said, "That's not my ass, Detective."

"You're sure?" Mathieu asked, surprised.

"Of course, I'm sure," Jacqueline said. "It's a nice ass, but it's not mine."

A half-hour later, Mathieu pulled up in front of Veronica Stonebridge's home on Hillside Drive in the Hollywood Hills. The maid once again escorted him upstairs to the music room on the second floor.

Mrs. Stonebridge sat at the piano wearing tan slacks and a white blouse, her long, loose brown hair reflecting the highlights of the afternoon sun streaming through the open window. She was playing a tune Mathieu recognized immediately, Hoagie Carmichael's haunting "Stardust Melody."

Sensing Mathieu's presence, Mrs. Stonebridge stopped playing and turned to him, "What is it, Detective? Have you found my husband's killer?"

"No, not yet, Mrs. Stonebridge," Mathieu said as he entered the room and sat across from her near the window. "But I have a few more questions for you."

"All right, "she said with a reluctant expression. "But I don't see how I can help. I've told you all I know."

"Does the name Travis Hays mean anything to you?"

"No," she said, looking confused.

"Your husband never mentioned his name to you?"

"No, not that I recall. Who is he?"

"His name is on the deed to a ranch along with your husband's and Lester Jensen's. Jensen thought there might be a huge oil deposit on it and was shopping it around."

"Do you think this Travis Hays killed my husband and Jensen to gain control of it?"

Mathieu shrugged. "I'm not sure, but it's possible."

Mrs. Stonebridge shook her head in dismay. "I know oil men can be vicious, but I never imagined any of them would kill to obtain oil rights."

"I could be wrong, Mrs. Stonebridge, but I have to check out all the possibilities."

"I understand, Detective."

"What about Arnold and Arlo Hays? Did your husband ever mention them?"

"No, are they related to Travis Hays?"

"They could be. They might have been the victims in the Texas oil field fire your husband was involved with."

Mrs. Stonebridge was silent for a moment, seemingly pondering the obvious implication. "Do you think this Travis Hays was getting revenge?"

Mathieu shrugged. "I'll know more when I'm sure who the victims were."

"But that was ages ago, and Reggie told me it wasn't his fault," Mrs. Stonebridge said, looking visibly upset. "Is there anything else?"

Mathieu hesitated for a moment, reluctant to show her the photo of the nude bather at the Chateau. "Just one more thing. I wonder if you could look at this photo," he said, handing it to her. "Does the setting look familiar to you?"

Mrs. Stonebridge studied it for a moment, then turned to Mathieu with a questioning look and asked, "Are you asking if this is me, Detective?"

"Yes, mam," Mathieu replied with an embarrassed expression.

Mrs. Stonebridge smiled. "It's nice of you to think it might be, Detective, but this woman's pert bottom is a little firmer than mine. Besides, I'd never wear that hat."

It was Mathieu's turn to look confused. "What hat?"

"That small hat on the chaise lounge behind the woman," she said, returning the photo to him.

Mathieu looked closely at the photo and spotted a small woman's hat lying beside the discarded clothes. "Thank you for pointing it out. I didn't notice it before," he said, sounding disappointed in himself.

Mrs. Stonebridge looked at Mathieu with almost maternal affection and said, "It's understandable, Detective. That's the difference between men and women. Men look at a woman's body while women look at their clothes."

40

The Hat

When Mathieu returned to headquarters, it was late. The office was empty, except for Enya, who was on the phone. He grabbed a magnifying glass, laid the photo of the nude bather on his desk, and peered through the lens. The out-of-focus hat lay in the shadows. Magnifying it didn't help define its shape; it just made it fuzzier.

Stymied, Mathieu pulled a flashlight from his drawer, turned off the desk lamp, and raked the flashlight beam across the photo, putting the hat in the hotspot. Then he laid a piece of tracing paper on top of it and began to outline the hat's shape, stopping several times to lift the paper and squint at the photo beneath.

As he worked, a shape began to emerge. After tracing the last contour line, he turned off the flashlight, turned on the desk lamp, and started filling in the outline with dark, heavy strokes.

The drawing he was left with looked like a small helmet. The shape looked familiar to him. He'd seen a woman's hat like that before. But where? Maybe at the Chateau Marmont, or the Santa Anita Racetrack, or perhaps at the Garden of Allah the first time he'd seen Lillian Hennessy.

The image of the small hat was like a word you can't remember, hanging tantalizingly just below the surface. The harder you try to grab it, the more it eludes you.

Mathieu pushed the drawing away, ran his palms across his face, and closed his eyes. He stayed that way for several minutes, rubbing his temples, trying to remember. And then it came to him, where he'd first seen the hat and who was wearing it.

Just then, Enya came to his desk, sat down beside him, and said, "It was difficult to find any information about the victims of the oil field fire in Desdemona, Texas, in 1918 because after the oil played out, Desdemona turned into a semi-ghost town.

"But I tracked down the woman who was the postmistress then, and she remembered the victims' names. I just got off the phone with her."

Mathieu sat up straight and asked, "Who were they?"

"Two people died, Arnold and Arlo Hays," Enya said. "Arnold was Arlo's father, and Arlo was his oldest son."

"Those are the same two names on the mass card I found in Harry Doyle's apartment," Mathieu said.

"By the way," Enya added. "I finally got a hold of Hank Laramie when he was sober. He confirmed that his friend who died in the fire was Arnold Hays."

Mathieu nodded. "Was anyone else injured?"

"Yes, Arnold's youngest son Travis. His face was badly burned. He disappeared soon after the fire. No one has heard from him in years. The mother, Ethel Hays, had died earlier that year from the Spanish Flu, leaving their fifteen-year-old daughter without a family.

"An uncle took the girl in, raised her until she was twenty, and then sent her to college in New York. The daughter's name was …"

"Florence," Mathieu said, stopping Enya before she could finish.

"How did you know?" Enya asked with a surprised expression.

"A hat," Mathieu said simply.

"A hat?" she asked in confusion.

"Yes, the one in this photo," Mathieu said, sliding it to Enya.

Enya picked it up and asked, "What hat? I don't see a hat. She's naked."

"The one on the chaise lounge next to the clothes."

Enya brought the photo close to her face and squinted. "I can barely see it. It's just a smudge."

"Yeah, I missed it, too," Mathieu said with chagrin, "until Mrs. Stonebridge pointed it out to me."

"But how does this hat help?"

"The day I interviewed Florence Drake, Jensen's office manager, she wore a hat like this. I think Florence Drake is Florence Hays."

"So, the naked woman in this photo is Florence Drake?" Enya asked.

"Yes, I think so," Mathieu said, nodding. "I suspect Florence had Jensen and Stonebridge killed because she believed they were responsible for maiming her younger brother Travis and killing her father and older brother. But perhaps for another reason also.

"Travis is on the deed for the El Saucito Ranch. Maybe Jensen and Stonebridge tried to have him declared dead because no one had seen him in years so that they could cut him out of any potential oil profits. And Florence found out about it. And if Edgar Mahoney agreed to go along with their scheme, he could be next on Florence's hit list."

"And you believe Jensen and Stonebridge were unaware Florence was related to the victims?"

"Yes," Mathieu said. "She was just a kid when it happened. They probably didn't even know she existed. By the time she applied for the job with Jensen, she was a grown woman and had changed her last name.

"There's no way Jensen could have known if she didn't tell him, which is unlikely. I suspect she seduced both Jensen and Mahoney so she could keep track of what they were up to."

"Where was this photo taken?" Enya asked.

"At the Chateau Marmont, where Mahoney lives."

"So, those are Mahoney's feet in the photo?"

"Probably," Mathieu said, nodding.

"Do you think Florence got the job with Jensen to seek revenge?"

"Most likely," Mathieu said. "It's doubtful it was a coincidence."

"My God!" Enya said in dismay. "What a tragic story."

"Yes, it is," Mathieu said with a somber expression. "Nevertheless, we have to bring Florence in and find out if I'm correct. Do you know where Travis went after he left Desdemona?"

"Like I said, no one has seen or heard from Travis in years. But just recently, someone from the town spotted him in Las Vegas."

"Where's Las Vegas?" Mathieu asked. "Is it in Texas?"

"No," Enya said, shaking her head. "It's a tiny town in the middle of the desert in Nevada. Apparently, the only reason it exists is because it's a water stop on the Los Angeles and Salt Lake Railroad where they take on water for the steam engines."

"How recently was Travis spotted in Las Vegas?"

"According to the former postmistress, he was seen there two weeks ago by her nephew."

Mathieu nodded. "Then we need to contact the sheriff in Las Vegas and see if he can locate Travis Hays."

"I can handle that," Enya said. "I'll let you know as soon as I get in touch with him."

"Thank you," Mathieu said.

When Enya left, Mathieu called Gus and asked him to send squad cars to Florence Drake's office and home and bring her in for questioning. He told Gus to tell his officers to be careful; he was pretty sure Florence was armed.

After he hung up, Mathieu got up and paced around the empty office, stopping to peer out the window at the streetlights below on Temple Street.

He thought about Florence Drake's demeanor the first time he'd met her. He remembered she seemed competent but cold. And he recalled what she said when he asked her if Lester Jensen had any enemies:

"I'm sure they counted in the thousands, but I doubt any of them had the courage or conviction to kill him. You have to be strong-willed to do something like that, and most of Lester's detractors are weaklings. Lester detested weaklings ... and so do I."

Mathieu had no doubt Florence was strong-willed and wasn't a weakling. But was she a killer? While he pondered that, the phone rang. He went back to his desk, picked up the handset, and said, "Detective Mathieu, LAPD Homicide."

"Detective, this is Martin Stroud," came the nervous voice over the line. "I'm the manager of the Chateau Marmont. Do you remember me?"

"Of course, Mr. Stroud," Mathieu said as he sat down. "You sound concerned. What's wrong?"

"Something strange occurred here at the hotel about an hour ago," Stroud said, letting out a sigh. "I might be making something out of nothing, but you did tell me to call if I learned anything."

"No need to apologize, Mr. Stroud. I'm glad you called. What happened?"

There was silence over the line, then Stroud said, "Around 8 p.m. I got a call from the garage attendant. He said he saw Edgar Mahoney and a young woman exit the elevator, walk to Mahoney's Cadillac, get in, and drive off.

"The attendant said Mahoney looked scared. 'White as a sheet' is how he described him to me. He told me the woman had a coat draped over her right arm. And he thought she had a gun underneath."

"Did he describe the woman to you?"

"Yes," Stroud said. "He said she was attractive in her early thirties, with dark hair, a slender build, and was wearing business clothes. Oh, and he said she had a very distinctive hat on."

"What kind of hat?"

"He said it looked almost like a 'brown felt helmet' were the words he used."

Mathieu stood and grabbed his coat. With urgency in his voice, he said, "I'll be there as soon as I can, Mr. Stroud. Please don't enter Mahoney's penthouse. You did the right thing to call. Thank you."

Mathieu toggled the cradle prong with his index finger, released it, and dialed Gus's number. When he answered, Mathieu brought him up to date, and they agreed to meet downstairs in five minutes.

On his way out of the office, Mathieu stopped by Enya's desk and said, "Sergeant Lombardi and I are going to the Chateau Marmont. It looks like Florence Drake kidnapped Edgar Mahoney. Call me there if you get ahold of the sheriff in Las Vegas."

"Okay," Enya said with concern, "but be careful. If you're right about Florence Drake, she won't hesitate to kill you, either."

41

Kidnapped?

When Mathieu and Sergeant Lombardi arrived at the Chateau Marmont a half-hour later, the manager was anxiously pacing up and down the cloister outside, waiting for them. Stroud escorted them inside to the elevator tower. They took the cramped elevator to the seventh floor, got off, and walked down the carpeted corridor to room 64—the penthouse.

Stroud reached for the doorknob to insert the key, but it was unlocked and turned easily in his hand. Mathieu gently pushed him aside and said, "Please stay here for a moment until we check the rooms."

Mathieu and Gus drew their revolvers as they entered. Mathieu shouted, "Police! Is anybody here?"

They paused in the marble entranceway for a second to listen for any sounds. Then Mathieu motioned for Gus to check the bedrooms on the left while he walked down the dark parquet floor toward the salon.

The salon was empty, as was the dining room to the left and the kitchen beyond it. Mathieu stepped out onto the deck and walked the periphery, but no one was there.

As Mathieu returned from the deck, Gus came down the hallway and said, "All clear in the bedrooms and bathrooms."

"Same here," Mathieu said as he holstered his Colt revolver. "Any signs of a struggle?"

"No," Gus said, shaking his head.

Mathieu looked around the living room and noticed a vintage mahogany desk with gold inlays to the right of the grand piano. The desk lamp was on. A single typewritten page sat on its surface, spotlighted in the lamp's glow.

He walked over to the desk, picked up the page, and began to read. Midway through, without lifting his eyes, Mathieu asked, "Gus, did you see a typewriter anywhere in the apartment?"

"No, why?"

"Could you get Mr. Stroud, please? I have a question for him."

"Sure," Gus said as he turned toward the door while Mathieu continued to read.

A moment later, Stroud entered the living room and asked, "What did you want to ask, Detective?"

Mathieu looked at him and asked, "Does the hotel have typewriters the guests can borrow?"

"No," Stroud said, shaking his head. "But we have several typists in the area who are on call to provide typing services to our guests on request."

"Did Mr. Mahoney request a typist recently?"

"I can check," Stroud said. "But I don't think so. Why?"

"Because this is a signed confession from Mahoney admitting that he hired Harry Doyle and Fred Fowler to kidnap and kill Lester Jensen and Reginald Stonebridge so he could obtain sole ownership to an undeveloped oil field they had the deed to. He admits to subsequently shooting Doyle to keep him quiet. Mahoney claims he was obsessed by greed but is now remorseful and intends to kill himself."

"Can I see the signature?" Stroud asked.

"Sure," Mathieu said, handing him the page.

Stroud squinted as he studied the signature. Mathieu watched as his eyes went back and forth over it. Finally, Stroud looked up and said, "Mr. Mahoney has lived here for over a year. I've seen his handwriting on notes, bank checks, and receipts countless times. His signature is rather flamboyant. This one looks cramped to me. I don't recognize it as his."

"What's your feeling, Gus?" Mathieu asked.

"A signed confession is a little too convenient, don't you think?"

Mathieu nodded. "Yeah, I agree. I'm not buying it, either. Mahoney isn't the type to confess to anything except at gunpoint. The question is, if Florence kidnapped him, where did she take him, and what does she intend to do with him?"

Just then, the phone rang, startling them. Stroud instinctively reached for it, but Mathieu stopped him. "Please don't touch the phone, Mr. Stroud. I'll get it."

Mathieu took out his handkerchief, picked up the receiver, and said, "Hello," then nodded as he listened.

A few seconds later, he turned to Gus and said, "It's Enya. The squad cars didn't have any luck at Florence Drake's home or office."

Then, speaking into the receiver, Mathieu said, "Enya, ask one of the cars to go up to Jensen's bungalow on the top of Lookout Mountain to see if there are any signs of life up there. Then have them radio back. But tell them not to approach the bungalow until they hear from us.

"After that, call Fred Wilson and have his team come to the hotel to dust for prints. Call me as soon as you hear back from the officers at Lookout Mountain."

Mathieu cradled the receiver, then looked at Stroud and asked, "Can you go down to the lobby and escort the forensic team up here when they arrive?"

"Certainly, Detective," Stroud said as he pivoted and hurried toward the door.

After Stroud left, Mathieu said, "Let's search the place again, Gus, and see if we can find any trace of Florence or any hint where she might have taken Mahoney."

"Okay," Gus said. "I'll take the bathroom and bedrooms."

"Thanks, I'll check out here."

When Gus left, Mathieu headed to the kitchen first. The place looked spotless, which didn't surprise him. He couldn't imagine Mahoney doing his own cooking despite the well-appointed kitchen. The same was true of the dining room. The polished table was empty except for two place settings on the surface.

Mathieu returned to the living room. He turned over the cushions on the couch and armchairs and searched underneath them. Not finding anything, he knelt down and scanned the floor, looking under the piano, desk, and the rest of the furniture. Then he stood, brushed off his pants, and walked over to the desk, where he sat down.

He opened the lone drawer and took out the contents. There was a stack of envelopes and stationery with the Chateau Marmont's logo, a black fountain pen, two pencils, a pencil sharpener, and a gum eraser. He shuffled through the pages; most were blank, but a few had random notes scratched in pencil.

Towards the bottom of the stack, Mathieu found a page that intrigued him. It looked like a hand-drawn map. He put the rest of the pages aside and studied it.

In the lower right-hand corner of the page, a diagonal line labeled Highway 33 started at a circle marked Taft. The line went northwest until it hit another line labeled Highway 58, which continued on the same heading.

At its apex, the line marked Highway 58 dropped sharply to the left in a southwest direction until it hit 7 Mile Road, which connected to Soda Lake Road on the west side of the lake. An unnamed spur road branched off of it, heading due south and ending at a square marked "El Saucito Ranch."

Mathieu thought the ranch would be a perfect place for Florence to get her revenge.

He wondered why the route went northwest, then circled back southwest instead of going due west from Taft.

But then he saw that Mahoney had drawn several large triangle shapes that signified mountains, which he annotated as the Temblor Range and a large heavy gash west of them that he marked as the San Andreas Fault, making the direct route rougher going.

As Mathieu studied the map, Gus came into the room and said, "I found a woman's gold bracelet on the floor beside the bed and a steel safe in the closet that's been emptied."

"Let me see the bracelet," Mathieu said, extending his hand.

He took a moment to examine it. It was a simple gold bracelet with a pendant that looked like an oil derrick. "This belongs to Florence. I saw her wearing it the first time I interviewed her."

"It looks like the catch is broken," Gus said. "Maybe Mahoney grabbed her, she pulled away, and it ripped off."

"That sounds likely," Mathieu said with a nod, then added, "I think I know where Florence is taking Mahoney."

"Where?" Gus asked.

"If she didn't take him to Jensen's bungalow on Lookout Mountain, I think she's going to take him to the El Saucito Ranch," Mathieu said, sliding the map to Gus.

They studied the map together, trying to determine how long it would take to get there and what route to take.

A few minutes later, the phone rang. It was Enya again. She told Mathieu that Jensen's bungalow on Lookout Mountain was deserted. She also told him that she'd tracked down Sheriff Wilkes in Las Vegas, and he had Travis Hays in his station.

Enya gave Mathieu the sheriff's number. Mathieu thanked her, hung up, then called the hotel operator, gave her the number, and asked her to make a long-distance call to Las Vegas, Nevada. As they waited for the operator to call back, Mathieu explained what happened to Gus.

A few minutes later, the phone rang. "I have your party on the line, Detective," the operator said as she transferred the call.

"Sheriff Wilkes, this is Detective Mathieu from the LAPD. I appreciate your help on this matter. I understand you were able to locate Travis Hays."

"Yes, he's here in the station with me. I found him in a brothel over on Ogden Street, as I expected."

"Is he sober?"

"Yes, Detective."

"Could you put him on the line, please?"

"Sure," Sheriff Wilkes said. "Here he is."

"This is ... Travis Hays," came the halting voice over the line.

"Travis, this is Detective Mathieu from the Los Angeles Police Department. Things are happening pretty fast here. I need your assistance in preventing a murder and helping your sister Florence."

"Florence is in Los Angeles?" Travis asked with surprise in his voice.

"Yes, she is."

"Is she in trouble?"

Mathieu hesitated, then said, "Yes ... I suspect she had two men killed to avenge the deaths of your father and older brother in the oil field fire in 1918."

"Who were they?"

"Lester Jensen and Reginald Stonebridge, although you probably knew the latter as Roger Stone."

"Oh, my god!" Travis said with anguish in his voice. "I had no idea Flo would do something like that. How can I help?"

"I'll tell you that in a moment," Mathieu began. "First tell me what happened the day of the oil field fire."

42

Dawn on the Plains

It was dawn when Mathieu and Sergeant Lombardi crested a slight rise to the north and spotted the farmhouse and outbuildings of the El Saucito Ranch in the distance. Mathieu immediately doused the headlights, killed the engine, and coasted down the dirt track to a tool shed just before the road curved southwest toward the house.

To the east, the sun was beginning to rise above the rounded peaks of the Temblor Range, casting long shadows behind the ranch house and its outbuildings.

The white two-story, clapboard farmhouse with a covered porch sat in a cluster of oaks on the west side of the property. Its long side was oriented on an east-west compass point, with the front facing east. The house had windows on all four sides, making approaching it undetected tricky.

Mathieu parked the Buick Phaeton behind the shed, out of sight of the farmhouse. He and Gus got out, grabbed their rifles from the back seat, then shook the kinks out of their legs from the long drive.

In a low voice, Mathieu said, "No heroics, Gus. But let's see if we can take her alive for her brother's sake."

"Got it," Gus said in agreement.

With Mathieu in the lead and the outbuildings and trees providing cover, they approached the farmhouse from the northeast. When they were twenty yards away, Mathieu motioned to Gus to set up behind a thick-trunked oak that provided good sightlines of the farmhouse.

Then Mathieu crept forward until he reached the back of the house. He crouched down against the wall and paused. There was a small window to his left and what looked like a kitchen door beyond it. Fortunately, the porch didn't wrap around in the back.

He listened for human sounds but heard only the sounds of the plains: the rustling of tall grass in the wind, the cacophonous chirping of grasshoppers, and the early morning calls of the sparrows who fed on them.

He spotted a prairie falcon soaring above the hills in the distance and a black crow perched in a nearby oak staring at him. He wondered if it would be the last crow he ever saw, then quickly shook the thought off. That kind of thinking could get you killed.

The tragic story Travis told Mathieu over the phone still haunted him. He'd replayed the images in his mind during the long night's drive. He wondered if the principals in this saga were villains or merely venal, victims of their own carelessness, drunkenness, greed, and revenge.

It was a tragedy that had multiplied like compound interest. And if Mathieu and Gus couldn't stop the cycle today, there would be even more hardship.

Mathieu assumed Florence had set up on high ground on the second floor. That's what he would have done. Or perhaps she'd gotten careless and thought no one would follow her here and was on the first floor.

Either way, he couldn't stay where he was. He had to find cover away from the house before she woke up. The longer he stayed here, the more he risked Florence waking up and discovering him if she hadn't already.

Staying low, Mathieu duck-walked under the window until he reached the kitchen door, where he stopped. He listened for any movement inside: footsteps, chairs scraping, water running.

Hearing none, Mathieu flashed past the door, then paused to peek down the covered porch on the south wall. Seeing it empty, he sprinted toward a cluster of dense oaks fifteen yards away to the west, where he dove into the tall grass behind the thickest trunk.

Mathieu put his back against the tree and slid up to full height. He paused to let his breathing calm and looked around.

He saw Mahoney's Cadillac parked to the right. Twenty yards past it was a large pond ringed by willow trees. Next to the pond was a metal windmill powering a sucker road that brought water up from an underground aquifer to a water tank.

At the base of the windmill, Edgar Mahoney stood tied to the steel struts, his arms out to the side, like Christ on the cross. Unlike Christ, Mahoney appeared to be alive. But barely. At his feet lay a bundle of three sticks of dynamite.

Mathieu looked toward the second-story windows on the south side of the house, which had the best sightlines to the pond and windmill. Not seeing any movement, he sprinted toward the windmill. He had gone about ten yards when a shot rang out, kicking up the dirt behind him. He dove for cover behind the nearest oak, then stood and looked toward the house.

Florence Drake was standing inside the now-open second-story window with a Winchester 45-70 lever action rifle at the ready—a rifle much more powerful than the ones he and Gus had.

"That was a warning shot, Detective," Florence called out. "I know how to shoot. I won't miss the next time if you try to free Mahoney."

Mathieu moved away from the oak with his rifle pointing down so Florence could see him easily. "I expected you to be here, Miss Drake."

"Why?"

"A hat," Mathieu said, standing in the open with his arms loose by his side.

"What are you talking about … what hat?"

"The brown one you wore when I first met you at your office."

"I don't understand," Florence said, lowering her rifle. "What does my hat have to do with anything?"

"It seems Freddy Fowler was spying on you at the Chateau Marmont the night you took a midnight swim with Mahoney. He took some photos of you getting out of the pool naked before you had sex with Mahoney. They didn't show your face, but your hat was on the chaise lounge. You remember Fat Freddy, don't you? You recommended him to Mahoney."

"Freddy was helping me keep tabs on Edgar," Florence said. "I seduced Mahoney to spy on him. He admitted to me that he killed Lester and Reggie one night when we were in bed. That's why I brought him here to get what he deserves. Mahoney left a signed confession at the Chateau. It was on the desk in his penthouse. Didn't you find it?"

"We found it, Miss Drake," Mathieu said. "But that confession is as phony as your New York accent. Or should I call you Miss Hays? That's your real name, isn't it, Flo."

Mathieu could see Florence shudder at the mention of her name.

"I don't know what you're talking about. My name is Florence Drake. I'm from New York, where I attended and graduated from Barnard College."

"I'm sure you did, Miss Hays, but you were born in a little town in central Texas called Desdemona, where your father, Arnold, your older brother, Arlo, and your youngest brother, Travis, all worked in the oil fields."

"That's an interesting story, Detective, but I've never heard of those people."

"You're lying, Miss Hays," Mathieu said as he moved closer to the house. "I talked to your brother Travis last night on the telephone. He certainly remembers you. He'll be arriving in Los Angeles this evening by train from Las Vegas, Nevada. I'm sure he'll be able to identify you."

"You're bluffing," Florence said in a conflicted voice.

"No, I'm not," Mathieu said, shaking his head. "Travis told me what happened the night of the oil field fire that killed your father and your brother Arlo and maimed Travis."

"You're making all this up!" Florence screamed as she fired another shot at Mathieu's feet.

Mathieu flinched but stood his ground. "I wish I were, Florence … because it was a horrible, senseless accident, but your brother Travis shares some of the blame."

"I don't believe you," Florence said, giving up any pretense of maintaining her story. "Lester and Reggie bullied him into thinking that."

"That's true. But that's only part of the story, according to what Travis told me."

"Prove to me you talked to him!" Florence said in a defiant voice.

"Travis told me that at twelve, you could outshoot everyone in the family, including your father and brothers. And that your favorite pet when you were a little girl was a goat named 'Sam Houston.'"

Florence stared at Mathieu in shock. "You *really* did talk to Travis, didn't you?"

"Yes," Mathieu said, nodding his head.

"No one has seen Travis in years," Florence said almost to herself.

"I know," Mathieu said. "We tracked down the former postmistress in Desdemona. She told us her nephew had seen Travis in Las Vegas recently."

"Travis never told me what happened that night," Florence said. "All I heard were rumors that it was Lester and Reggie's fault, but they tried to blame Travis because he was new to the job and inexperienced. What did Travis tell you?"

"Are you sure you want to hear it? It's a disturbing story."

Florence hesitated, then said, "Yes ... I'm sure."

In a somber tone, Mathieu began the story.

"Travis told me that Lester, Reggie, and himself had night watch the evening of the fire. Lester was the crew chief. Their job was to keep watch over the field and sound the alarm if there was any trouble. They set up in a little guard shack on top of a ridge on the east side of the field.

"From their vantage point, they had the best sightlines across the dense forest of wood oil derricks in the field. It was windy that night; the winds blew east to west, and a dry thunderstorm was predicted. The rest of the crew, including your father and your brother Arlo, were asleep downwind in the bunkhouse on the west side of the field.

"Lester had brought some whiskey, and they'd all been drinking. At one point, to pass the time, they decided to have a shooting contest. They all had rifles with them to scare off the coyotes. Next to the shack was a small garbage dump of discarded tin cans previous crews had tossed away.

"Lester picked up three cans and carried them to a wooden fence in front of them. He was so drunk he had trouble holding the cans steady enough to put them on the rail.

"Below them, at eye level, about twenty yards away, were power poles with transformers holding the power lines that ran north to south across the eastern edge of the field to drive the generators.

"They stood three abreast about fifteen yards from the fence, and Lester shouted, 'One, two, three ... fire!' And they all fired at once, and they all missed.

"They started laughing just as one of the bullets hit a transformer on the nearest power pole and exploded in flames. The dry winds blew the fire downslope, and when it hit the first wood derrick, it went up in flames, starting a chain reaction that quickly spread across the field heading west.

"The sight of the conflagration sobered them up quick. Travis sounded the alarm bell, then they all charged down the hill toward the bunkhouse on the western edge of the field. But they couldn't outrun the flames; the winds whipped through the field at over thirty miles an hour. By the time they reached the bunkhouse, it was totally engulfed in flames.

"Most of the men had escaped and were milling around outside. But Travis didn't see his father or brother, so he ran inside the burning building. Rafters were falling all around him, and there was so much smoke he couldn't see a foot in front of his face.

"Part of the roof fell on him, and his clothes and hat caught fire. Travis stumbled around in the dark, disoriented, then, seeing an opening, ran for the door and rolled on the ground outside to smother the flames. But it was too late; his face had been badly burned. Your father and older brother were the only two that died.

"Even though none of them knew for sure which of their bullets hit the transformer, Lester and Reggie convinced Travis it was his fault.

"After talking to Travis on the phone, I think Lester and Reggie bullied him into believing that by cynically playing on his guilt over the deaths of his father and brother. But I suspect you already know that, Florence, and that's why you had Lester and Reggie killed.

"In the official report, Lester claimed lightning had struck the power pole, causing the fire. Reggie and Travis backed up his story. Lester went back to Colorado, and Reggie returned to Canada soon after. Your brother, wracked with guilt, left a few weeks later.

"Travis wandered around West Texas for a few years before he crossed into Nevada and ended up in a hole-in-the-wall town in the desert called Las Vegas. Lester has been sending Travis money all these years to make sure he kept quiet. Both Lester and Reggie knew Travis was still alive."

After finishing the story, Mathieu watched Florence. She looked lost and conflicted, unsure what to do with her rage. She stepped back into the shadows, and he lost sight of her.

Mathieu saw Gus approach the farmhouse from the north and set up behind a tree ten yards from the covered porch. Gus raised his rifle to signal if he should fire. Mathieu shook his head no and pushed his palms toward the ground to signal Gus to hold off, which he did. But Gus remained vigilant and ready to fire from his covered position.

Mathieu stayed where he was. A few minutes later, Florence reappeared at the window with her rifle ready to fire and shouted, "I don't care what happened that night! Mahoney deserves to die anyway!

"He was in on the scheme with Lester and Reggie to have Travis's name taken off the deed so they wouldn't have to share the profits with him. Mahoney had a Beverly Hills lawyer all set to file a motion to declare Travis legally dead."

"Please, don't do this, Florence," Mathieu pleaded. "We have you surrounded. You'll never live to see your brother."

"You're lying," Florence shouted back. "There's no one with you."

"I'm telling you the truth," Mathieu pleaded. "My sergeant is with me."

"I don't believe you," Florence said.

Mathieu turned to Gus and yelled, "Gus, fire a warning shot through the north window!"

When Gus fired his first shot, Florence ducked out of sight. Mathieu dropped his rifle and sprinted toward the windmill as fast as he could. As he got closer, he could hear the exchange of rifle fire in the background.

Reaching the windmill, Mathieu grabbed a folding knife from his coat pocket and slashed violently at the ropes that bound

Mahoney to the frame; then, he yanked Mahoney's arm as they ran toward the pond.

They dove into the water just as a bullet from Florence's rifle ignited the dynamite, rocking the air behind them. The windmill creaked and groaned as the supports gave way and buckled. Then, in seeming slow motion, the windmill toppled over, its propeller blades spinning wildly as it fell across the pond with a thundering crash.

Gus heard the explosion and saw the windmill crash into the pond. He stepped away from the tree and took aim at Florence, who was staring open-mouthed at the sight. He fired, and the bullet smashed into her left shoulder, causing her to spin around and drop the rifle out of the window. It slid down the porch roof and fell to the ground.

Gus ran toward the farmhouse, tossed Florence's rifle into the brush, then entered through the French doors. Once inside, he went up the stairs with his rifle at the ready.

Florence was lying on the floor, writhing in pain from the gunshot wound. He handcuffed her, tied a sheet around her shoulder to stop the bleeding, then hurried down the steps and ran outside toward the pond.

As Gus got closer, his heart sank; he couldn't see Mathieu or Mahoney anywhere.

43

Florence's Story

When Gus reached the pond, he frantically scanned the shoreline, looking for Mathieu. Not seeing him, he peered into the water through the tangled wreckage. But the crash had kicked up tons of silt, and he couldn't see anything.

The demolished windmill blocked the south side of the pond, so Gus searched along the northern edge, glancing into the water and high reeds, but saw no signs of either of them.

As he approached the western shore, Gus looked to his left and spotted Mathieu and Mahoney lying motionless on their backs in the deep willows.

He ran to Mathieu and shook him. "Are you all right, Theo? You scared the hell out of me."

Mathieu squinted into the bright sun as he nodded at Gus. "Yeah, just knocked the wind out of me. I needed a moment to recover."

"What about him?" Gus asked, pointing to Mahoney, lying next to him.

"Yeah, he's all right," Mathieu said. "He just passed out from fear and exhaustion. I can't say I blame him. Did you apprehend Florence?"

"Yes."

"Is she alive?"

"Yeah."

"Good work," Mathieu sighed as he started to get up. "Let's get Mahoney and Florence back to the cars and go back to LA. I've had enough of country life for one day."

On their way back to LA, they stopped in Taft to have Florence's wound tended to, then continued on. Mathieu thought Gus deserved a luxurious ride home, so he had him drive Mahoney back in his Cadillac.

Mathieu drove a handcuffed Florence in the Buick Phaeton. They rode in silence up the steep, twisting grade of the Grapevine until they reached the crest of the Tejon Pass just north of Gorman at over 4,000 feet. The air was crisp and fresh here. They could see for miles as they looked south toward the rugged, sensuous folds of the Liebre Mountains.

It was here, without prompting, that Florence began her story. By the time they'd traveled the snaking thirty-six miles of the Ridge Route and descended into Castaic, Mathieu understood, without condoning, what had motivated her.

"I was fifteen at the time of the fire," Florence began, "and suddenly without a family. My Uncle Walt took me in and cared for me with a gentleness you don't usually expect from men. When I turned twenty, he felt I was mature enough to live on my own, so he sent me to New York to go to school, where I enrolled at Barnard College.

"The oil had played out in Desdemona by then, and it was turning into a ghost town. But my uncle had made a lot of money in oil stocks. He thought I needed a fresh start, away from all the sad memories, so he financed my trip, paid for college, and set up a modest trust fund for me.

"I was an ambitious, motivated student and did well in school. I dropped my Texas drawl and became a New Yorker. I blocked out most of the memories of what had happened. I became so enamored with my new life that I legally changed my last name to Drake.

"I graduated Summa cum Laude with a bachelor's in economics and then began working on my master's. One day during my final year, I went into the library to study. I stopped by the desk to peruse the newspapers hanging on the wooden dowels next to the counter. All the major newspapers were displayed there: the *New York Times*, *Washington Post*, *Herald Examiner*, and others.

"On the front page of the *Los Angeles Times* was a huge headline over a quarter-page photo of a man in a gray suit. The headline read, 'Lester Jensen strikes it rich with oil find in the Rincon Oil Field.' When I saw it, I froze.

"All the terrible memories came flooding back. I'd heard rumors after the oil field fire that Jensen and Reginald Stone were responsible for starting it, but it was hard to know if that was true. Suddenly, I felt like a powerless fifteen-year-old girl again, and I hated it. I was in turmoil; my hands were shaking. I took the newspaper over to a table and sat down to read it.

"Here was the man I thought might be responsible for my father and brother's deaths, and he's smiling at the camera with a smug expression, looking happy and successful. The injustice of it enraged me. That's the day I decided to find out the truth. I finished grad school with honors, took the first train west, strode into Jensen's office with confidence, and got the job after the first interview."

"Did you sleep with him?" Mathieu asked without looking at her.

"What do you think?" Florence said in a flat voice. "It was the price of admission."

"Did you know for sure he was guilty?"

"No, I'd only heard the rumors. I wanted to be sure, so I bided my time like a fly on the wall."

"Did Jensen have any idea you were related to the victims?"

"No," Florence said, shaking her head. "Why would he? I'd changed my last name to Drake, and I was only a teenager at the time of the fire.

"Lester and Reggie probably didn't even know I existed. I never met either of them until I moved to Los Angeles as a grown woman. Lester had no idea my real name was Hays.

"He just thought I was as savvy and ruthless in business as he was. People see what they want to see, Detective," Florence said as she gazed out the passenger-side window at the passing landscape.

"Does that apply to you, too, Florence?" Mathieu asked as he glanced over at her and caught her eye. "Did you see what you wanted to see in Jensen?"

"Yes, I guess I did in retrospect," Florence said with a shrug. "But at the time, I felt powerful. It was wonderful. I was in control for the first time in my life. Lester had no idea who I really was. I was pulling the strings. He was my puppet. I knew he'd screw up eventually. I just had to be patient."

"How long did you have to wait?"

"About six months after I started working at Jensen Petroleum, Lester and I were out drinking at Musso and Frank's one evening after work. He leaned close to me in the booth with his sour breath and said, 'Florence, let me give you some advice, sweetheart. No matter what you do in business, even if you cause someone's death, never admit it.'

"I asked him if he ever had caused someone's death, and he responded with a drunken grin, 'What do you think?'"

"That's pretty cold," Mathieu said. "What did you do?"

"I toasted him for his savvy," Florence said with hard eyes. "And we continued drinking, then afterward we went to my place, and I slept with him."

"Did you intend to kill Jensen and Stonebridge from the beginning?"

"No, initially, I just wanted to find out the truth."

Mathieu knew they were at a critical juncture. He wondered if Florence would continue. He'd been watching her out of the corner of his eye as they carved their way up the ridge. Each curve brought a new revelation. It seemed like the mountains had become her confessional; he slowed the car to allow her time to finish.

"What happened that changed that?" Mathieu asked.

"One night at work, I was in the backroom going through some files. It was late; everyone else had gone home. Lester and Reggie were in his office with the door open. They were sitting around bullshitting, smoking cigars, and drinking. I don't think they realized I was still there.

"At one point, I overheard them talking about the oil field fire in Desdemona, so I stopped what I was doing and moved a little closer to Lester's office. They started bragging about getting away with it by blaming it on a lightning strike and then bullying Travis into believing it was his fault.

"They called Travis a sap and belittled him for running into the burning bunkhouse to try to save his father and brother. They said anyone that stupid deserved to be burnt.

"My brother ran into that burning building and was horribly scarred for life while they stood around outside and did nothing. And yet they were the adults; Travis was a kid. He was only eighteen. They were responsible for what happened, not Travis.

"Afterward, they discussed their plan to cut Travis out of the El Saucito deal by having him declared dead because no one had seen him in years, even though they knew he was still alive. Lester even wondered aloud if they could encourage Travis to kill himself.

"That night, I realized what callous bastards they both were. They had no remorse at all for the deaths of my dad and Arlo. So, I began to plot my revenge. I took my time putting the pieces in place, finding Fowler and later Harry Doyle."

Mathieu glanced at Florence and asked, "Before you overheard their conversation, did you know Travis was still alive?"

"No," Florence said. "I hoped he was, but I wasn't sure. I feared he might have committed suicide. I had no idea where he went. He disappeared without a word soon after the tragedy. I've always felt guilty about how I reacted the first time I saw his face after he'd been burnt. I was too shocked to give him the comfort he needed. I've never forgiven myself for that.

"We were close as kids. Travis looked after me when Mom died. We had a special bond. My father didn't know how to raise a teenage girl and Arlo was married by then. I've felt a responsibility to stick up for Travis ever since—dead or alive."

"Did you know everything Travis told me on the phone?"

"No," Florence said, shaking her head. "Not all the details about the drinking and the shooting contest. I didn't realize Travis might have been responsible, too. I just assumed from the way Lester and Reggie talked that they had bullied him into believing he was."

"Why did you have Lester and Reggie killed in such a dramatic way?"

"Simple," Florence said, "to deflect attention away from myself. That was the main reason. Thousands of people hated Lester already because he'd ruined their lives by cheating them out of their life savings with his phony oil stock schemes. So, it was believable that one of them might want to kill him. That's why I had Doyle stuff one of the worthless Jensen Petroleum stock certificates in Lester's mouth.

"The other reason was personal. I wanted their deaths to be as grizzly as my father and brother's to tell the world that whoever killed them hated them so intensely that they must have deserved it."

"When did you first visit Edgar Mahoney?"

"Soon after I learned their scheme to pitch the development of the El Saucito Ranch to him, I wanted to confirm Mahoney intended to invest in it. I lied and told him they were shopping it around to other oil barons, too, but they were keeping me and him in the dark. Mahoney and I agreed to a side deal. I'd spy on Jensen and Stonebridge in return for getting a piece of the action if he won the bid."

"Where did you meet Freddy?"

"At the crap tables at La Bohème. I'd heard a lot of questionable thugs and ex-cops hung out there who would do anything for the right price. Freddy lost big the night I was there. I paid off his debt and told him I could help him out.

"Soon after, I introduced him to Edgar, who helped get him a job at the Chateau. Then, I paid Freddy to spy on Edgar," Florence said, then laughing to herself, added, "It's kind of ironic that Freddy ended up spying on me, and that helped you catch me."

Mathieu shrugged. "We would have got you eventually once I realized the motive was revenge for the oil field fire."

Florence sighed. "Yeah, I know. Everybody I asked about you said you were smart, but I didn't realize just how smart until it was too late."

"Did Freddy hook you up with Doyle to do the actual killings?"

"Yeah," Florence said, nodding her head. "Freddy was too squeamish to kill someone himself."

"How did you convince Freddy and Doyle to murder Jensen and Stonebridge?"

"With money, of course. Plus, I told them the truth that it was revenge for killing my father and brother in the oil field fire. They were both sentimental slobs. I even gave them mass cards to seal the deal."

"I found Doyle's in his room," Mathieu said.

Florence scoffed.

"Why did you kill Doyle?"

"To keep him quiet," Florence said with a shrug. "I was tying up all the loose ends that pointed to me. You'd already spooked Freddy into getting himself killed at the racetrack."

"Why did Freddy and Doyle kill Eddie Hennessy?"

"That had nothing to do with me," Florence said, shaking her head. "That was Freddy's idea. Eddie was blackmailing him about the Jensen killing."

"Why did you kidnap Mahoney?"

"Because he's as guilty and cynical as Lester and Reggie were. He was just fine about having Travis removed from the deed by declaring him dead. And because after you started sniffing around, Mahoney got suspicious that I had something to do with Lester and Reggie's deaths. He threatened to tell you, so I had to act fast."

"What were you going to do after you killed him?" Mathieu asked, glancing at her.

"Disappear somewhere, probably Mexico or Baja," Florence said with a shrug. "I have a lot of money saved up. I could have lived in exile for a long time. Then, after things died down, reemerge with a new identity."

Mathieu didn't have any other questions. Florence had filled in most of the blanks for him. He had plenty to convict her. He was sure they'd eventually find the gun she'd used to kill Doyle, and that would seal it even if she reneged on her confession.

Neither spoke for the next few miles until Florence asked, "Is Travis really coming to LA?"

"Yes."

"Will I get to see him?" Florence asked, staring at him with her large brown eyes.

"Yes," Mathieu said. "As soon as we get back."

"I regret firing at the dynamite," Florence said, sounding contrite. "I didn't want to hurt you, only Mahoney."

"I know," Mathieu said with a nod as he glanced at her. It was hard to imagine that such a delicate creature had been the mastermind behind these heinous crimes. But he remained wary. He remembered what she'd said before: "People see what they want to see."

A few minutes later, as they came down the steep grade toward Castaic, the car picked up speed. Mathieu tapped the brakes to bleed some off, then looked toward the next curve. He saw the road drop precipitously to the left. He downshifted to control the car's momentum as they entered the hairpin turn.

At that moment, Florence lunged at the steering wheel, pulling it to the right. The car lurched toward the cliff's edge. Mathieu wrested control, yanking it back to the left. The rear of the Phaeton fishtailed over the gravel verge at the lip of the cliff, then back onto the pavement.

Mathieu ripped Florence's wrists off the steering wheel with his right hand, raising them until she screamed in pain from her wound. Then he shoved her toward the passenger door, where she curled up in a ball and sobbed.

They rode the rest of the way back as they had begun, in silence.

44

A Parting in the Moonlight

It was three weeks after the trial. Mathieu angle-parked his Buick Phaeton in front of the La Grande Train Station on Santa Fe Avenue.

Moonlight reflected off the depot's onion-shaped dome. The exotic Moorish-style station, with its dark sandstone façade and fanciful turrets, looked like it belonged in North Africa or on a Hollywood backlot.

A casual passerby wouldn't have been surprised to see Berber tribesmen riding up to the depot on camels, if it wasn't for the Yellow Car trolleys running down the middle of the street.

Mathieu got out of the Phaeton and retrieved two suitcases from the back seat. A lot had happened since the case ended.

Upon returning to headquarters from the El Saucito Ranch, Mathieu booked Florence Drake into custody on three charges of first-degree murder. Before taking her to the cells, he let Florence see her brother Travis, who had been waiting patiently in the detectives' office.

Then, Mathieu called Julia and said he would swing by in the morning to pick up Marilyn Lane. He thanked Julia for keeping her safe. Julia replied that Marilyn had been a delight, pitching in willingly when asked without putting on any airs.

But Marilyn's roommate must have alerted the press because when Mathieu pulled up to the Fleur de Lis apartments the next morning to drop Marilyn off, photographers lined the sidewalk.

Mathieu escorted Marilyn past the popping flashbulbs into the building's lobby and left soon after. The evening *Herald* ran front-page photos of Marilyn and Mathieu with the headline: "Handsome Detective Saves Actress Marilyn Lane's Life."

Mathieu cringed when he saw the headline, but there was a positive outcome for Marilyn. A week later, she got a part in a movie. Despite the heady publicity, Marilyn denied all rumors of an affair and, honoring Mathieu's request, never mentioned what happened the night they escaped from Idyllwild.

Florence pled guilty at the trial and threw herself on the mercy of the court. At the sentencing hearing, the judge, while sympathetic to what happened to Florence's family, seemed initially reluctant to spare her life. That changed when her brother Travis took the stand to testify on her behalf.

Despite Travis's disfigurement, everyone in court that day, Mathieu included, seemed taken by his quiet dignity. While admitting his own part in the oil field fire, he spoke with measured anger about the callous way Lester Jensen and Reginald Stonebridge had avoided any responsibility for his father and brother's death.

Travis told the court Jensen and Stonebridge had instigated the drinking and later the shooting contest. And yet, after the fire spread, they did nothing to try to save their coworkers in the burning bunkhouse.

Subsequently, they lied to the examining board and bullied an eighteen-year-old Travis into believing it was his fault. Travis spoke of his lonely fifteen-year exile when wracked with guilt he attempted suicide multiple times.

While not condoning what Florence had done, Travis begged the judge to spare the only family member he had left, his sister. Travis further stated to the court that he had no intention of benefiting from Jensen's and Stonebridge's deaths. He'd decided to donate the El Saucito Ranch to the State of California under the condition that it never be developed for oil.

The judge took two days to deliberate and, in the end, sentenced Florence Drake to life imprisonment without the possibility of parole.

Bull gave Mathieu some time off after the trial. Mathieu escorted Lillian to her brother's funeral. Afterward, he asked her if she'd like to get out of town for a few days and go to Santa Barbara, and she accepted. They stayed in a cabin belonging to his friend Detective Barnes near the Botanical Gardens.

On the day they arrived, they took a hike up San Ysidro Canyon in Montecito along a beautiful, boulder-strewn creek flush with cool mountain water from the recent rains. They found a small pool a few miles up where it was safe to swim. Then, afterward, they lay beside each other on a boulder to dry in the sun.

That evening, back at the cabin, ravenous from the day's hike, they devoured two huge omelets Lillian had cooked on the wood-burning stove. After helping to clean up, Mathieu struck the opening chords to "Georgia on My Mind" on the cabin's ancient upright piano. Lillian retrieved her practice violin from her rucksack, and they began to play.

Mathieu was initially nervous about playing with her, but Lillian gently encouraged him. Several hours, which seemed like minutes, went by as they played together.

Near midnight, Lillian put the violin down and walked over to the piano. She stared into Mathieu's eyes and offered her hand. He took it, and she led him into the bedroom. They didn't go hiking the next day or the one after.

It was a dizzyingly wonderful three days. Neither wanted to leave the other's side. They clung together naturally. No words were needed. But it was also frightening. Mathieu knew this kind of bliss couldn't last, and it didn't.

On the third morning, as they were packing to leave, Lillian told Mathieu she'd recently received an invitation to play a three-month engagement with the Chicago Philharmonic Orchestra. It was the opportunity of a lifetime for her. She asked him what he thought.

Mathieu gazed open-mouthed at Lillian, unsure how to reply. His stomach dropped. His vision constricted. He stood for several seconds, paralyzed with fear at the thought of losing her. He took a deep breath to calm himself. Despite how he felt, he knew in his heart there was only one answer.

"You have to grab this opportunity … Lily," Mathieu said in a halting voice.

"Will you wait for me?" Lillian asked, seemingly unsure of herself now.

"Yes, of course," he said in turmoil. "You can't pass this up."

Now, a week later, Mathieu carried Lillian's luggage while she carried her violin case. It was unseasonably cold. Both wore coats and scarves. The station's dark façade looked rather ominous at night, softened somewhat by the warm glow of light coming through the mullioned windows.

Noticing Mathieu's far-off expression, Lillian hooked her arm through his as they walked under the arched entrance and down the central concourse. Once inside, Lillian went to the ticket office to purchase her reserved roomette for the evening's Santa Fe Chief to Chicago.

Afterward, they walked toward the edge of the concourse and stopped under a horseshoe-shaped Moorish arch. Mathieu put the suitcases down. Lillian leaned against him. He wrapped his arms around her while they silently watched the porters and engineers ready the train for departure.

The passenger rail yard sat just west of the LA River, roughly between 1st and 4th streets. The yard had four passenger platforms and eight sets of tracks. Lillian's train was on track 3, in plain view from where they stood.

They could hear the hissing sound of steam escaping from the smokestack of the massive Baldwin steam locomotive idling in front of them. Engineers busied themselves lubricating the wheel trucks and piston arms while porters pushed dollies stacked with luggage and clean linen toward the sleeping cars. Except for a dining car, the trainset consisted entirely of Pullman sleepers.

As they stood huddled together watching the activity, Mathieu said, "I need your advice."

"About what?" she asked in a soft voice.

"About a girl I met recently."

"What's her name?"

"Lillian."

"Where did you meet her?"

"At the Garden of Allah Hotel. I was there for work to talk to a source. She was playing violin with a quartet near the pool. I was mesmerized by her playing."

"What is she like?"

"Quiet, reserved, beautiful, with red hair and wistful dark eyes. The kind you never tire gazing at, the kind you can be silent around."

"She sounds wonderful," Lillian said, burrowing into his chest. "What's the problem?"

"She's going away, and I don't want to lose her."

"How can I help?"

"I don't want to mess this up," Mathieu said with a sigh. "I'm good at my job, but I don't know a lot about love. I want to love her without smothering her. And in truth, I don't want to be smothered either. I need my space. I suspect she does, too. So, I need some advice."

"Can you be more specific, Detective?" Lillian asked as she looked up at him.

"For example," Mathieu said, "if I write her one letter a week while she's away, do you think that would be too much?"

"Handwritten or typed?"

"Handwritten."

"In that case, I think one would be fine," Lillian said with a smile. "How many do you want?"

"Whatever she has time for?"

"What if she writes every day?"

"I can handle that."

"What if she misses a day?"

"I'll assume she's run off with the drummer."

"I don't like drummers," Lillian said as she turned to him in mock seriousness. "I prefer pianists. They know how to use their hands."

"That's comforting to know," Mathieu said with a grin.

"What if you run off with some beautiful damsel in distress like Marilyn Lane and forget all about me?" Lillian asked.

"You saw that headline?" Mathieu asked with chagrin.

"The whole town saw it, Detective."

"That's not going to happen?"

"Why not?"

"A good violinist is hard to find."

"Is that the only reason you like me?"

"No," Mathieu said.

"What do you like most about me?" Lillian asked.

"The way you make toast."

Lillian laughed. "The way I make toast?"

"Yes, I watched you in the cabin. You spread the butter all the way to the edges on all four sides before you handed it to me. I felt very loved at that moment."

Lillian's eyes softened. "You're very easy to please, Detective."

"Not really."

"Anything else you like about me?"

"Besides your beautiful face and great legs?"

"Yes, besides that," Lillian said, challenging him.

Mathieu hesitated a moment. His expression turned serious as he said, "Those moments when you drop your guard and let me in. It makes me feel that I'm special to you and that you trust me."

Lillian was silent as she gazed into his eyes. "Do you know what I love about you besides your beautiful, intense brown eyes?"

Mathieu shook his head no, blushing.

"That you don't back away when I do," Lillian said in a soft voice.

Mathieu brought her closer and kissed her hair.

"What else do you like about me, Detective?" Lillian asked in a muffled voice.

"If I listed them all … you'd miss your train."

"Do you want me to leave?" Lillian asked as she took a step back and stared at him.

"No," Mathieu said, returning her gaze. "I want you to fulfill your dreams."

"Even though it means leaving?" she asked cocking her head to one side.

"That appears to be the tradeoff," Mathieu said with a shrug.

"It's going to be tricky, isn't it," Lillian said.

"Yes," Mathieu said with a pensive look.

"This isn't going to be easy for either of us," Lillian said.

"Do you know anything worthwhile in life that is?" Mathieu asked.

"I thought you said you didn't know anything about love, Detective?"

"I don't … but I know that much. I just need help with the details."

Lillian grinned at him. "Remember to put the toilet seat down."

"Yes, miss," Mathieu said with a laugh. "You taught me that in the cabin."

"Pick up my mail while I'm gone."

"Done. Anything else?"

"I need your touch," Lillian said.

"That's easy. How often?"

"Everyday."

"How's that going to work if you're in Chicago?" Mathieu asked with a quizzical look.

"You're the detective ... figure it out," Lillian said as she playfully poked him in the chest with her index finger.

Just then, they called her train for boarding.

Neither moved as they gazed at each other. After a moment, Mathieu tugged at his scarf, then gently placed it around Lillian's neck. "Maybe this will remind you of me while you're away."

Inhaling his scent, Lillian removed her scarf, put it around his neck, and kissed him. "Perhaps in some ancient culture, exchanging scarves was a marriage ceremony."

"If it was, it beats a church wedding any day," Mathieu said with a smile.

The final boarding call came over the loudspeakers. "All aboard for the Santa Fe Chief to Chicago departing on Track 3."

Mathieu picked up her suitcases. They walked arm-in-arm across the tracks to the second-to-last Pullman sleeper. Mathieu handed her luggage up to the porter.

Lillian looked at Mathieu, put her arms around his neck and whispered, "This is going to be a long three months, Detective."

"I know, but I'll be here when you return, Lily. You're going to be fantastic in Chicago. Savor it!" Mathieu said with pride.

They pressed together in an intense, hungry kiss, then separated. Mathieu helped Lily up the steps. She turned to him with a wistful smile. He nodded back to reassure her. Then, reluctantly, she followed the porter into the sleeping car.

Stepping back, Mathieu strained to catch a glimpse of her through the Pullman sleeper's windows. He craned his neck as he walked along the edge of the car, then stopped when he saw her come to a window midway down. Lillian tightened the scarf around her neck and kissed it. He smiled back.

Soon after, the train whistle blew, the air brakes released, and the chugging sound of the pistons intensified as the train lurched forward and began to move. He stayed where he was, waving to her as the train slowly picked up momentum.

Two minutes later, all he could see were the red lights of the last car receding in the distance. He was already missing her. He hoped he'd get a challenging case to distract him while she was away.

About The Author

Mr. Nicholas lives and writes in Los Angeles, California.

"Black Gold" is the fourth in a series of novels featuring Detective Mathieu.